# THE LADY AND HER CHAMPION

## SARA R. TURNQUIST

**If you would like to stay up-to-date on this and all other series from Sara:**

https://saraturnquist.com/list

*To my daughter, who makes me smile.*

# PROLOGUE

The year is 1420, five years after the martyrdom of Jan Hus and the start of the Hussite Wars. Pope Martin V called for Royalist forces to retake Bohemia and stop the heretics in what would later be known as the First Anti-Hussite Crusade. This effort culminated in the Battle of Vitkov Hill. The ensuing Hussite victory put an end to Royalist rule over the Kingdom of Bohemia. The Royalist Catholic army, commanded by Holy Roman Emperor Sigismund, has been thwarted...for now. Sigismund's desire to claim the Czech lands as his has not been quashed.

Pavel Krejik, along with his friends Zdenek Ambroz and Radek Miklas, have served in the Hussite army, figthing for the freedom of their brethren. However, Radek has had reservations about the Hussite leader, General Jan Zizka, and some of his military tactics. In the end, Radek defected to the Royalist camp.

Their other friend, Stepan Dvorak, struggles with the ghastly things he has had to do and witness in the course of combat. Especially what the mercenaries and foreign soldiers fighting on the side of the Royalists have intended for the Czech people. He becomes increasingly uncomfortable with the side he has chosen.

Pavel and Karin are still learning what it means to be man and wife. They have weathered the loss of their child to miscarriage. Despite this struggle, they have discovered they are stronger together than apart. But General Zizka called Pavel back to the front, thus separating them once more. And then Pavel's family home, the Krejik castle, was burned to the ground. Those behind it have yet to be identified.

Zdenek and Eva found one another even as the Hussite army has been engaged in conflict. The spark between them upon first meeting has developed into a deep love. After a decisive victory at the Battle of Vitkov Hill, Zdenek asks Eva to be his wife.

*And now, the continuation...*

# THE KINGDOM OF BOHEMIA DURING THE HUSSITE WARS

# CHAPTER I

Pavel Krejick closed his eyes. Karin's face was before him. How long would it be before they were together again? He and his wife—separated by this war—would they ever know what it was to live together?

That should not be such a far-fetched hope.

The Hussites had prevailed. Once things were settled in Prague, he could return to Tabor. Then he and Karin could truly begin their life as a married couple.

Leaning back, Pavel allowed the sting of the recent loss of their child to wash over him. Had he truly grieved? Or would he yet be swept away by it? What of Karin? How did she fare?

A hand landed on his shoulder.

He jerked to attention, eyes wide, reaching for his sword's hilt.

A young man crouched beside him. How had he come upon Pavel without notice?

"Excuse me, my lord." The young man's eyes were clear. "General Zizka sends for you."

Zizka? What might he want?

Pavel nodded and rose. Whatever the general needed, it would certainly be important.

The short walk through camp to Zizka's tent seemed longer than it could have possibly been.

Though the hour was late, and nearly all the men had long since surrendered to sleep, Zizka still worked over a table, pouring over maps illuminated by candles. The flame flickered across his features, casting shadows and drawing attention to different angles in alternating patterns. His stern expression became all the more severe.

Pavel halted a few steps short of the simple desk.

Moments passed and still Zizka's gaze did not divert toward him. Was the man so focused? Surely, he must have realized he had company. But Pavel did not find offense in it—he had long since accepted that the good of the majority was more important than his own needs. He could wait for Zizka to finish whatever strategic planning he had engaged in.

Once his eye fell on Pavel, Zizka set his tools to the side and stepped around the table, moving toward the man, who was several years his junior.

"Pavel," he began, his voice low and his words measured. "Thank you for coming."

"Of course, General."

Zizka stopped a couple arms' lengths short of Pavel. He nodded in acknowledgment at the other men around them, and they moved several paces away.

Pavel worked to keep his features neutral. What could this mean? What manner of news did Zizka have? Or was there some task he wished Pavel to perform? Some delicate or dangerous matter? Did Pavel have more fight in him?

The man's steely gaze leveled on Pavel once more. It seemed to bore into him. Certainly, it saw more than Pavel wanted it to.

"There is news. From Tabor."

Karin! Was she unsafe? His heart raced, and his chest tightened. He suddenly had great difficulty moving air. Forcing a breath in and then pushing it out, he worked to calm his body. This was no time to fall apart.

"Your parents—the baron and baroness—their home has burned to the ground."

Now, it was impossible to take air in. Nothing would move. Then his breaths came in and out rapidly. He had no ability to control them. Nor a care to try. His vision became hazy.

No. Not now. Not like this.

Once again forcing rhythm to his breathing, he brought stability to his body. And clarity to his mind.

"And what of my parents? My...wife? Are they...?" He drew in a deep breath. He would stand. He would maintain his hold on himself. "Do they live?"

Zizka's mouth, now a thin line, hardened. "We have word from the Baroness Krejikova. She is well and in Tabor."

"The others?"

The larger man's head dipped. "Nothing."

The ground opened, and Pavel's stomach fell through.

Zizka laid a large hand on Pavel's shoulder. "That means only that there was not news at the time the messenger was dispatched. Nothing is certain."

Pavel nodded, swallowing hard. He wished to speak, but his emotions were too close to the surface. Surely, they would spill out.

Zizka's brow rose.

"May I...?" A lump in Pavel's throat caught his words and cut off his request. He drew in a breath and pressed on. "General, may I take my leave to return to Tabor?"

"God be with you." The man squeezed Pavel's arm, and the one good eye caught Pavel's gaze. What was that in his regard? Sadness? Regret?

It would be of little gain to attempt to decipher Zizka's emotions when Pavel's own rushed and tumbled through him, cluttering his mind and heart.

And only one thing was clear: he had to get to Karin.

Radek stirred. His mind came to awareness, but he kept his eyes sealed. Did he want to open them and accept this day? What had transpired on the day past? Had he truly left the Hussites? Left Pavel and Zdenek?

He rolled onto his back and groaned. There had been reasons. And they were good. Noble. Strong enough that he had made the difficult decision to abandon his friends. His brethren.

No. Not abandon. He'd had no choice. General Zizka had left him none. Not after all he had seen. After what he had done at the general's behest.

"Will you sleep all day?"

The voice loomed over him. Familiar, yet strange somehow.

He let his eyes open at last to confirm what he suspected.

A figure looked down, but the sun behind silhouetted him. His features were not discernable.

It was no matter. Radek did not need to see the man to know his identity.

The only thing amiss was that his voice held no hint of joviality. Only tension. Not for the first time, but it had been uncommon.

Before now.

"Are you unwell?" Stepan spoke again as he folded his arms across his chest.

Did he inquire out of concern or impatience? It was difficult to determine.

"I am well enough."

Now fully awake, Radek's senses were bombarded with his surroundings.

As he came to a seated position, he gagged. "What is that...?" Was there a word to describe the foul odor assaulting him?

Stepan looked off toward the horizon. Was he becoming irritated with Radek?

It had been nearly nightfall when Radek had made his way to

camp after defecting, and several hours later, Stepan had helped him find bedding and a place to lie down.

But now, the true state of the place was laid bare in the morning light. Unspeakable things littered the ground. And the bugs...they were everywhere.

Radek glared at Stepan. "Were there no latrines dug? Or do Germans simply not care?" Pressing the back of his hand to his mouth, another wave of nausea rose and threatened Radek's tightly held control. What could this be?

"One does what one must in war." Stepan set narrowed eyes on him.

Radek quirked a brow. An easy excuse.

Stepan held out a hand toward him. "Come, we must make good of our day."

Still uncertain his stomach would hold, he gripped the proffered hand and hoisted himself up. It did not help his uneasiness.

"This way." Stepan indicated that they would go in the direction in which the tents were thicker.

Closing his eyes and forcing down a hard swallow, Radek followed.

The walk through camp did not improve Radek's impression of the Royalists. He was careful with his steps, avoiding placing his feet in...areas he did not wish them to be.

Germans and other foreign soldiers were being roused around him. Some of them suffered from having imbibed too much drink the previous evening. Their boisterous speech pulled at his attention more than once.

"Watch yourself!" Stepan's voice cut into Radek's wandering thoughts.

His foot hit something hard, and he became unsteady—his body moved forward, but his legs were held back.

Stepan caught his arm. That was the only thing keeping him upright.

He nodded to his friend. And then looked down at what had halted his momentum.

A dead a horse lay across the path.

How had he not smelled it? The animal had been dead for some time. But it was not a sick stomach welling up in him now, it was anger.

"How long until this is moved?" He glared openly at Stepan.

His friend gave him a sharp look. "Lower your voice."

"What manner of insanity is this?" Dead carcasses left to rot in the hot sun, human waste left wherever anyone cared to leave it, both attracting the multitude of bugs that covered the grounds.

Why? Why would they choose to live this way?

Stepan closed the distance between them. "You will do well to check yourself and silence your objections."

"Check *my*self? What about the—?"

Stepan grabbed his arm and pulled him to the side, glancing about. Was he fearful of those listening? Would those within this encampment turn on their own?

"This is not the place to air out your grievances against the Germans," Stepan seethed.

What? Could Stepan not see that the conditions of the camp were deplorable? Not because they were Germans, but because they were negligent. "It's not about—"

"Just keep your opinions to yourself." Stepan turned and moved farther into the camp.

Radek watched him go. Should he follow? Dare he stay behind? Drawing in a painfully acrid breath, he stretched out his stride and attempted to catch his friend.

Eva shifted. Slowly, her mind drifted toward the brink of awareness. Had she been asleep? For how long? Where was she?

As her senses trailed behind her thoughts, she took in what information she could.

The ground. Only a thin pile of blankets separated her from it. Her hip ached from being pressed into the hard surface for so long. Indeed, she smelled the earth—the dirt and the grass—quite well.

She opened her eyes. The sun shone down upon her. Morning?

Indeed, the night had gone.

Yes, she recalled having bedded down for the night in the women's camp in Prague. Days past rushed into her memory. Must she always wake so? Unknowing of her circumstances?

Sitting up, she put a hand to her forehead.

The battle had been fought. And the Hussites had won. By some miracle, they had prevailed!

Rubbing sleep from her eyes, she turned. Movement off to her right indicated she was not alone.

Turning to take it in, she noted the women and girls shuffling about this way and that. What were they doing? Was she the only one still abed?

She stood. A little uneasy at first, but soon her legs became confident and strong. Walking toward the cluster of chattering ladies closest her position, she laid a hand to a shoulder.

The brunette turned, and a brow arched in her direction. "Up at last, I see."

"Huh? Oh, yes." Her face warmed. "I am."

The young woman stared at her, a slight smile crossing her features.

"Can you tell me…where I might find my sister, Patricie?"

"For certain, she does as everyone else does." The woman appeared to hold back an amused laugh.

What had tasked everyone? Eva was ignorant of such. Should she know? Meeting the woman's eyes once more, she dared voice her confusion. "I fear I do not understand what that might be."

"Preparing for this evening's feast!" The young woman took her hands. "The likes of which you have never seen!"

The corners of Eva's mouth rose and spread until her cheeks ached. Still, she could not help the moisture that filled her eyes. "God has been good to us!"

"He's been more than good. He has shone His favor upon us. For sooth, there is nothing we won't accomplish now."

The women around the young lady spoke, adding their agreement, excitement filling their voices.

As the young woman loosed Eva's hands and turned back to the others, Eva reminisced on the victory—the fear she had experienced in the bunker and, just as keenly, the comfort of Zdenek's strength and love. And, after all was done, the words he spoke to her.

Did he mean them? Or had they been the product of a celebratory spirit? Of life restored where it had been thought forfeit?

*Her* professions had been heartfelt. What if his had not? Could she bear it? She must know.

Zdenek. Where was he?

Coming back to herself, she looked around. The men's camp. That's where he would have lain for the night. But where had they set up? To the north? Yes.

Eva touched the brunette's elbow. "I thank you." She put on her best smile. "I shall return to assist after I am finished with my ablutions."

The woman did not much acknowledge Eva as the group moved farther into the camp.

Eva slipped around other small gatherings and pairs of women busying themselves with the preparations. A pang pricked in her chest as she did not stop to assist—after all, it was her duty. But, she could no more delay her errand than she could put off the beating of her heart.

Making her way to the outskirts of the camp, she spotted two men standing guard. Was their charge to prevent anyone from entering the camp? Or watching the comings and goings of its inhabitants?

She scanned the area. A bucket sat nearby among some grasses.

It had eluded her until now. Now she homed in on it—salvation! Taking a step toward it, she reached into the brush and lifted the handle.

Why would anyone leave such a resource behind? Had it been thrown or kicked and been hidden from its owner?

Drawing it to herself, she spotted the ground, quite visible through the interior of the bucket...due to a rather large hole. Oh yes —this must be the reason. Of what use was a bucket that could no longer carry?

Ah, but it would be of great use to her. If she held it near enough to her dark brown skirt, the guards may not see the hole. Why would they see something they were not looking for?

With great effort, she slowed as she walked the remaining distance to the camp's entry point.

The shorter of the two men, still a full head taller than she, noticed her first. He dipped his head in her direction. *"Dobry den."*

*"Dobry den,"* she returned his greeting of a good day, bending in a slight curtsy.

"Off to fetch something?" His tone remained pleasant. Did he merely wish to make conversation?

What might she need that she could not secure within the boundaries of the camp? Why did she not think this far ahead? They had water, foodstuffs...

She looked at the soldier.

His brows, once raised as if curious, dropped. Her lack of response also drew the attention of the larger man.

"Bread!" she said, a bit louder than she'd intended.

The men glanced at each other.

"Yes," she softened her tone and offered a coy smile. "I am charged with fetching fresh bread from the baker and delivering it to General Zizka."

The smaller soldier scratched his head, but the larger man appeared skeptical.

He stepped forward, his manner threatening, his size overwhelming her small frame. Would he stop her now? Before she had even gotten started?

Scratching at his jaw, his deep voice thundered. "What is your name?"

Raising her chin, she halted, determined she would not back down. "Eva of Hradec Kralove."

"Well then, Eva of Hradek Kralove," he said, his eyes leveling on her.

Had he seen through her ruse? Would he force her back into the camp? Turn her in to some authority? Would she be expelled from the Hussite army for lying? Though she maintained her firm stance, she shook within.

"Tell the General that we are well pleased to fight under his sword." The man put a fist to his chest.

She forced her mouth to remain closed, lest it fall open. The full force of the chance she took had fallen over her. Would there be more such instances? What was she doing? The warmth drained from her face. Was it too late to take it back?

Nodding, she looked up at the soldier. "Of course, I will let the general know of the two brave men who watch the women's camp and how much they respect his leadership."

The man, who loomed over her by much, made a slight bow at the waist. Even still, his head bent only to her shoulder. Was it due to his massive size or her petite one?

She gripped at her skirt with her free hand and forced her steps to remain steady as she walked away. Though she couldn't deny her relief that they weren't able to see her face. For certainly, it had become all the more pale.

Karin's lungs burned. And her eyes. Dry. So dry. She blinked several times as she opened them. Would moisture ever return? Everything in her had become parched of the smallest hint of liquid.

Would that she could stay asleep. Perhaps then she would not feel so arid. Was there water nearby?

She coughed. A pained gesture. For every move was effort. Great effort.

As she sat up, she looked around. Where was she? Her head hated her for the simple movement, pounding in response. Had someone driven a spike through her temple? For certainly it felt that way.

Her hands covered the sides of her head, and she pressed as if a vise. It offered but small respite.

Rustling grass to her right assaulted her senses but also told of another nearby. She jerked in that direction. Her vision followed. Slowly.

Baron Alex Krejik shifted to a sitting position.

Why were she and her father-in-law sleeping on the ground in the forest line? Unsheltered?

The piercing slice of pain in her head fractured her thoughts. But images flashed before her. Memories?

Danger. Much haste. Nicol's attempts to hurry her away. There had been a fire. The castle!

Turning toward the open grounds where the grand structure once sat, her eyes fell on the debris that remained.

Her memories returned in full force. A torrent of emotion with them. And tears.

She drew her knees to her chest and rested her head in the pocket created there. The pressure within only increased. How much pain could she endure?

A hand fell to her back.

Without looking, she knew it was the baron.

"It will be all right." His voice broke.

How could she believe him? "Who..." She pushed the word out through her sobs. "Who could have done this?"

The baron was silent for several moments.

It drove her sorrow to greater intensity.

"I do not know." His hand drew back.

The loss of what little comfort he offered saddened her more than she'd expected. Biting her lip, she worked to quiet her tears. They did not serve him, or her.

"And the baroness? Did she make it to safety?" Karin peered to the side, over her shoulder.

The baron crouched beside her and ran a hand down his face.

Despite her best efforts, Karin's eyes watered anew. He didn't know. What were they to do? Should they seek out the baroness? Find a safe place for themselves? Would the baron make rebuilding a priority? Or would finding the one responsible be more important? Would she, then, lose him, as well, to the villain?

Where was Pavel? She needed him. Her tears burned hot.

So many days and nights she had been strong. But no more. There was no strength left in her. She had failed him.

Curling into herself again, she quieted her sobs but let her tears flow.

# CHAPTER 2

Zdenek stretched. He hadn't been awake but for a few hours. The late-night celebrations did not negate the camp routines. And those started early. But he had finished his assigned tasks.

If only it were possible for him to rest for a few moments more. The sun had been up for only two hours, and yet he already longed for his mat. Except...

Except for the hope of seeing Eva today. The words spoken between them had made it rather difficult for him to find sleep the night before. Yet another reason for his weariness.

As he approached the place his mat had been for the night, he was pleased to discover his horse had been given something more than just grasses to graze upon.

A gentle slap on the animal's side alerted her to her master's presence.

He muttered soothing words as he crossed behind, keeping a hand to her body, and around to the other side.

She appeared well and in good health.

Rubbing her muzzle, he whispered to her. "Thank you, my steadfast friend. You have served me well."

The horse sputtered in response and stepped slightly to the side. Did she find some displeasure in him? Had he wronged her?

Then he heard it—the clomp of boots, the rustle of grass. Someone approached.

He turned, hand on the hilt of his sword. Why must he always be on guard? Was he not safe even in this camp?

A farmer-turned-soldier approached, perhaps a year or so older than Zdenek at the most.

Zdenek attempted to read his features. What manner of news did he bear?

The man's face offered no clues. But in moments, he stood before Zdenek.

"Dobry den, my lord." He bowed his head briefly.

"Dobry den." Zdenek returned the greeting. "Why have you sought me out?"

"General Zizka must see you."

Zdenek furrowed his brows. The general? Why? But he need not show this man any reluctance, lest it be thought he questioned General Zizka. The general was now a hero to all Hussites, far and near. That would likely not be tolerated so well.

Zdenek nodded. "I will come."

The man turned and walked in the direction from whence he had come.

And not long after, Zdenek found himself approaching the general's tent.

Zizka's booming voice was audible from even these few feet away. And there was another—a woman. It almost sounded like...

But it couldn't be.

He bit his lip and continued forward even as his guide paused. Striding to the tent's opening, he then halted and listened. He did not wish to step in on the general entertaining company. But was that so appropriate? That was not for him to judge.

As he turned to leave the woman's voice grew louder. And,

though he could not make out the words, he became much more certain of who the voice belonged to—Eva. But what would she be doing with General Zizka?

Unless...

His heart stopped. What if she had not truly cared for him at all but sought the attentions of the general? It didn't make sense. Yet it fit with what he now witnessed.

Zdenek's heart sank into his stomach. But he refused to lose his constitution in front of the soldiers surrounding the tent. What could he do? Walk in and make his humiliation complete? Run away from her, from the general, from this war?

Perhaps...

He blinked as he stared at the tent flap over his shoulder.

Could he?

Dare he?

His insides tensed, and his face heated. Yes, he could give in to this anger and storm into the tent. Make them the fools.

He spun and marched into the tent.

Those within were indeed startled.

But not as much as he.

The general stood nearby, with three other nobles looking on. They shifted their focus to him as he entered. But it was Eva who drew Zdenek's eyes.

She stood in what made for the center of the tent, poised as if with a sword. Nothing improper.

Nothing.

Improper.

Except that he had forced his way into his general's privacy without announcing himself.

Eva's eyes went wide as she looked upon him, fighting to maintain her balance.

"I take it, Eva of Hradec Kralove, that this is the man of whom you speak?"

Zdenek shot a glance in Zizka's direction.

The man shook with barely contained laughter.

Zdenek's stomach felt uneasy and, though his mouth moved, nothing came forth.

"Yes, General! This is he." She straightened her posture and smiled in Zdenek's direction. Yet something in her eyes held back. Why? Had she any idea of his earlier thoughts? He prayed not.

"Zdenek," Zizka said, stepping toward him. "Have you any knowledge of why you were sent for?"

He must choose his words carefully. "I did not, sir, until I saw the lady. Now, I am left to assume it is to do with her."

Zizka smacked him on the shoulder. "Can you imagine that this lady was discovered trying to sneak into the men's camp?"

Zdenek caught Eva's eye, his brow arched. Was it his imagination, or did her cheeks redden?

"She said she came looking for you. Some important message or some such nonsense."

What should he do? Take the blame? Or speak the truth that he knew nothing of it? He opened his mouth, but before he could speak, Zizka interjected.

"I would have had her thrown out into the streets, but something about her manner gave me pause. Can you think of what that might be?"

Zdenek swallowed against a thickness in his throat. "N-no, sir."

"She speaks of love. Have you ever heard of such a silly notion? Love!" He laughed.

Eva's features deepened in color.

Zdenek's hands curled into fists. How dare the man, especially a general, make light of her...of *their* plight! Turning, he thrust himself toward Zizka.

Two men appeared at his sides and held him back.

"Calm yourself, Zdenek." Zizka's laughter was gone. Replaced by drawn features. Wearied by too many days of concern? "I see you have a care for her. And no harm will come to her. She is simply delightful."

Zdenek blinked as the men released him.

"This young lady has been entertaining us with the oddest tale—of dressing as a man and fighting in battle. Can you even imagine?"

Zdenek remained silent but poised as Zizka stepped toward Eva.

The general offered her a hand.

She hesitated but soon slid her hand into his.

He escorted her toward Zdenek. "The question is...what am I to do with a maiden who prances about, alone, in the morning hours... lying to my guards and sneaking around barriers?"

Zdenek ached to take Eva's hand from his, to pull her behind himself and ensure no harm came to her.

"Shall I send her back to Hradec Kralove?"

Eva opened her mouth.

Zdenek shot her a warning look.

She clamped her lips shut.

Turning back to Zizka, Zdenek garnered what courage he had and offered what he could. "General, I am fully prepared to marry this young woman."

"You are?" Though his words sounded surprised, Zizka's features told another story.

"If you will bless it." Zdenek shifted his body to face Zizka.

"I will do more than that." Zizka smiled. He tugged Eva forward and laid her hand in Zdenek's waiting one. "I can have a priest readied within the hour."

Zdenek forced the determined expression to remain on his face lest it fall. Marry? Now? Today? Was he ready?

He looked at Eva. In her eyes, he found peace, love, and hope.

"Be certain he makes haste," Zdenek said, his words soft as his gaze rested only on Eva. "For it cannot be soon enough."

Hana ducked. Could she become invisible? There was nowhere left to hide. Nowhere to run. No *way* to run.

The Germans had taken all away.

She pulled against the rope binding her wrists to no avail. The coarse rub of the material against her skin was her only reward. Grimacing against the burn, she pressed her face all the more against her shoulder.

Was this all that was left to her? Could anyone survive this?

At least for now, the soldier that had glanced her way returned to the joviality of his small group. She was safe. For now. But for how long?

Her stomach ached. When was the last time they had fed her? Fed was perhaps too generous a word for the act of tossing scraps her way. She wasn't an animal.

Still, she could not help herself as she lunged for the morsels. And the sneers and laughter from her captors made her burn much deeper than the ropes ever could.

What did they intend to do with her? Thus far, she had been little more than a source of amusement. But she was not ignorant. They would tire of their play, use her as they pleased, and toss her away. And there was little she could do to stop them.

That didn't mean she wouldn't try.

Peering at the group of men drinking and laughing, she wondered how much they had consumed. Would they soon be passed out? Perhaps then she might work on the knots again. Her jaw ached at the mere thought. But she had to try.

Hana Novakova would not go peaceably. That was certain.

The men became louder, drawing her attention back in their direction.

Two soldiers faced each other, nearly nose-to-nose. The others had drawn back, creating a circle around them. Those surrounding chanted in German while the two men locked their foreheads together, putting their hands on the other's shoulders and jerking the other closer. What had their drunkenness drawn them to now?

If only she weren't secured to this tree, she might take advantage of this opportunity. Dare she creep closer to the oak and work the knot?

The voices grew louder, and the circle tightened until she could no longer see the combatants.

She had to try. Pushing herself to a standing position, she bit her lip against the pain in her leg. How badly was she injured? If she hadn't been slowed by the sprain, she might not be in this situation at all. Easy prey.

She sniffed back her frustrated tears. They would not serve her. Refocusing on her task, she crouched and limped toward the tree, keeping careful watch on the men.

They seemed wholly unaware of her movements. Just a few more inches, and she would be there. Letting loose her leg, she reached for the portion of rope that bound her to the trunk.

It had been secured tightly. Did she expect anything less?

As she slid her fingers around the rope, she frowned at the state of her once fine skin. Cuts and reddened patches marred her fair skin. What would her mother think?

She pushed that thought back in her mind. There wasn't time for that. This was her life she was trying to preserve.

But the ties wouldn't give. Still, she worked. There was no other option.

The sounds of the men cheering on the two locked in some sort of game increased. What did that mean?

She didn't have the time to stop and investigate. Jerking on the thick, rough hemp, it gave a little. She almost cried out. But stopped herself.

Holding her breath, she then became aware that the nearby noises had ceased. Dare she turn?

The hair on the back of her neck stood on end. Was someone behind her? She pushed out a ragged breath and closed her eyes.

A rough voice spoke in German.

Others laughed.

They were close. Too close.

"It seems, my lady, the cat has caught the mouselette. And she has been very naughty," the roughened tenor said in her language.

Her head swam with a million thoughts. Should she comply? Drop her arms and turn? Would that make it better for her? Or was she correct in thinking they would end her life when they were done with her? Might there be a chance for her to escape? Would she want to live after they were done?

Or should she resist? A part of Hana was scared and thought perhaps she might escape if she did not fight. But, that was not who Hana Novakova was. Not now. Not ever.

The grass crunched behind her. Did the man step closer?

She thought to pray briefly. But only a few words for strength and boldness. Then she intertwined her fingers, pulling her hands together.

One more step.

"What has the mouselette to say for herself?" He was close. So close, she felt the heat from his body.

Gripping her hands together, she spun, pivoting on her good leg, arms outstretched and firm. They connected with the soldier's face.

Though she had not the strength of a man, God must have heard her prayer. The blow knocked the man to the side. He fought for balance.

But there was nowhere for her to run, and there were too many men surrounding her. Hands gripped her from all sides, fingers digging into her skin.

She kicked out in any and every direction she could.

The soldiers forced her into a kneeling position, pinning her arms to her sides, her bound hands in front of her.

Where was the man she had hit? Had she done any damage?

Movement off to the side caught her attention. The man was hunched over, a cloth to his face. He looked in her direction. And she saw...

The cloth was pressed to his bloodied nose.

She could not help the warmth in her chest that caused her to square her shoulders and straighten her back, straining against the hands that held her. "German pig!"

From somewhere a hand hit her across the face. Her world became darker. And as her vision returned, everything seemed a little blurry.

The soldier she had assaulted was now masked in naked outrage. His features were set and stony. He took a step toward her, his own hand raised.

She turned her head. What more was she to endure?

"Stop!" a voice a bit farther away demanded.

A hush ended the soldiers' grumblings.

She peered in the direction of this new voice without exposing herself fully.

A man, medium build, with a beard and a rather gentle voice, stood in defiance to these men. And he spoke with a Czech accent. Could he be? Either that or he was a German who had studied excellently.

But was there any chance he could offer her salvation?

Pavel pushed his horse onward. The animal was weary. As well she should be. Wasn't Pavel himself in need of respite? How he had ached to bed down in the last inn they had passed. But his desire to see Karin safe had given him ample reason to push through these last couple of hours to Tabor.

The last four days had left him disgruntled and overwhelmed. Both the worry for his wife and problems encountered as he traveled served to darken his mood. He should have been able to make the trip in half the time; however, trouble with his horse and difficulty finding a proper blacksmith had delayed him more than he would have liked. It frustrated his every move until he fairly burned with desperation. All the more as he neared the quiet hamlet.

Now upon approaching the village in the middling of the night, he loathed his earlier decision. The town was at rest. How would he learn anything at this hour? He would be forced to find a place to spend the night and begin his search in the morning.

Unless...

Dare he go beyond the good sense of what his horse could withstand and journey to the next barony? Or seek out his father's castle?

Nonsense!

What would ash and smolder reveal in the darkness but that there had been a fire?

The horse slowed.

If Pavel wished to retain the destrier, he best not test if the animal could go beyond the limits of reason.

Pavel would have to find a place to lay his head in the small village. Scanning the buildings, he settled on the larger inn. The one he was more familiar with. What was the keeper's name again? His tired mind could not produce it. It was no matter.

Dropping from the horse, his knees buckled. How had he become so ignorant to the cries from his body? He should have long since stopped for rest.

Still, if he had any hope, any lead on where Karin might be, he would return to the saddle and push onward. Perhaps to his own detriment.

His heart ached for her. To hold her. To know that she was well.

Surely, she lived. Wouldn't he know if she didn't? For certain, a gaping hole would have opened where his heart had been.

Yes, she must still be alive. He had to believe that. As tired as his arms were, they would have held her with renewed strength if he could have but found her.

But as it were, he wondered if he could hold his sword if necessary. He prayed it would not be necessary. Why would it?

His steps drew him nearer the inn. The destrier just behind him.

A stable hand rushed to assist him.

Pavel did not hesitate as the eager lad took hold of the reins.

"There'll be leftover goulash from dinner inside. My mistress always keeps some warm for late-night arrivals."

Nodding, Pavel turned to the entrance, wishing he had the energy to thank the boy. Once inside the dimly lit inn, he was greeted by the aforementioned mistress.

"Oh, sire, you do look a sight!"

He could only offer a nod as he deflated into a chair.

"I was just about to turn in myself, but I'll get you a bowl of me goulash."

Pavel's mouth moistened. Had it been so dry? "Water?" He managed.

"Oh, yes, my lord." She poured liquid from a pitcher and brought it to him with a bowl of the thick stew, which was not hot, but not cold either.

He gulped the temperate liquid from the cup, not minding any sense of propriety. And then shoveled a spoonful of the meaty concoction into his mouth. The goulash was blander than he was used to. But it was still delicious. And he relished the nourishment after his impossibly long ride.

As he came to the last of the meal, he became aware that the innkeeper's wife still stood nearby, watching him. "Where is your husband, good lady?"

"Died. Last winter."

Pavel nodded.

"And I fear I must say that the drink and stew are all I can offer a fine nobleman such as yourself."

Pavel furrowed his brows.

"A lady has come to my inn just earlier today. A baroness. And taken all me spare rooms."

"Baroness, you say?" Could it be?

"Yes, my lord. The baroness what's lived in the castle not a half day's ride from here. Burned down it did."

Pavel rose, surprised at the strength in his legs. "Good lady, you must take me to the baroness. Immediately."

"My lord!" The woman held a hand over her heart. "Please, don't ask me to..."

"It is imperative." Pavel stepped toward her.

She drew back. Were his eyes as wild as he imagined?

"Good lady, the baroness of which you speak...is my mother."

Eva barely heard anything the priest said as he spoke the words of marriage over her and Zdenek. Was this actually happening? In truth, she could hardly breathe. The only thing anchoring her to the moment was Zdenek's hands enclosing hers.

His eyes held her gaze steady and sure. Was he so certain? Hadn't it only been moments ago that she questioned the reality of his feelings for her? And now they were being joined for life before God. Taking sacred vows.

Tugging on their joined hands, Zdenek pulled her ever nearer. What had the priest said? Had the ceremony ended? Was it time to seal their union with a kiss?

Zdenek's lips pressed hers, and all thoughts left her mind. There was only she and he and this moment. She forgot herself and her hands gripped his arms, certain she would float away or fall—one or the other.

He pulled back.

Still, the moment between them was thick.

Would it always be like this? This lightness? This loveliness? This intensity?

"Eva?"

She opened her eyes. The world seemed hazy.

Zdenek's mouth was bent in a crooked smile. Was he so amused?

A gentle tug on her hand drew her to face away from the priest. At the same time, Zdenek looped her hand through his elbow.

He then led her through the small gathering of Hussites and women, cheering for their comrade and his lady.

Her face warmed. Did she deserve such laud? Such celebration?

One glance at Zdenek proved to reinforce it. His green eyes shone with pride as he gazed at her.

Dare she hope that he would always look at her thusly?

She prayed he would.

Oh, how she prayed.

# CHAPTER 3

Radek stared at the scene before him. What had he said? Did he dare speak out against this group of burly men? His stomach churned. Whatever boldness had made him intrude began to diminish.

As he took it all in, his resolve strengthened. Dare he not? How could he let the men continue to brutalize this woman? Though from the looks of it, she was hardly as helpless as she seemed. For one of the soldiers held a bloodied cloth to his nose.

And her eyes, now on Radek, had a fire in them. But there was something else...

Hope. For him? Did she think he could help her?

His heart beat with more vigor. Somehow. Yes, he would do what he could to help her.

"What?" one of the men spat. The shock of Radek's appearance must have worn off. "Do you speak for a Hussite?"

What could he say that would not bring his life to the same precipice from which hers now hung? He had his weapons, but even if Stepan were to aid his fight, of what use would it be? A quick and easy defeat was all but certain.

The man with the cloth shook off his companion and stepped toward Radek. "What say you? Do we have a Hussite sympathizer among us? A snake in the grass?"

"Of course not." Stepan came forward, now standing shoulder-to-shoulder with Radek.

Did his friend wish to assist him? That was unexpected. Stepan had seemed all too ready to abandon him earlier when he spoke out about the conditions of the camp. Now he would stand beside Radek with danger so near? Maybe something of his friend still remained.

"We wish only to offer a trade. My friend here," he clapped Radek's shoulder. "Has spied this lady and wishes to make an exchange."

"There is nothing you could offer that would entice us to..."

The largest of the men stepped toward them, pressing blood-nose back with a thick arm. "I will to hear what you offer. And I may consider your desire to...entertain the lady for the evening. Under my watch."

Stepan's gaze was intent on Radek.

What did he have to trade? Radek had little to call his own on his person. There *was* his horse. He prayed that would not be necessary. That would be an unfortuitous move. How could he manage without his mare? Nor did he think relinquishing his sword, though it bore a fine hilt and boasted sturdy construction, would be ideal.

Rubbing his hands against his outer thighs, damp from sweat, Radek worried. His right hand struck his sheathed dagger—a family heirloom. Encrusted with gems, it was valuable indeed. However, its worth to Radek was far more than the jewels embellishing the hilt. It had belonged to his father, his grandfather, and many others before. But it might well be the only thing that would save this woman's life.

He pulled it free, lifting it slowly.

The large man grabbed for it, jerking it free from Radek's grasp.

Radek hadn't a moment to react before the priceless piece was gone. Perhaps forever.

The man examined the dagger as one would any object in a marketplace.

Radek's core burned. His family did not deserve for this, a constant companion in untold skirmishes and battles, to be treated like some common ware.

As the oversized German ran a hand over the gems, he smiled. Then he clasped the small weapon and gave Radek his back.

"What of our arrangement?" Radek could not help but speak out.

"You may have the woman for the night." The broad shoulders continued to be Radek's only view as the man stepped farther away. He laid a hand on the shoulders of one of his men. Only then did he stop. Making eye contact with the man who was only a half-foot shorter than he, the leader said, "You shall maintain vigil over my prisoner. Take their swords. But they may have them back when you return to the camp."

"But..." the bloodied nose German said, his voice rising.

The larger man shot him a look, and the protesting man hung his head.

As the leader continued to move away, so did his men. All but the one he had appointed to keep watch.

In a matter of moments, Radek and Stepan stood in front of the woman, relieved of all weapons and alone but for their overseer.

Her head fell. What did she expect of him? Did she think he intended to violate her? Or did she suspect his ruse? It was difficult to discern.

He stepped to her and took a knee just short of her bowed stance. Her features were difficult to see. He could only stare at the top of her head. "My lady?"

All too aware that they were being watched, Radek glanced in the direction of the man who was still larger than he.

Their overseer's features were set. Stony.

Radek reached forth, touching the side of the woman's face.

She jerked away. As she did so, her piercing gaze caught his. A portion of her light brown hair fell across her face, unhindered by pins and gatherings. But through the strands, her blue eyes found his. There was nothing pleasant about the way she attempted to stab at him with her glare. She did have spirit.

They had not broken her. He thanked heaven for that.

"Come with me."

Her breathing became harsh and more rapid. And her eyes narrowed. "I will not go without a fight."

That defiance, that resilience stirred something in Radek. Something he wasn't sure he had felt before.

"This," he said, his voice low. "I know."

Karin jolted awake. Her gaze searched out her surroundings. They were the same as when she had closed her eyes. Green, treed hills stretched out before them. How long would they ride before stopping? Even as they had set off, she struggled to maintain her hold on consciousness. Perhaps the ground had not been as welcoming a bed as she had thought. Glancing toward her father-in-law, she wished for his regard.

But his eyes were trained forward. Did he seek their destination? Or was he wary of danger that may befall them? How real was that concern?

Would brigands leap from the bushes and set upon them at any moment? Or perhaps whomever had so hated the baron's family they lit fire to his home in the middling of night would set upon them?

She forced her eyes to remain open as she scanned the area. The shrubs were still but for the movement of the wind. And all around there seemed only the sounds of nature—nothing amiss. But dare she, or the baron, read it false, it could be to the detriment of them all. She allowed herself another glance in his direction.

His jaw clenched, the muscles rippling underneath. Was he so tense?

For it was a mannerism she knew all too well. How many times had she noted the same tightening of Pavel's features. And always when he would be deep in thought about an unpleasant situation or inevitable danger.

Swirls of color gave way to his face in her mind's eye. Pavel. Why did he have to leave them? They needed him. *She* needed him.

Biting her lip as hot tears formed beneath her eyelids, she fought a wave of emotion. Why couldn't she stamp out this anger? She *loved* him. And yet she harbored resentment.

But was it not deserved? A voice, so like her own, but not quite, whispered into her mind. Hadn't she begged him not to go? And he had chosen his duty to the people over her, his wife. Look what happened.

Drawing in a deep breath and pushing it out slowly, she examined that thought. No, there was no way to know if Pavel's presence at the castle would have made any difference. Still...

No. She would not think such things.

The horses around hers halted.

She pulled back on her reins, searching for the baron.

His arm was at shoulder level. Had he bidden his men stop?

Before them, a castle stretched out upon the open land. They had made it! This must be the home of Duke Novak. Here, her father-in-law had said, they would find shelter. And they would send word to Pavel.

Would he come? She prayed so. What could possibly keep him?

The drawbridge lowered and, in due time, Baron Krejik and Karin were escorted into the inner bailey and into the waiting company of Duke Novak.

"I cannot imagine what you have been through," Duke Novak said as Karin dismounted. The man's features were drawn. Did he empathize? Or were they just words for propriety's sake?

"It...has been a trial, my friend," Baron Krejik said. Did he trust the man with all?

She would listen and discover just how deep that trust went.

"I shall see baths are drawn at once." Duke Novak signaled to one of his men.

That did sound heavenly. Karin could only imagine the sight she must present. To be clean...and in clean clothes soon thereafter.

Duke Novak turned to Baron Krejik, pressing a hand to his shoulder. "But before you depart, there is something I must share."

Her father-in-law's brows came together, his mouth drooping.

"The baroness."

The grooves in Baron Krejik's forehead deepened. "What do you know of my wife? Is she here?"

"She *was*." Duke Novak released on a breath. "But no more."

Baron Krejik turned on his friend. "What is this you speak of?"

"There is no reason to think she is unwell." Duke Novak waved an arm between them. "She left, fraught with concern after you, Baron. And you, Lady Karin." He turned his gaze on her at last.

"And you let her go?" Baron Krejik's eyes narrowed.

"I did what I could to delay her. And, indeed, I sent a contingency of my men to ensure her safety."

Baron Krejik's shoulders relaxed.

As did Duke Novak's.

"Do you know where she went?"

"The village of Tabor."

"Then that is where I will go." Baron Krejik spun.

"Please," Karin interjected. This was madness. "You must take me with you."

He looked down at her, at his friend, and then to her again. "Duke Novak will care for you. It has been a long ride. You must rest. It would be unforgivable for me to put you back in the saddle again this day."

Karin's lips moved, but she forced the words to die there. She wished to protest, but this was not the place. It would be unseemly for her to question her father-in-law. Instead, she stepped closer and put a hand to his arm. "Please, make swift your journey. And be safe." Her words were but a whisper.

He drew her to his chest. And, as hands pressed against her back, he spoke. "All will be well," his kind, deep voice said near her ear.

With great reluctance, she released him and stepped back.

He turned, shouting commands to his man-at-arms.

When he'd disappeared, Karin drew her arms across her chest.

She was alone, isolated...again.

Zdenek sensed movement beside him. He jerked awake, grabbing for his sword.

But as he reached forth, he caught a fistful of the rough blanket covering him. And small, fragile hands moved from his chest to his shoulders.

He glanced down.

It was no attacker prepared to overcome him, rather it was his Eva who drew closer to him, even as she remained in peaceful slumber. Resting back against the thin palette upon the hard earth, he relaxed and let his gaze wander over the face of his wife.

Her lashes swept over her cheeks, impossibly long. And her lips were parted but the slightest as she slept. Dark hair framed ivory features before falling over her shoulder—an angel, surely.

And she was his. Had pledged to be his for the remainder of their earthly lives. Could it be?

A powerful emotion pressed through his core and up into his throat. Could he swallow against it? He feared not.

What was this strong feeling? Pride? Love? He was uncertain. But it overwhelmed him. And he wished to give himself over to the warm and pleasant sensation. He could not help but pull her closer and press his lips into the soft mused hair atop her head.

"Please, tell me the morning has not come," she groaned.

Leaning away, he met her eyes. What should he say? How could he speak with such emotion as this filling his being?

She raised a hand and touched the side of his face. Her smile fell, and her brows drew together. "Are you unwell, Zdenek?"

He touched his forehead to hers, letting his eyes close. "No," he choked out. "I am but..." What words would encompass all he felt? What had happened between them? A word whispered into his mind. And it fit. "Blessed."

"Mmmm." The murmur escaped her.

His hands sensed the vibration in her body as she did so. His arms ached to crush her to himself, to hold her such that they would become one as seamlessly as God had promised they would. But he dare not.

"Can we not remain like this the entirety of the day?"

Moving his head, he pressed a kiss to the side of her face then to her neck. They were not going anywhere anytime soon.

Hana struggled against the two men. Who were they? Though she tried to fight her tears, they squeezed out through her eyelids. Must she betray her vulnerability? Why?

What she had hoped to be salvation had been nothing more than another opportunistic ravisher. Would she have to resist both men? Or would the bearded man be the one who...who...

She wanted to give up. To send her mind elsewhere and pretend none of this were happening. But she refused to give in. To let them take any part of her without every bit of resistance she had. So fight, she must. And push through this weariness, as well.

They pulled her into the wood. The German soldier followed... closely. Fresh air filled her senses.

At least there was that. Would it reinvigorate her? Give her that extra measure of strength?

"That's quite far enough," came the gruff voice of the German.

The men half dragging her halted. They exchanged a look. What did they communicate?

The beardless one looked at the soldier. "My friend is a bit... uneasy with you watching."

Even so, the soldier offered the bearded man a narrow-eyed glare, followed by a thin-lipped grimace. He took a step forward and ground out, "He will have to get over this...uneasiness."

Beardless one held his hands up and stepped away.

She pulled against the bearded one, pain screaming at her from her right ankle. But even alone, he was too strong. It took little effort on his part to keep her secured.

More tears. And more hopeless thoughts poured through her mind.

The soldier stepped closer to her new captors. "I tire of this. Now."

"I was told my dagger purchased the whole night." Bearded one's voice was firm but softer than the others. As if he weren't used to violence. Indeed, perhaps he was accustomed to a more gentile sort of life. Then what had brought him to participate in something so repugnant?

"And I tell you, the bargain has changed," the soldier barked. He closed the distance and gripped Hana's other arm painfully. "Shall I take her back now? Is that what you would prefer?"

What would Bearded one do now? Would that rile him up?

"No. I have kept my part of the bargain. I expect you to uphold yours." His voice remained steady and set—no tremor or nervousness in it at all. How could that be? This soldier was bigger, stronger, and more prepared to work violence upon them. Still, the Czech man did not show any hint of fear—or any other emotion.

The soldier blinked a couple of times. Did he not know what to do when others did not cower before him?

If her situation were not so dire, with her virtue and very life at stake, she might even find his reaction humorous. And perhaps this bearded man's calmness something to admire. *If.*

The soldier continued to push out heavy breaths in lieu of

responding, the bearded man pulled her free of the iron grasp, which had loosened without her notice.

"What say you?" Bearded one's eyes narrowed.

The soldier opened his mouth.

*Thonk.*

The soldier's eyes rolled back in his head, and he fell.

What? Who? *The beardless Czech.*

Had he truly surprised the man? Yes, there he stood, a large branch in his hands.

Why would he do that? His life would be forfeit when the Germans discovered what he had done.

"Make haste, Radek! We must tie him to a tree."

The bearded one, Radek he was called, looked to her.

"Please, forgive me." He tied the end of her rope about his waist. Then he stepped over, with her in tow, and helped his friend secure the soldier to a nearby tree.

It required both men to drag the hefty soldier toward the base of the trunk he was so large. Then, the beardless Czech sat on the other side of the trunk. "Now, me."

The one called Radek seemed confused.

As was she. How could he stay? Would not the Germans figure out what had occurred?

"No," Radek protested. "You must away with us."

*Away?* He would take her away from this place? Was he intent on saving her after all then? This was but a ruse? Dare she hope him the hero he seemed?

"I shall not, friend. This is where I belong. There is nothing for me with the Hussites. Perhaps, I will convince them you tricked me. It is possible."

"It is also possible they will kill you."

The beardless one shrugged. "I daresay not. My father's money will appeal if not my story."

Radek's raised brow and down-curved mouth spoke of his doubt and concern.

"Your time is short, Radek. Make haste. Tie me up and then away with you! Save yourself. Save the girl."

Then this *had* been a plan to save her life. How many Hussite prisoners had died at the hands of these foreign soldiers, bitter with the outcome of the skirmish at Vitkov Hill? And yet, she would be saved. Why?

Radek let out a breath. "I cannot make you come with me. And I will do as you wish, only because you ask it."

The man's downcast features told of the war within as he completed the task he'd been charged with. Something within her wanted to offer comfort. Where did that come from? She wasn't even certain she could trust the man.

He tied the end of the rope and crouched before his friend. Laying a hand on the man's shoulder, he spoke too softly to be understood.

The beardless one nodded and looked to the side. "Please, go. Lest you be caught."

Radek stood, grabbed his sword that had been tossed to the side along the way, and shifted his focus to Hana. "Do not fight me. We have much to do."

As he came near, her mind screamed to back away—the captive within wishing to thwart any advance. She stepped several paces back.

He frowned.

She wanted to look away, but as his eyes met hers, she found she could not. There was a depth she could not pull away from.

"Your leg, it is injured?"

She hesitated. How much to share? How vulnerable dare she risk being with this man?

"My lady, your leg?"

"It is...not bad," she lied. In truth, it throbbed terribly from her constant movements, and the sharp pain shed doubt on her words. How long could she travel on it? How far?

Radek turned before she could, gripping the length of rope

attached to her bindings and pulling her along as he headed into the dark of the forest and into the night.

# CHAPTER 4

Pavel was not accustomed to being put off. And his patience wore thin.

The innkeeper's indecisiveness drove him near mad.

She chewed at the side of her lip so aggressively it seemed as if it would bleed.

His hands, now in fists by his side, fairly shook with frustration no longer contained. "Good woman, I beg you, what will you do?"

Her gaze shot to him, her eyes peering in his direction from their corners, as she would not turn her head. She only then seemed to become aware that she wrung her hands. So, she pressed them into the folds of her apron and she smoothed over the linen. "You are certain, my lord, that it cannot wait until the morning?"

Pavel resisted the urge to sigh. He had answered this question in many ways. "I fear not. It is not for my own sake I ask, but for the lady's." He let out a long breath and leaned against the nearest table. "As well, her husband and my lady wife." Why did he give her these bits of information? He owed her naught.

One of her brows quirked. "Yer wife?"

He met her open stare, now that her face turned toward him.

"Yes, my wife. She had stayed with my parents as I went to war. I did not wish her to be near the fighting."

The woman jerked back, her features hidden as she faced the floor. "Well, now, that makes a difference. I don't have a mind to be keepin' a man from his wife."

Pavel stood and stepped toward her. "Is my wife with the baroness?"

Features devoid of color found his. "N-no, my lord. That is, I only discerned the one lady among the party. I—" She glanced toward the stairs.

"What?" Pavel advanced one step farther.

The woman didn't seem to notice.

"What say you, good woman?"

She passed a hand over her face. "I only meant to say I might have been mistaken. But I have a keen eye, I do." As she met Pavel's gaze, she backed away.

He had gone a step too far. It was no matter. This needed to be settled.

And now.

He opened his mouth to speak.

"I have your assurance you take full blame for wakin' the baroness?" The woman called over her shoulder as her stout frame maneuvered through the small room and toward the stairs.

Was it possible? He dare not test it. "Yes. A thousand times, yes."

She turned and gave him a curious look.

He tightened his hold on his tongue.

A moment more, and she preceded him up the stairs and down a hallway so small it could hardly be called such.

A man at arms stood watch outside one of the doors. That must be their destination. For sooth, they would not leave his mother vulnerable.

But as they neared, he saw no recognition in the man's eyes, nor did he see anything familiar about the guard. Had he been wrong? Why would a man unknown to him be outside his mother's temporary chambers? Certainly, he was right to assume he would have seen the man before.

He touched the innkeeper's shoulder. "Did you not say it was the baroness of the castle not a half day's ride from here? The one which was burned to the ground."

"Aye." Her brows furrowed.

Pavel laid a hand to the hilt of his sword and calmed. This would all be laid out—one way or the other.

They paused before the man standing some few inches taller than Pavel.

"Yes?" the man spoke gruffly.

"This man claims to be the baroness's son and wishes an immediate audience."

The man eyed Pavel up and down. Was he sizing up how he would fare should they cross swords? That would be unwise. How could anyone measure the skill of the hand by the appearance of the body? In Pavel's case, he was more than confident in his own capabilities with his blade.

"Is that so?"

Pavel held his tongue. Would it not be best to let the scene unfold?

"How can I be sure he is a son and not a villain come to steal her ladyship's last breath?"

The innkeeper's eyes shot to Pavel. Had she not considered the same?

Pavel worked to keep his features placid, his words even. "And how do I know the same of you, sir knight? I have not seen you performing as my mother's protector in all my years upon the barony."

The man's head jerked back on oversized shoulders. Then it settled into place once more. "Ah, but you do know something, then. Or else you think you do. I have been charged by Duke Novak with keeping the lady safe until she could be found of her kin."

Pavel ground his teeth. Were they at an impasse? Would this man not concede? "How would I know you are unfamiliar to the baroness if she, in fact, is not known to me?"

The man's eyes rolled up and to the right as he seemed to consider Pavel's question. "Perhaps. But perhaps you simply guessed well."

"I will see the lady. I insist upon it."

The man took a step closer to Pavel. They were now perhaps two inches apart. "And I insist that you leave. Since I cannot account for your veracity, I will not allow you to disturb her ladyship. No matter what tidings you bring."

Pavel's face warmed. His hands tightened into fists. Dare he strike at this man?

*Creak.*

"My lady!"

The cry came from the innkeeper, but it drew the attention of both men toward the doorway. There, in the gentle light provided by the moon and the few flickering torches, stood the Baroness Marketa Krejikova, his mother.

"What goes here?" she demanded.

The guard turned, all but blocking Pavel with his massive size. "It is nothing to concern yourself with. A small disruption that I am more than capable of—"

"If you are so capable, sir knight, then why have I been roused by the interchange?"

Pavel peered around the large man.

His mother glared at the large guard.

The man fairly shrunk at her scolding.

"I shall remedy the situation, my lady," he insisted.

Was her consideration of him so important? Why?

"Meanwhile," she put out her arm and pressed the guard to the side. "What kind of brigand has attempted to trespass..."

Her eyes met Pavel's. And she was frozen. Did she think him an apparition?

"Mother?"

She stepped around the less than helpful guard and laid a hand to the side of Pavel's face. "Is it truly you? Pavel?"

He pressed his hand over hers. "Yes, Mother. It is I."

The baroness, who had just given a tongue-lashing to the massive guard, fell into Pavel's waiting arms. And for a moment, all was right with the world.

But just for a moment.

Radek's legs ached. How long had they walked? Certainly, they had covered several miles of rough terrain. It would have been much easier without the girl to contend with. Even though he had removed her bindings, it did nothing to silence her complaints.

He groaned inwardly as the litany of protests she had all but lashed him with played through his mind like a sickening dirge. The tumbling words were broken by the sounds of water, tripping over stones. A stream?

Perhaps they could stop and refresh themselves. Even sleep. But as the thoughts tempting him to stop broke upon the edge of his mind, he remembered what they had left and the likelihood of those pursuing to catch them. Then he picked up his pace once more.

"Wait!" She laid a hand to his shoulder.

Had she come up so close behind him? He afforded her but a glance as he continued to push his feet forward.

She halted.

*Bless it all!* He paused. A growl caught in his throat. "What?"

Her eyes widened.

Had the word come out so harshly? Had he wanted it to?

"Do you hear that?" She tilted her head. "A stream. We might find respite there."

He took in a ragged breath and let it out. Must he explain every decision to her? "Yes. We might. But we cannot."

One perfect brow rose. "No? I suppose you—"

*Here it comes. Her list of reasons why I'm wrong.* Radek stepped toward her and held up a hand. "I need you to listen. Now."

They stood only inches apart. Something hot seemed to move in the space between them. Perhaps from their mutual ire.

"We cannot stop. Our pursuers still may gain the advantage we have won if we give them the opportunity."

"Our pursuers?" She crossed her arms, shifting her weight to pull away from him. Or perhaps to remove her weight from her right leg. She had more than favored it as they traveled. His concern grew for the injury. How bad was it truly? Would it soon impede their progress further? How much?

Regardless, her movement relieved some of the tension between their bodies. Radek could breathe again. "Yes, my *lady,*" he stressed the last word as if swearing. "Our pursuers."

"And just who would be pursuing us?" Her eyes narrowed. "You disarmed and bound the only men who knew of our leaving."

"Don't be foolish," he said, his tone on edge. "I only deterred that soldier for perhaps a half hour. He will have come around and made his situation known forthwith. And do not be mistaken...our *pursuers* will come by horse. As you see, my lady, we are on foot."

Her features dropped, as did her arms. Had she not considered these things? And why should she have? Outside of this war, a lady of her beauty and grace should never know such hardship. Should never have faced such abuse...or been threatened with more violence.

It wasn't right.

Even now, disarmed as she seemed, she appeared lost.

He longed to take the couple of steps between them and offer her the comfort she was due.

But he could not. She was not his betrothed, and he would not take such liberties. No matter how fitting the action seemed.

She glanced to the side. "I see."

He wished she would look at him. Would this lead to one of the female hysterics he had heard tales of? What would he do then?

But she breathed in deeply and then turned her face toward him.

"Then we must go. And make haste."

He nodded. And something warm and pleasant blossomed in the center of his chest. What was it? Admiration? Relief? Something else? There was no way to know for certain. He did appreciate her drive to push onward and do her best to disguise her anguish. He was well aware of her pain at each step. But, verbose as she had been and many her words, none had been on such.

Without knowing quite why, he held a hand out to her.

She walked past it, brushing against his arm.

It stung.

But he wasn't sure why it should.

"Don't lag behind, my lord. If we're going to make any progress with this mess of a journey, we cannot linger."

*And so, we continue.*

"I don't understand why we must travel this unmarked way. We'll fall to our death on one of these inclines — I just know it."

*Why? Why must I endure such?*

"Are you listening to me?"

Eva pulled the last garment from the water and squeezed, twisting the cloth until the excess moisture had been pressed out.

Tossing it into the waiting basket, she lifted the load easily and, balancing it on her hip, moved away from the stream.

She had volunteered for laundry duty every day this week. It allowed ample opportunity for her to daydream. It seemed that was all she had done since she and Zdenek had married. How could one help it?

It had become impossible to think on anything else. Her mind set on his face, his manner, his eyes, his smile...and the way things had changed between them. Truly, it had been a dream—better than any dream she'd ever known.

For certain, the other women's whispers and giggles were of her newfound happiness and resulting inability to concentrate. But it mattered not. This was love.

She neared camp and scanned for the best place to dry the garments entrusted to her. Her favorite spot by the big oak had not been taken. Could this day get better?

Stringing a simple line, she hung the clothing, humming. Where did the song come from? She thought on the melody as it came forth. Though familiar, it did not strike her as significant.

Still, she continued to let the notes flow as she worked. She had nearly finished her work when it struck her—the ball at the Viscount's chateau. This song had been her first dance with Zdenek. That was the tune's origin. Smiling, the song filled her senses as she closed her eyes and swayed to the rhythm of an orchestra only she could hear.

Something caught her arm.

*Who? What?* She opened her eyes.

A pair of bright blue eyes met hers. Patricie.

Eva's face heated as her sister's lips widened into a smile.

"It would serve you well not to sneak up on people." Eva grabbed for the now-empty basket. What could Patricie be thinking? Embarrassing her like that.

"Eva," Patricie plead. "I did no such thing!"

Stopping, Eva turned on her sister. "Did you not?"

"No. I announced myself. I tapped your shoulder. But you were... distracted."

"Oh." Eva dropped her gaze, wishing her face wasn't warming again. How could she have been so caught up?

Patricie laid a hand on Eva's arm. "It must have been a nice daydream." Laughter laced through her words.

Eva glanced at her sister's features. The amused expression was not one of jest but more of support. Was Patricie so happy for her?

Allowing a smile in return, Eva pulled her sister into an embrace. "How can it be that I am so blessed?"

"Because you are you," Patricie whispered into Eva's hair. "Gracious and kind. And deserving of every good thing."

Eva fought a tear as she pulled back and put a hand to the side of her sister's face. "As are you, sister dear. Your time will come."

Patricie gave Eva another amused look but did not contradict her.

"Come." Eva linked an arm in Patricie's, excitement bursting within her. "Let us make merry, for we know not what tomorrow may bring."

Eva tugged her sister forward, but Patricie didn't move. Why? Why would she not come? Turning back, a question in her eyes, Eva said, "Is something amiss?"

Patricie shook her head. "I hope not. But I have just remembered—I was sent to collect you. Zdenek seeks you."

*Zdenek?* Eva's heart fluttered in response. What might he need? She drew a breath in and let it out. "I must go to him."

"Of course." Patricie lifted the basket from Eva's arms. "I will await what tidings he brings." Then she winked. "If words are what he seeks to give you."

Eva swatted at her sister. "Patricie! Such things are unseemly for you to say!"

Patricie shrugged and turned back to the laundry.

Eva took another deeper breath. What did Zdenek want? A few stolen kisses as Patricie suspected? Or did he have something of import to say?

Karin read the words before her on the page, but they made no sense. The letters ran together and blurred. It was no use. Why even try?

Her mind was not, and had not been, on this book. Not since the first page. She wasn't even sure what the main characters' names were...or what they were seeking. Oh, what did it matter anyway?

She looked out the window, surprised when the countryside did nothing to lighten her mood. What was this heaviness?

Why would she ask herself such a question? As if she didn't know.

Pavel.

Where was he? Had he heard of their plight? Was he concerned after her? Did he remain with the Hussites at war? Or had he come after her? If he had, where was he? Why hadn't he found her?

Her eyes pricked with hot tears. No, she would not think like that. Of course, Pavel would come for her. But it would take time. He had naught but guesswork as to her location. Yes, she must at least give him that—time.

How long had it been since she had been in his arms? Two months? Three? And that short time together had been spent grieving the loss of their child. It had threatened to pull them apart. But by God's grace, their love held strong, and they clung to each other amidst the pain.

Alas, Pavel had all too soon returned to battle. Of course, she understood. Didn't she?

The time after had passed slowly. Too slowly. Long months. Longer than they should have been.

She paused.

Other than the movement of the days, nothing had marked the passing of the months. Nothing. Was it even possible? Or was this some effect...something caused by the loss? Would she now be barren?

She shuddered to her core.

But there was peace within. All seemed well. Did that mean...?

She had not been ill or uneasy in her stomach as she had been before. Maybe she made too much of it. Yet, the mark of each month passing had never failed to come, except when she carried a child.

Should she discretely send for a healer? How? Approach the Duchess Novakova? Would the woman hold her confidence? She hardly knew her.

Did she have a choice?

She did not relish the idea of sneaking from the castle into the village to visit a physician.

Perhaps it was nothing, but it may well prove dangerous to carry another child so soon. If only she had someone here she trusted to ask. If only she wasn't alone in this place.

If only...

Dropping her head into her hands, raised by her elbows on her knees, she pressed the heel of her palms into her forehead.

*God, how do I find myself in these predicaments? Show me, Father. Show me what You would have me do. Who I should trust.*

A stillness fell over her. She didn't quite know what else to pray. But somehow, that was all right. Because, if nothing else, she could trust Him.

# CHAPTER 5

Zdenek attached his bedroll to his saddle. What was he going to do? How would he answer such tidings as these? And Eva...where did she fit in?

Could he be without her for days, perhaps months? But he dare not ask her to come with him. It just simply wasn't possible.

Placing his arm on the saddle, he rested his forehead on his forearm. *Are You listening? Are You there?*

"Zdenek!" The voice of his beloved called to him.

He turned as she approached. And, forcing his lips to curve upward, he managed the best smile he could.

She moved into his embrace, falling against his chest as he wrapped his arms around her.

"Zdenek, I worried!"

"Worried?" What would concern her so? Had someone spoken to her about the letter? Who would know?

"When I heard you needed to speak to me, I thought something must be amiss."

He pulled her to his chest again. "Oh, my love, it was not my intent to cause you undue stress. All is well."

She released a long breath and melted into him.

Kissing the top of her head, he lingered in the moment. Perhaps longer than he should. But he refused to allow guilt to steal his joy in it. They deserved this happiness.

After some moments in his embrace, Eva whispered, "Why did you send for me?"

He closed his eyes. Must he speak of it? Would it tear this sweetness apart?

She pulled far enough away to meet his eyes. Confusion and concern shown in hers.

He cupped the side of her face.

She blinked at his caress but did not lean into it. Rather, she watched him.

Dropping his head for a moment, he sighed and then lifted his gaze to hers once more. "I received a letter from my father."

She stared into his eyes, unmoving. "Your father?"

"Yes. He has requested my presence." He examined her features for changes.

Her brows rose. "Perhaps he is unwell. Yes, we must prepare to leave at once." She pulled against his arms as if she would away to camp to make ready.

He held her. "You do not understand. My father..."

Her eyes seemed to deepen as they questioned what he had withheld. "Your father...?"

Why had he spoken? Opened this Pandora's box?

"What is it, Zdenek?" Her voice held a slight tremor.

He closed his eyes at the truth he must share. "My father will not approve of our marriage."

Her brows furrowed. "And you would hide it then? Am I only good enough for you here?" She jerked harder against him, freeing her arms.

"No!" He grabbed for a firmer hold. Then when she turned her back toward him, he spoke more gently, "No, Eva. That is not in my mind. It is only my concern for your well-being that keeps me from wishing you to accompany me. My father can be rather...harsh. And I cannot...I *will* not ask you to endure it."

She swallowed. Then met his gaze again as she placed a hand on his arm. "Is that not for me to decide? We are husband and wife. Where you go, I will go. Your people will be my people."

Zdenek's voice seemed caught in his throat. Her quote from the book of Ruth was well-placed. And beautiful. He marveled that she would be willing to go with him anywhere, even accept his family and whatever they might put her through. Indeed, she was brave.

He tugged at her hand and drew her into his arms. "And may God deal with me, ever so severely, if anything but death should part me from you."

Hana collapsed upon her knees. She could go no further. And that was not of her choice...but rather due to the failings of her body. Long had she surrendered her ability to hide her injury. Long had she struggled desperately to maintain any semblance of keeping up.

She stared at Radek's back as it moved away. Dare she call out? What would he think if she made plain her weakness? Had she any other option? Perhaps she fooled herself to think he did not know already.

Opening her mouth, she pressed her voice forth, but a ragged squeak was all that came. She had become parched some time ago, but truly to the point she'd lost her voice?

Radek turned—whether from the pitiful noise she'd emitted or some sense she no longer followed him, she was not certain.

But she attempted to sit straighter and prepared to bite back at his retort.

Though that was not what she found. Rather, compassion and perhaps some measure of sadness shone from his eyes. It stilled her heart. Would she prefer to find frustration there? Pity?

That may have been easier to respond to. For in that moment, she could not hold his gaze. Instead, she settled her focus on her hands, folded in her lap.

Grass crunched once more. Most likely it was because his footfalls brought him closer. Would he now levy upon her the words she anticipated? His tongue every bit as sharp as hers had been throughout this day. Perhaps she deserved such.

He stood over her now. Though he remained silent.

Too silent.

How she wished he would speak!

Any manner of words she could endure much better than this.

For several drawn out moments more his even breathing tortured her. Were his eyes upon her? Did he look into the distance? Which did she wish?

Her heart beat hard, thundering in her ears. Was it truly so loud? Or did the tension of the stillness only make it seem so?

"It is too much, my lady."

*Words! Precious words!* But...

Oh, that he had not said anything.

Too much? Did he mean to say that she was too much? That traveling with her was too much trouble? She wanted to be angry, but she could not deny the truth of it. He had endangered himself to aid her escape, and now she would become his downfall. Any fire remaining within was stamped out...save the burn of tears she fought to hold back.

He pushed a breath out. "Forgive me. I ask too much."

*What?* She looked up.

His features had contorted into a grimace.

Could it be? Was it so? The regret he felt was not with her, but in pressing so furiously onward? In truth, a worry after her well-being?

He looked at her as she turned her face upward. His lips, tight and thin, drooped into a frown. And his eyes...his deep, thoughtful eyes, softened as his brows lowered. "My lady?"

Falling to his knees, he lifted tentative fingers toward her but stopped just short of her skin. Something made her want to lean forward, just that couple of inches separating her from his touch.

"Are you unwell?"

Why would he think…?

A tear slid down the side of her face. She wiped at it without a care for how it might appear. How could she have been so weak?

Her emotions had betrayed her. Now, she appeared to him nothing more than a weeping mess.

"I am well." She met his gaze once more, forcing more confidence into her demeanor than she truly possessed.

His eyes moved as he examined her features, watching the lines of her face.

She wanted to shrink back from such scrutiny, but that would only prove that she was intimidated.

After a few moments, he pulled back and scanned the area. "I think we should rest."

She resisted the urge to close her eyes and praise God. Her limbs would have to return the silent accolades for her.

"If you can continue for a little while longer, I think we must find better cover inside the forest line." He rose and glanced to the right.

Turning in that direction as well, she noted the thickening of the trees. A sound plan. There seemed only one problem—she would need to walk an additional ten yards or so. Did she have that in her? Would her legs even obey? Would her right ankle support her weight for another step?

Radek extended his hand.

Dare she take it? Just how much should she allow opportunity for this softening within her toward him? How much should she instead keep him at a distance?

Lifting a leg and placing her left foot in front so that she was in position to push her body up, she attempted to straighten herself. But her muscles protested.

What must he think of her struggle? And her stubbornness.

She peered at him.

The soft brown of his eyes filled with concern.

She slid her hand into his before she could stop herself. For his sake? Or hers?

But with his help, she was on her feet soon thereafter. Though her legs wobbled a bit and her right ankle ached at the pressure she placed on it.

Radek gave a quick nod and released her before turning.

She stepped after him, and her aching muscles threatened to give way. Reaching out, she grabbed for his arm.

He twisted his torso and caught her arms, assisting her balance in time to keep her upright. Something darkened in his gaze. Was he upset? Or simply concerned? His lips parted. Would he speak?

"I..." she said, cutting him off "...seem to be a bit...unsteady on my feet."

His lips thinned. *Was* he angry with her? Or perhaps with himself? It became difficult to discern.

She closed her eyes, unable to look at him any longer. He had every right to be irritated. Even so, she couldn't bear it.

What would he do? Leave her? Settle her somewhere and disappear into the night while she slept? She deserved as much.

Her feet came out from under her. Opening her eyes, she braced herself for the hard stop of the ground.

It was not the dirt-packed earth, but firm arms and a solid chest that her body soon fell against.

*Radek?* She sought his gaze.

But his eyes were focused on the wooded area. Was he still angry with her?

She bit her lip to keep her words in and fought the urge to bury her head in his neck. Even as she allowed herself the truth of how much this caring act meant to her. Even if he only did so to gain time until nightfall.

She closed her eyes and swore she'd find a way to understand.

Pavel checked the straps on his horse's saddle for perhaps the tenth time.

"Dearest, where will you go?" his mother asked from somewhere behind him. The angst in her voice pulled at his heart.

He stopped and drew in a deep breath as he turned his head to the side. "I do not know, but I cannot sit by and do nothing. I must try."

The baroness looked to the ground. "How long will you search? Anything..." Her breath caught.

He could not keep his gaze from cutting to her. But his anger dissipated soon enough. For he saw the deep sorrow in her eyes.

"Say it." His words were but a breath.

She lifted her face only enough to meet his eyes. "We must believe they are alive."

A quick jerk of his head was his only response. "I shall ride to... see what remains of...the structure first."

She nodded.

Was it not strange that they had not received word from the survivors? Or were there none? Had the flames engulfed all brave enough who attempted to fight the rage of the fire? His hand cramped. Splaying it open, he realized he'd been gripping the saddle rather tightly.

He lifted his regard to his mother. But her gaze was not on him. Her eyes were downcast, with sorrow pooling within.

Did she now regret her flight to save herself the night of the incident?

How might he speak...to tell her that she mustn't. If she hadn't, her fate would be the same as...

*No.*

Karin *was* alive. Had to be. In his heart, he knew it.

Grasping the pommel, Pavel pulled himself up and into the saddle in one fluid motion.

He then sensed his mother's gaze on him. But he could not give her his—that would only make it more difficult to leave her.

She had already begged him to stay. Had been...from the moment she became aware of his plans. It wore on him.

But Karin. She was out there. Perhaps hurting. Maybe in danger.

He had no choice.

Without another consideration for his mother's grief, but carrying with him an ache born of it, he pressed his heels into the horse's flank and urged the animal into action.

A wail filled the air behind him, carried on the wind. It threatened to crack his determined exterior. But his mission was not one he dare take so lightly.

And not one he was so apt to abandon.

Not now. Not ever.

Eva sensed Zdenek shift beside her. Was he so tense? He had been like this most of the journey. It had made these last days stretch longer than they, in truth, were.

She leaned against his shoulder and rubbed a hand along his forearm. Many times, this simple gesture had soothed him, but this time it did not. Instead, he stiffened under her touch. What had bothered him so? She sought his eyes.

His gaze had become fixed out the window of the fine carriage. There, in the distance, one of the larger manors she had ever seen appeared on the horizon. Was this the landowner of the village? Or could it possibly be the home of Zdenek's parents?

Yes, she knew he was a nobleman. But this was more than she had imagined possible. It was not the first thing today that had taken her by surprise. The carriage, which had met them not far into their journey, had also been unexpected. Such opulence used only for a mode of transportation awed her.

Yet Zdenek had waved off the magnificence of the carriage and the laud of the footmen accompanying it. He merely handed over their horses' reins and assisted her into the small, but fine enclosed space.

Was he so blind to her shock? He certainly seemed to be.

Settled back against the bench, he appeared rather bored with the whole matter. And she was all but forgotten. Was this the man she married? The man who but hours before pressed his lips to hers with a tenderness that melted her and touched her cheek with a reverence she had never known? As if he cherished her above all things?

Impossible. This bored nobleman beside her did not bear much resemblance to her husband of a day ago. But then...

He continued to watch the grand house as they neared. Was that a slight tremble within him?

As she watched, he swallowed. Hard. So much so, she also heard it.

Without turning, his fingers curled around hers, gripping her smaller hand as if he needed it to steady himself.

She covered their clasped hands with her other one.

Only then did he pull his regard from the window to look at her. His gaze upon her pierced her outer defenses, searching the idiosyncrasies of her person.

"What is it?" She worked to keep her rising trepidations beneath the surface.

He looked at their hands, locked together.

"Please, Zdenek, I am your wife." She ducked her head as she leaned forward, attempting to catch his eyes.

"I...do not know what we will find. My father is not so...easy as yours. Not as...accepting of everyone and everything."

She pressed her lips together, trying to process his words. Not as accepting? Not as easy? Did he wish to tell her they would face opposition?

Hadn't she known this? Hadn't they both? From the moment he called on her after that first dance at the Viscount's ball in Hradec Kralove so long ago. But the war had changed many things. For certain, as far as the Hussites were concerned, she and Zdenek were no longer unequal.

In that, there was hope. She just had to help him see that.

"Zdenek," she said, waiting until he met her gaze before she continued. "After what has happened in Bohemia, things are different. The nobility, the merchant, the peasant...it is not what it was."

He glanced back at the now, much closer, rather looming structure. Then back at her. A slight nod was all he offered.

She smiled at him and squeezed his fingers. "All will be well. You will see. Who knows? Perhaps your father has summoned us to congratulate you on your accomplishments at war and on our nuptials."

His features were still drawn, but after a couple of seconds the left corner of his lips lifted.

Was it for her benefit though? Or because he had become convinced?

Even as she shared his smile, a heaviness settled in her stomach. Perhaps she had not done a good job convincing herself.

# CHAPTER 6

Radek wished for a blanket, a bed roll...anything that would increase Hana's comfort. She had become overtired on their journey. Why hadn't she told him?

Would he have listened? Or continued to push her? He doubted himself.

Though these last couple of days they had pressed on through much and rested little, the distance they had covered was vital for their survival. Still...

He glanced at her, lying on the ground, curled into herself, her hands folded between her knees. The night brought with it a cool breeze. No one would consider it cold, but still Hana shivered. Was she afraid?

Her face turned toward his. A sadness lay deep in her eyes.

She looked away, as if she did not wish him to see. Or did she prefer not to look upon him?

Perhaps, she processed her capture and the things that had been done to her. What *had* happened before he and Stepan found her? His gaze dropped to the ground, and his jaw clenched as he gritted his teeth. Heat filled him, threading through his veins. Monsters. That's what they were—monsters.

The stick he held snapped in two.

Her eyes shot to his again. And fell to the broken twig. She arched a brow.

He prayed the question remained unspoken. How could he answer her?

Turning away, he leaned against a nearby tree. He tossed the piece of wood to the side and then folded his arms across his chest. Where did this rage come from? Why did he care so much?

It must stop. He could not continue like this. Closing his eyes, he took several breaths and, with each exhale, he let loose a little more of the tension from his body. When his spirit found peace again, he heard the lightest whimpering.

He jerked around. Was she injured? Scared?

She lay in the grass as before, but she had tucked her face into her shoulder.

Dare he go to her? Would she push him away? Or did she need him? If she relived the things done to her, she may require a strength beyond herself. A strength, were he honest with himself, he wished to provide.

He stepped toward her.

Her shoulders shook, but she made no other motion.

Two more steps and he was beside her. It was a simple matter to kneel. He reached a tentative hand toward her shoulder. Warmth emanated from her body. Was she ill?

Undeterred, he laid his hand upon her.

She jerked back. Her eyes, reddened and raw from tears, found his. And as their gazes collided, her shoulders relaxed, if only slightly.

"I do not mind your tears, my lady. Let them come."

Confusion crossed her features.

He settled onto his knees.

"Know that you are safe. You are far from that camp and those..."

He searched for a word that would not make matters worse. "...soldiers. They cannot touch you now."

Her head dipped.

He ducked his head in an attempt to catch her eyes. "I promise. The tears will pass...in time."

Silence fell between them. But despite his assurances, she continued to sniffle and her tears flowed with no sign of stopping.

She took a few more ragged breaths and whispered.

He could not discern her words, they were soft and too broken. "What, my lady?"

She met his gaze, her eyes gleamed, shimmering with the moisture built up there. "As will you."

"I will?"

"Pass. In time."

His brows furrowed. What did she speak of? Did she mean that he would not always be with her? Did she wish him to be?

"Don't you think I know? You intend to leave. As soon as night falls, and I am asleep."

A fire lit in the center of his chest. "Why would you think such a thing?"

She turned away, looking toward the grasses to her left.

He reached forth and tugged at her chin until she met his gaze once more. "Why?"

Her eyes slid shut. But that did nothing to prevent more tears from coming. "Don't you see? I will mean the death of you. The manner in which I have slowed you this day will only be worse come the morrow. My ankle...it is bad. Worse than I thought. I know not how it will fare. What could you possibly gain from abiding me but a blade run through you?"

Leave her? While her argument may have its own sound reason, it did not shine a good light on his character.

"Look at me." He kept his tone even and soft.

She kept her eyes closed.

"Look at me." He spoke a bit louder but still with softness.

Her lids opened. The blue eyes that found his were sorrowful. And reddened. Had she lost all hope?

"I will get you home. That is my word, and that is my bond."

"But what about—"

"Trust me," he said, his voice firm. "I will not leave you. Not tonight, not tomorrow...not until you are safe within your father's walls."

She studied him. Something played behind the brilliance of the azure pools. Emotions at war. Did she gauge whether or not to believe him? Or how much?

After several moments, her eyes cleared and she fell into him.

Surprised at her movement, he was slow to respond. But after some seconds, he wrapped his arms around her. He could not deny how well she fit in his embrace. Or how much it warmed his body to have her so close. And that even something so chaste stirred his heart. A piece of him he thought no longer existed.

But he didn't want to overthink this moment.

He shut off his mind and just held her.

The gardens were rather peaceful. Karin wandered there for nigh two hours. For there was much on her mind. So much so, she could hardly make two thoughts come together.

She had been right to trust Lady Novakova. It may have taken more time than she would have liked. But within a week's time, the mistress of the castle had secreted the healer within the walls to see Karin.

And now it was certain. A babe grew within.

What was she to feel? To think? A child? Again? And so soon? How was one to manage such emotions? It took her breath away. She needed Pavel. He should be here. To hold her, to help her make sense of it all.

And he should know.

But where was he? Still at war? Or had he come for her? Was he searching even now? She prayed he was. And what of Baron Krejik? For certain by now, he should have made it to the village and collected his wife. He could have made it there and back thrice.

So, where were they? Had something happened to them? To him?

The direction her thoughts moved only dampened her mood further. She must not think such things. There *must* be hope. Had to be.

Movement behind drew her attention. She turned in that direction.

A servant girl made haste across the garden path.

"My lady," the girl's out of breath words came as she curtsied.

Karin banished all traces of her trepidation and addressed the girl. "Yes?"

"Duke Novak has sent for ye."

The duke? What might he need? Karin kept her musings to herself and rose. With the wave of her hand, she indicated that she would follow the girl. Though as she gripped her skirt to avoid tripping on her hem, it proved difficult to keep up with the girl's quick strides. Had the servant been told to bring Karin with such speed? Karin had to lengthen her stride to keep up.

They moved into the castle and through the halls until they arrived at the Great Hall. There Duke Novak stood. He seemed placid and content. Was he so unfazed by whatever errand he had sent the poor girl on?

As Karin approached, the duke waved his hand and dismissed the young woman. "That will be all."

Karin laid a hand to her midriff. Her breaths coming more shallow than she would like. "My lord, you wished to see me?"

A brow arched. "A man has come. A man claiming to be your husband."

Pavel? Here? Her eyes widened. Where could he be? She resisted the urge to scan the room.

"I have sent him to appropriate chambers. For now." The duke's features stiffened. "But I have no way of verifying that he is who he claims to be."

Karin dared not move, she feared even breathing. What might become of Pavel?

"You alone can confirm his identity."

After only a moment of silence, she nodded. "I can do so, my lord, and I will. If you can but show me to where—"

The duke held up a hand. "I should tell you that I am rather concerned after Baron Krejik. He has not returned as expected. In fact, he is well overdue."

Karin nodded.

"And now this man appears, claiming to be your husband. It is all rather suspicious. I hesitate to allow you near the man. You are, after all, under my protection."

"My lord, if I may...this man...if he is, in fact, my husband, he would not harm me..."

"If he is an imposter, he might very well do that and much more," Duke Novak interjected.

Karin nodded. What he said was true. She considered his words. What could she do? How would she stand being separated from Pavel one hour longer? "Are we at such an impasse? You must have a plan, else you would have him in the dungeon."

The duke's lips tipped upward on one side. "Well spoken. You are clever, my lady."

She dipped her head. "What must I do to satisfy your conscience that this man is who he says he is?"

The duke's lips thinned and his brows furrowed. He scrutinized Karin for a moment. "I do have a thought in that regard. But you must be agreeable to do as I say."

What would he ask? For the chance to be reunited with her husband, she would do most anything.

The pause became so extended that Karin feared he wouldn't continue.

Duke Novak motioned a couple of his servants forward.

As he began to share his plan, Karin's eyes widened. She would have to trust Duke Novak...if not, trust that God would be with her, with Pavel...with them.

Zdenek and Eva stood in the dining hall, awaiting the lord of the manor—Zdenek's father.

Eva slipped a hand into her husband's.

He responded with a gentle squeeze. She offered him a strength that was beyond himself, a strength he didn't know he possessed. Perhaps with her by his side, he could face his father. Perhaps.

Footfalls sounded in the hall just beyond the large room. Drawing nearer each second.

Zdenek's heart pounded to the same beat as the rhythm of the steps. Was that even possible?

The footfalls became louder.

And that same fear from his boyhood crept through Zdenek— filling him, threatening to overwhelm him. What exactly was that? Did he fear his father's hand? Surely not. He did not need to fear for his life. Something more then?

The doorway darkened. A man's figure filled the space.

And all thoughts left his mind.

The man's height rivaled Zdenek's tall frame. But there was more girth upon this man's stature. He stepped into the room.

The din of voices, servants milling about, halted. Were they, too, fearful?

As the great lord stepped forth, his face became better illuminated.

Zdenek attempted to discern his father's thoughts from his features. But they were impassive. Would that his mother were here. Where was she?

His father stopped in front of him and Eva.

Eva moved closer to him. But only slightly.

Father looked her over, eyes settling on their clasped hands. He grimaced.

Zdenek let loose her hand.

"I am...relieved that you have come, Zdenek."

"Of course, Father." Was his voice as weak as it seemed?

Zdenek sensed Eva's eyes on him. Perhaps his tone needed strength.

"We have much to discuss," the larger man boomed.

"Yes, Father." A tug on his shirtsleeve reminded him that Eva was beside him. He had not introduced her. "Father, I would like you to meet my wife, Eva."

"Yes. I had heard," the great man said.

There was something dismissive about Father's tone. Glancing at his bride, Zdenek could not mistake the hurt in her eyes. What was he to do? Speak up for Eva and anger Father further? "Father, I don't think—"

Zdenek's father made a motion for one of the servants across the room to come forward.

The small woman obeyed.

"Please, take my son's...wife...to her chambers."

"*Her* chambers?" Zdenek spit out. "Are we not to share as man and wife?

His father's eyes were hard. "I only expected you would wish to bed down in your old chambers. As you may remember, it only accommodates one." The man's lips twisted before righting into a smile.

Zdenek swallowed. Hard. He resisted the urge to look toward Eva. Though he sensed her eyes boring into him. Dare he speak up? Dare he not? "I appreciate the consideration. However, I...if it can be accommodated, I wish that my wife and I be able to stay together."

His father's eyes became stony. "My most sincere apologies. It cannot."

Zdenek became aware of a layer of sweat on his body. And he was no better off for his forthrightness. He let his shoulders fall, only then realizing he had tensed them. "We thank you for your hospitality."

Father's features relaxed, and his lips turned upward at the corners. "It is good to have you home."

Hana did not want to open her eyes. She had slept fitfully, still not able to accustom herself to bedding down on the ground. She wished this to be the reason she delayed in waking. But for many days she had resisted each coming day, wanting so much for her eyes to open and find her captivity a horrid nightmare and herself safe in her father's fine home.

Only it never came true.

And on this day, a new wish was birthed—to find Radek nearby when she awoke. She wanted it so badly, she resisted the coming day. So great was her desire for it, she didn't care that the morning would bring with it another long journey. If only she could have Radek with her.

Yet, he said he wouldn't leave her. He promised he would remain. Would she find him true to his word? Or only another man who had disappointed her?

She drew in a breath. Letting it out with a prayer. And, braving what may come, she allowed her eyes to open and adjust to the soft light of the early morning.

There was no Radek beside her.

But then, that would not be appropriate. Where had he lain for the night? She could not remember. Only...

Ah, yes. He had held her until she surrendered to sleep. She could still feel the warmth of his arms. But then where did he go? He would have stayed near her, wouldn't he?

She sat up and scanned the area. A patch of flattened grass several feet away caught her eye. Was this where he had slept? And now there no more. Where had he gone?

Had he slumbered only briefly? Just enough to regain enough strength to push on?

Her heart dropped. He had left her. Tears came so forcefully they nearly choked her. She pulled her knees around that she might lay her head atop them.

Grass crunched.

Jerking her head in that direction, she shifted, preparing herself for an attack. She rose, moving with uneven steps toward some bushes and crouching behind them. To what? Run? What for? She was hopeless. Would she ever make it home on her own?

She might as well let the wild animal or enemy soldier have her. And hope they were quick. But her body would not release its tension.

The footsteps measured two. A soldier then.

She looked for a weapon. A branch perhaps? Nothing looked promising.

The steps were not rushed.

Waiting for her fate was torturous.

But when the figure took shape and stepped from the thickness of the trees, she gasped. It was not her enemy, but Radek. She collapsed onto her hands and knees.

He rushed for her. "Hana!"

She held a hand out. "I am well."

He remained on his knees in front of her. Did he not believe her?

"I am simply...relieved."

"Relieved?"

What of her part should she tell? That she hadn't trusted him? She must say something. "When I heard you coming, I feared a soldier had found me."

He drew in a long breath. "I should have thought. I am sorry." His hands were on her arms then.

She let him help her to her feet.

As her eyes met his, she saw his care and consideration as much as felt it in his touch on her, the way he handled her. And she regretted her thoughts of him. Her lack of faith. She couldn't take it anymore and turned her face to the side.

As she broke eye contact, he shifted his attention. "I found berries and nuts nearby. I brought some for you." He released his gentle hold on her arms, leaving her oddly cold in the heat of the summer sun.

He moved back to where he had first appeared in the opening of the trees and gathered the dropped foodstuffs.

"I seem to have forgotten about eating." Her face warmed as she realized what she said. And she was thankful his back had been turned.

"You must be in need of nourishment." He brought the precious items near and held them out. "I can't imagine you were well cared for at that camp."

She took a couple of nuts, hesitating. Though her stomach grumbled for all the things he offered, she didn't wish to appear greedy. He would need to eat, too. Looking up, she spoke, "Please, eat."

"I had some as I gathered. These are for you."

Now, he would watch her eat?

"Here." He indicated she should hold out her hands. Dumping the items into them, he then moved off toward the edge of the forest.

She popped a berry into her mouth. Though tart, it satisfied. Her stomach ached for more. But, looking at the bounty Radek had brought, she sighed. There was plenty.

Even as she wondered what he might be doing, she no longer feared he would leave. Remembering her earlier thoughts brought a heaviness to her midsection. How could she think such? Radek had proved himself to be good, kind, and faithful.

Yes, and he would see her to safety.

*Thank you, Lord, for sending this man. For saving me from a deplorable situation. And for giving me hope.*

# CHAPTER 7

Pavel paced in the large chamber. It was no matter. He was not here for a fine room. No, he was here for his wife. And he was determined. Even as he set his mind that she was here, he prayed that it was true. For there were not any more trails for him to follow. Short of barging into every establishment, home, and castle this side of the Krokonose Mountains.

But the reception he had received had only served to raise his suspicion. What manner of game was Duke Novak playing, if a game at all? Why would he keep Pavel from his wife?

Pavel paused at the window and gazed at the mountains beyond. She was here, wasn't she? His muscles trembled with the effort to contain himself. He ran a mental sweep of the makeup of the castle —the rooms and floors of the keep. Where might she be? Could he not slip free from this chamber and eliminate any remaining doubt? As he consoled himself with these imaginings, it was as if his skin confined him, preventing him from going everywhere and searching every nook and corner.

He groaned. How long must he wait?

*Knock, knock, knock.*

"Come." He moved toward the door as he spoke. Would she be on the other side? His breath caught, and his heart stopped.

A man-at-arms appeared as the heavy wooden barrier opened.

Pavel's whole being faltered, the air within rushing out.

"Duke Novak is ready to see you."

Pavel stopped the harsh words that threatened to spill out. They would not further his cause. He nodded, not trusting his tongue even for simple pleasantries.

The man-at-arms widened the door opening and then led him from the chambers, down a stairway, and to the Great Hall.

Duke Novak sat at the high table as if to preside over a trial.

Pavel stepped into the room with two guards flanking him as the man-at-arms joined the duke. The guards prodded Pavel to step forward and stand directly before the duke.

Silence fell over the room.

Would the duke wait for Pavel to speak first? Or should he wait for the duke?

Just as Pavel prepared to break the stillness, Duke Novak spoke. "We are here to determine if you are, in fact, the Baron Krejik's son or someone sent to work harm upon the Lady Karin."

At the mention of her name, Pavel's heartbeat quickened.

"I will take any test, answer any question, provide any information you require to prove my identity. For I am Pavel Krejik, son of Baron Alexander Krejik and husband of the Lady Karin Krejikova."

Duke Novak smiled. "Your forthrightness is appreciated. The nooning meal approaches. Shall we dine and discuss the matter?"

Pavel held the duke's eyes. He did not doubt that his own gaze was hard. "Will my wife be joining us?"

"If you wish it."

Pavel's heart thudded so loud he was certain the guards beside him could hear it. "I do."

Duke Novak smiled and then indicated the chair to his right. "I would have you sit then, Lord Krejik." The address was tight. Did the duke trust him or not? Why wouldn't he?

Resisting the urge to glance about the Hall, Pavel stepped forward to the proffered seat.

The duke then leaned back and to the opposite side, speaking with his man-at-arms. Pavel took the time to scan the area. There was no sign of Karin anywhere. Only a scattering of men and servants about the space.

As the duke concluded his words with his man, he shifted his focus forward. The Hall began to fill as other inhabitants of the castle anticipated the meal.

Pavel's gaze moved over every individual that entered the room.

"Patience, Lord Krejik, patience." Duke Novak's voice broke through. "I am certain the Lady Karin will join us soon. Perhaps she only wishes to look her best for her lord husband."

Pavel offered the man a curt nod. That did not seem likely. He doubted anything would keep Karin from coming to him at the earliest possible moment. They had been apart too long.

Or was that just wishful thinking? Mayhap they had been separated *far* too long. Was she accustomed to being without him? Did she not ache for him the same as he did for her?

"Ah," Duke Novak uttered, once again pulling Pavel from his thoughts. "Here is the lady now."

Pavel turned in the direction the duke faced—the stairway. Karin's footfalls on the stairs were light and elegant. She all but floated down. His heart hammered at seeing her, but a piece of him hurt. These were not the actions of a woman desperate for him. Not as much as he had known of his Karin. Things between them may have changed. Because of the loss of the baby? Because he wasn't there when she needed him after the fire?

Guilt filled him. And he felt sick.

As more and more of his wife became visible, he became increasingly uneasy. It wasn't just the way she walked. There was something else. She...moved differently. Held herself in an odd way. He couldn't quite describe it.

Could their separation due to the war, the loss of their child, and the fallout of the fire have changed his wife so much?

Once the entirety of Karin's figure came into view, he gasped. Her face was covered in part. Why? What had happened.

He moved to step around the duke and go to her.

Duke Novak put a hand to Pavel's chest, halting him, and the duke's man-at-arms dropped his hand on his sword's hilt.

"Do not make this worse," the duke said low.

"Why is she covered?" Pavel's whisper was harsh. His eyes bored into the woman's face. There was more wrong here than the covering and the awkward movements. Was this his wife at all?

The duke leaned closer but slightly. "She suffered some...burns."

Pavel's gaze landed on the duke's eyes then. Only to find that Duke Novak had averted them. "And you did not warn me?"

"I thought you knew."

Anger boiled within Pavel. How would he have known? Did the duke assume the missive he received held such details? That was over-reaching. The man should have told him.

But why, even now, did the man prevent Pavel from going to his wife? She needed him. Needed his assurances.

Still, Duke Novak indicated Pavel's seat.

Pavel narrowed his eyes.

The man-at-arms stepped forward.

He did not like it, but Pavel would need to play this Novak's way. He would not risk any further injury to his beloved. As he sat, his gaze turned back to Karin. Though, her eyes would not meet his. She kept her regard on the floor before her steps.

As she approached, she took the seat on the other side of the duke. Another affront! Would he not share a trencher with his wife? How could he stand for this? The words rose in his throat, but one look at Duke Novak and he decided to hold his ire and let things fall as they may. But one thing was certain: he was not leaving here without his wife.

Throughout the meal, Pavel maneuvered this way and that,

trying to catch Karin's eye. Was she no more intent on him than this? He was not able to see her beyond the duke, who seemed to purposefully block Pavel. This was impossible.

But then, something moved in him. His heart was at peace, at home, and aflutter all at once. It was the same thing he felt when Karin was near. So, it must be true.

He shifted his focus to the trencher before him. But his appetite had long since abandoned him.

A flash to the left caught his attention. It was a servant girl, pouring drinks on the lower level. And what clumsy service she provided. She knocked over goblets and spilled mead more often than she poured.

The people grumbled, but no one chastised her appropriately. Then again...

Her movements, too, seemed out of place. Was that what had drawn his attention? Pulled his thoughts from his wife?

Then it struck him...he was thinking of this servant girl and her plight when he should be set on his wife and her predicament. How distasteful of him. *Lord, forgive my wandering eye.*

He shut his eyes and dropped his face toward the table.

But the image of the serving girl would not leave his mind. The way her movements were fluid and smooth, how gentle she was even in her clumsiness, and how familiar the strands of red-blonde hair that fell from her hair wrap was.

Red-blonde hair.

His eyes popped open.

It couldn't be.

He looked down at the serving girl. She was now flustered and facing off with a rather angry guard. Heat rose within Pavel.

The duke leaned forward beside him. Why?

But Pavel could not tear his eyes from this woman, no matter how he tried. Would that she could turn around!

The guard grabbed the woman's wrist.

Pavel and the duke were on their feet.

Duke Novak barked at his man-at-arms, but the man was already on the move. The solid man-at-arms separated the guard from the servant before Pavel could take a full breath and right his vision. For it had become hazy.

Pavel glanced to his right at the duke, now on his feet, and at the lady beyond. Her gaze was set forth to the activity below as well. Her hazel eyes focused on what transpired. Hazel eyes.

Stepping around the others beside him at the high table, Pavel rushed to the lower floor. As he set foot on the lower level, he ignored the duke's beckons and looked to see that the guard had been taken out and the serving girl was being escorted to the kitchen. Was she injured?

Pavel would not have it. He would not be separated from his wife for one minute more. Lengthening his stride, he was by the woman's side in a moment. But there were no words. He'd not had the time, nor the thought to construct any such fine words.

He turned the woman toward himself, severing the helping hand of the other woman servant. Then he found the familiar green eyes of his wife looking up at him.

His Karin. His wife.

Her eyes went to his. As their gazes locked, he had no more fear. But for the bruises on her wrist, for which that guard would answer, she appeared to have not been harmed or mistreated.

He was not certain what game the duke played, but Karin was whole and well.

"Karin," Pavel breathed. If he thought his skin had restrained him before, it did doubly so now.

"What is the meaning of this?" The duke's words rang out from behind Pavel. "Why would you accost one of my servants? And with your wife naught but five feet..."

"Enough," Pavel ground out. He broke his connection with Karin only long enough to address Duke Novak. "I know not what you play at, but it is over. *This* is my wife. Not that imposter." Pavel jerked his head toward the raised table.

But the duke did not seem surprised in the least. Who was fooling whom here?

"Lady Karin," the duke began, addressing the woman in front of him, the woman Pavel knew to be his wife. "I do not wish you to be intimidated. You are protected and safe within these walls. This man cannot harm you. Is this your husband?"

Karin's eyes glistened as Pavel's gaze fell on her again.

"If you need to make a closer inspection, I can have my men restrain him."

She shot a hard look at the duke. "Please, don't. I need nothing further. My heart knows this man better than my eyes. This is my husband. And he bears me no ill will nor will he bring harm upon me."

"And you are certain?"

She met Pavel's eyes again. "As certain as I am about my own identity."

Was this real? Was Karin in front of him?

She came into his embrace. There was much more he wanted to do than hold her, but that would have to be sufficient for now with so many onlookers.

"Praise God!" he whispered in her ear.

"I am whole again," she said, warming his ear with her breath.

It took all he had in him not to lift her and carry her to his chamber right then.

He raised his head to lock gazes with Duke Novak, who watched them intently. Did he still fear that Pavel might hurt his wife?

"Forgive me, Lord Krejik, but we had to be certain. You and I have much to discuss." The duke's features darkened.

What more was there to tell? No matter...it must wait.

"I beg you a reprieve." Pavel did not regret his boldness. "My wife and I have spent much time apart."

Duke Novak held Pavel's gaze for several moments before he smiled. "Granted."

Pavel looked at Karin. Her cheeks colored—his blushing bride still.

Keeping an arm around her, he led her from the many eyes in the Great Hall and toward her chamber where he intended they have a proper reunion.

The journey on foot was impossibly longer than it had taken on horse. The days had melted into more than a sennight. Had they been misled? Had he turned them the wrong direction? Radek followed the sun across the sky to gauge which was east and where was west. But he was fallible. And this he knew all too well.

Zdenek had been the directionally gifted among their group of friends. And Radek the challenged. Should he share this with Hana? Would it only worry her?

She had continued speaking...did she expect an answer of him?

"It is a wonder that the Hussites prevailed at the Battle of Vitkov Hill, don't you think? I cannot work it out. All I truly know are those things muttered under breath in the Royalist camp."

"Yes," Radek said, breaking into her monologue. "It was a wonder. Indeed. Perhaps even a miracle."

"You were there?" She paused in her step. Her stride had been eased much by a less hurried pace and by the splint he had pieced together before they started out that morn. The added support to her ankle had proved to aid her such that they covered more ground with fewer stops.

Gaining a few paces on her, he, too, halted, looking back on her. Had he said too much? He did not want to speak of that time...open doors to pieces of his life he didn't wish her to know. Still, he did not see any benefit in a lie. "I was."

He picked up his step again, and she followed once more.

"What happened?" Her words were awed. "Do you have anything to say that may make plain the mystery of this?"

What might he share? What could he share without becoming too entangled? He was not prepared to share the entirety of his experience. Decidedly not.

He glanced at her.

She watched him with wide eyes.

No, it would not behoove him to shift the subject. He would have to provide something for her curiosity, should he wish for any semblance of peace on this journey. And he did.

"I was in Prague when the battle started. And it was not long into the exchange when I became aware that the Royalists had attacked the hill."

Should he speak of Zdenek in the bunker? It had been paramount for him, for the way he followed through. Only...it seemed as if it would expose a piece of himself he didn't wish to.

"...were you?" She stared at him expecting.

Had she spoken? And now she awaited a response. "Was I what, my lady?"

Her brows furrowed. Not so much in anger, but in concern. Though he preferred her features not to be creased in worry, it touched him that she would be so moved. As he watched her, the lines on her face deepened. Was he staring?

He looked away. "I am sorry. It seems I was lost in a memory."

"It is not my wish to plague you with unfortunate things." Her gaze dropped to the ground.

A pang snagged at his heart. And in that moment, he wanted to tell her. To ease her distress. Even if it meant exposing places he'd rather leave be. "No, my lady. I will answer."

Her eyes met his and they were clear. But he noted that they held a depth...one that knew pain. Did she truly wish to share his?

"My friend was in the bunker on Vitkov Hill." His shoulders tensed at the thought of what almost happened to Zdenek. What, by all rights, should have happened.

Her eyes widened again.

"They were besieged and outnumbered...with little weaponry to defend themselves."

Her mouth became a thin line.

He forced his regard elsewhere—the hillside, the distance, the sky—anywhere but that perfect mouth. "I rushed to alert General Zizka, but he was already aware and had rallied forces to march into the fray. I, too, joined him. But as we did so, we discovered that we were few to the Royalist cavalry. The rescue, even if successful, would be at a great loss. We were not deterred, but prepared to fight to the last man." As he finished his statement, he couldn't help but peer at her.

Her concern had melted into a look of confusion. "But it wasn't a victory for the Royalists—did not they experience the great loss. How?"

"We did see losses to the cavalry. Only..." He allowed his voice to trail off. Could he even explain what happened? Was he entirely certain himself?

"Yes?"

He'd forgotten it was she who sought the tale for a moment. Letting out a sigh, he then continued. "Hussite soldiers on foot mounted the hill, the second wave to our attempt. And they were singing praises." He wanted to scoff. Had even been angered at the time. But he couldn't anymore. Not after what had followed.

"The Royalist army they...it's...difficult to put words to." Why couldn't he admit he struggled to explain because he still couldn't make sense of it himself? "They became mad. Some sort of mass hysteria. Many just fell to their deaths off the steep slope. It was simply madness. I...cannot explain it."

Several moments of silence filled the space between them. After those minutes passed, he glanced at her, hoping for, wanting for something...some kind of reassurance that he wasn't completely mad himself.

She focused on their path. And, perhaps sensing his gaze on her, she spoke. "Because there is no explanation."

"But how can—"

"Don't you see? God confused them."

"God?" How could she think such a thing? Was she as empty-headed as the rest of them?

"Yes! He brought the Hussites this great victory. Surely His hand is upon them."

What was he to say to that? Pavel had talked often of the all-knowing, all-mighty God. For certain, he believed as Hana did. And Zdenek had turned his thoughts as well. Was he, even now, speaking accolades and singing praises to God as well?

"But there is one thing I don't understand." Her eyes met his again.

*Just one?* He kept his retort to himself and waited for her to voice her thoughts.

"Why were you in the Hussite camp at that time, fighting alongside your brethren, and in the Royalist camp when you found me?" The blue of her eyes now pierced into him, no longer soothing, but seeking, peering into his soul.

Not certain he liked that, he swallowed and looked away—off to where the ground met the sky.

Still, she waited.

"I was not...well-placed in the Hussite camp."

"Not well-placed?" Her words were soft, as if she only sought understanding.

He stopped and turned to face her. "I found, after some time, that I could not submit to the authority of General Zizka."

She remained silent, just watching him, listening. Her eyes had softened. Was that compassion?

"Hana, I saw things. I...*did* things under Zizka's orders that I'm not proud of."

"And you thought you might find a place in the Royalist camp?"

He glanced off, squinting against the sun. "I don't know."

"What does God say to you?"

He let out a breath. "God."

"Yes—God."

Meeting her eyes again, he matched her fervor. "God has never been more to me than a story."

Everything in her seemed to deflate. She blinked several times. Would she cry? *Please, no.*

"I apologize if that is difficult for you to hear. But I see no reason to disguise myself."

"I wouldn't want you to." Her voice broke.

"And I see no reason for us to delay our progress any longer." He turned and resumed walking, hoping she would do so as well. Because he refused to look back.

Eva lay in her bed. Alone. She couldn't quite grasp what had happened. One minute, she had a husband. And the next, it was as if she didn't.

Hadn't she known Zdenek's father could be a sore spot? Still, be that as it may, she never imagined it would be like this...that Zdenek would let the man separate them. Make it appear as if they were not even man and wife.

What host would not allow a husband to lie at night with his wife? She, born of a merchant, had not enough experience with the nobility to know what infraction this might be...if any at all. But within a township, it would not be done. Anyone would give up his own bed rather than deny a man and his wife the privilege of each other's company.

A tap on her door startled her.

Was it on the door? She turned in that direction, inclining her ear. Nothing.

She lay back down. It must be her imagination.

*Tap, tap, tap.*

There it was again. Louder. But only just.

She moved to the edge of the bed, slid her legs off, and stepped to the door. Dare she open it? What if it were someone who meant her harm?

"Who is it?" she whispered harshly.

"It is I, my love."

Zdenek's voice.

She opened the door.

He fell into the room and sealed the door behind himself.

Gathering her into his arms, he held her to himself. "I am sorry it has to be this way. Please, know that."

She let him enclose her within his embrace and even enjoyed the comfort it brought. After the chilling reception and a dinner that had been an equally cold event, brightened only a little by the appearance of Zdenek's mother, Eva was desperate for the warmth she found in his arms.

In fact, Eva had longed for Zdenek's arms in those moments—for his protection from his father's steely gazes. But it was not to be had. Even now, as he held her, the solace she sought was not there. And the war in her was not soothed. She still ached.

"What is it?" Zdenek pulled back.

Had he sensed her resistance? She looked toward the window.

"Eva," he said, smoothing back a stray hair. "Tell me."

Her eyes met his. "How could you not know?"

The dimness of the room, lit only by the moonbeams seeping in, made it difficult to discern the minutia of his features.

He became silent. His hands slid down her arms, but kept hold of her hands. "You don't understand."

"Then help me."

Zdenek released his hold altogether and stepped to the edge of the bed. He sat there, rested his head in his hand, propped on a knee.

She stepped across the space, stopping just in front of him. "We are one now. Share this with me."

"My father is...difficult."

"I can see this."

He shot her a glance that rivaled those of his father's.

She leaned away.

Standing, he pulled her into himself once more. "I am sorry. I just...I can't put it into words."

She wanted to resist his arms, but as stung as she was, she needed them.

"I love you," he said on a breath.

Pressing her face into the crook of his neck, she bit her lip.

"You do believe me, don't you?" His voice was insistent.

She shut her eyes as tight as she could. Would the tears stay in?

"Of course." Her voice was shaky. Perhaps he wouldn't notice.

"Come, my love, let us rest." He tugged her toward the bed and sat.

"But—" She did not let herself be pulled down beside him.

"I don't care what he may think." He continued to urge her onto the bed.

She gave in. For she was weary and much in need of her husband to be with her.

"My father may put us in separate rooms, but he cannot keep me from my wife's side."

Eva tried to push aside the thoughts of how strange this all was. Because she wanted her husband beside her as she slept. She *needed* him with her.

So, she no longer resisted as he helped her lie down.

And seconds later, he stretched out beside her and pulled her to himself.

Sleep found her moments later.

Karin allowed Pavel to lead her through the halls. As they topped the stairs, she pulled him toward the chambers assigned to her.

His brows furrowed, but she offered him a reassuring smile as she tugged him to the door that remained the last barrier between them and the privacy the room afforded.

He opened the door, swept her in, and shut it soundly behind them. Then she was against his chest, his lips pressed to hers.

Heaven.

Her hands, against his chest, moved into his hair. It was longer and tinted even more blond from the sun, and she reveled in the thickness.

He held her impossibly closer as his mouth moved against hers. And when he broke contact, he buried his face against her shoulder, his lips pressing kisses there and to the tender places on her neck he knew she liked.

"I missed you," he groaned.

"And I you," she sighed.

He drew her to the bed.

She wanted to get lost in the wonderful feelings he stirred in her and in the fullness of his love...but he needed to know.

Moving her hands to his face, she placed one on each side of his mouth, stroking his jawline.

He slowed his caresses.

She pulled back to look into his amazingly blue eyes. "I must tell you something."

"What is it?" He searched her face. Did he seek whether the tidings were happy or worrisome? He need not bother; her news would not be long in coming.

"I am with child."

All was still. He was as a statue.

"Pavel?" What was the matter? Was this not happy news? Why wasn't he embracing her again? Celebrating?

He dropped his head to her shoulder.

She wrapped an arm around him and put a hand behind his head. "What is it?"

"I cannot."

"Cannot what?" She became concerned.

"It is too difficult." He lifted his face to catch her eyes. "I cannot walk this road again. It was too painful. What if...what if I lost you, too? I could not bear it."

Yes, she had thought this. After the loss of their first baby... nothing about this would be easy. Still, she wanted to be happy, to thank God for the new life.

"There is no reason to think this baby will..." She found she could not say it. "That God will not give us a healthy baby."

The pain in Pavel's eyes was naked and raw.

"The healer said the pregnancy is good. That the baby is well. That I am well. There is no reason to worry."

He watched her, searching her features.

"We must be happy when we can. God has blessed us!"

Still nothing.

She grabbed his hand and pressed it over her abdomen, already slightly swollen.

His eyes lit at the swell even he could discern.

"That?" His voice came so gentle, it was almost a whisper. "Is our child?"

She nodded.

He knelt. Placing both hands on the sides of her abdomen, he put the side of his face to her belly.

She wondered at his connection. The babe had not yet made itself known with movements she could feel, but she could tell this was still meaningful for him. And she blinked at the moisture in her own eyes.

He stood and drew her face to his again, a kiss that held both promise and passion.

She reached for his tunic and held him to her as she deepened the kiss.

He pulled her toward the bed once more then paused just short of the mattress. "Wait. Is it wise for us to..."

Wise for them to...? What could he mean? But the look in his eyes said it all. "I have the healer's blessing."

He grinned and kissed her. "Good."

"And you have mine." She smiled then kissed him again.

That was all the reassurance Pavel seemed to need. And their reunion would soon be complete.

# CHAPTER 8

Zdenek urged his horse up the hill before him. Why did his father insist on turning everything into a competition? There would be no peace if he won. Though it wouldn't be much better if his father returned the victor either. What was the right choice?

He steadied his mare and allowed his father's horse a better start going down the hill. That was the only real option.

When they met at the base, Father's face flashed with pride. "How does it feel to know that your old sire can still best you?"

"It gives me hope that I will one day grow in skill." Zdenek pressed on one of his more charming smiles.

Father nodded. "That is true. If you will take heed."

"Yes, my lord."

Had he and Eva been with his parents a fortnight? It did not seem possible. And in that time, he had made no progress with the man. His father had not been in any hurry to play out whatever plan he had, either. Why had he summoned Zdenek? What was yet to be revealed?

His father glanced into the distance. What held his attention so?

Zdenek turned. There, on another hilltop, stood the neighboring manor not too far off. But it couldn't be so close. How long had they ridden?

Zdenek knew this place. The baron, only a few years his father's junior, had a daughter but a few years younger than Zdenek himself. They had been thrust together often, but never quite took a liking to one another.

"I wonder how Lucia fares?" Father gave Zdenek a hard look.

"I know not." Zdenek turned his horse and worked his brows downward. Would that communicate his disinterest? Hint to his father that he should venture no farther? Instead, Zdenek set his eyes back the way they had come. "Shall we return? I am certain Mother and Eva will be—"

"I believe she has grown into a rather lovely maiden."

What did his father play at? He feared he knew. And he did not like it. Not one bit.

"I think we best return to my *wife*."

Father waved a hand. "Your mother can entertain the little Hussite girl."

It was as if Zdenek had been struck solid in the chest by a thick pole. The shock and pain of it reverberated from his center in all directions.

*Little Hussite girl?* Is that what his father thought of Eva? Zdenek's mouth moved, but he couldn't form the words. He swallowed.

"Perhaps we should visit our fine neighbor? We are old friends, after all."

His father's words were muffled, as if he heard them through thick wool. He heard them, yes, but they lacked sense. There was, too, the great difficulty putting his own words together.

His father seemed to take that as assent. Shifting his larger body, his father angled his darker horse toward the manor and launched the animal in that direction.

"Father—" Zdenek called.

But the man neither halted nor slowed.

What could Zdenek do? Return to his father's home, collect Eva, and never see his parents again? Didn't Eva agree that he should reconcile with his father? What might become of his mother if Zdenek left her to face Father's anger? No, he must do what was necessary to make things right.

He turned his horse once more and followed. Only this time, he cared not about letting his father win. Zdenek poured his frustration, his anger into driving the horse.

Pressing his legs and heels into the animal's flank, he urged even greater speed. As he closed in on his father's horse, his blood pumped harder, thudding in his ears. Yes, he would best his father. And he would not regret it.

But was he pushing the mare too far? She continued to give him the speed he asked for. Could she give more?

As he neared his father, he pressed the horse again with his boots, begging for a last burst of energy.

The mare shot forth, leaving Zdenek's father behind. How long would it take before Father would consider just how many races his son had let him win?

Hana bit her lip to keep from crying out as Radek worked out a splinter in her hand.

"Aren't you going to remind me that you warned me away from the broken branch?"

Radek, intent on her injury, did not so much as shake his head.

"I appreciate your chivalry."

Although, with his hands holding hers and his face so near, her thoughts were certainly not of his being chivalrous.

What was wrong with her? She had to stop these vile thoughts. Now. Before she said or did something she would regret.

"*Ow!*"

"My apologies, my lady." His eyes sought hers.

It didn't help that his face was only inches from hers.

Her features warmed. Indeed, all of her seemed a bit heated. Then again, it *was* mid-day in the summer.

His brows furrowed. "Are you holding your breath?"

She was. Letting loose the pent-up air, she then drew in freshness, relishing the relief as it filled her lungs. It was pure and clean and...warm. Like his eyes.

Something changed in Radek's gaze. "Maybe it would be best if I not—"

"No!" She put her uninjured hand on his arm. "You must. I cannot abide the sight of blood, and it stings."

He watched her. Perhaps too intently.

"I'll be calm. I'll hold my tongue and keep breathing."

A curious look fit onto his features.

"I assure you."

He dipped his head over her palm again.

She imagined if he pressed his lips to it. A warm puddle filled her middle.

*Stop it!*

She turned her mind to the stick, tossed by the side and to the right, that had caused the injury.

Why had she insisted she needed it? Her ankle had fared well in the wrapping Radek had made. True it was sore, but it did not pain her as it had before. Still, when she happened upon the broken limb an hour earlier, she thought it might be useful, helpful even. But Radek's warning that the branch, in the places it was broken, may cause her injury, rang in her ears.

She had gloated for nearly the full hour, happy to throw his words back at him...until this shard of wood embedded deeply in her flesh as she leaned on the staff coming up the last hill.

Now, here she was, thinking things about Radek she had no right to while he attempted to rid her of the foreign object.

"I have it," he said, a calm sound. "Don't move."

She forced herself to stay as still as possible. That's when the burning began. And it continued for a few seconds.

"It is done," he announced before letting out a breath and leaning away. He held the offending object in the palm of his hand. A tiny piece of wood.

She widened her eyes. How could something so small cause such injury?

"You are still in pain?" His brow creased.

She shook her head, not trusting her tongue as his eyes, his lips were still quite close.

He lifted her hand once more and blew, lightly, on the injured place.

She could not tear her eyes away, nor stop the bumps rising on her flesh nor the hairs on the back of her neck standing on end as evidence of his effect on her.

He watched her face.

The wisp of air halted.

"And now?" His voice had a husky quality.

She nodded. Or did she? There was no way to be certain.

He brought the reddened flesh to his lips and pressed a kiss to it.

A small cry escaped. She wanted to pull away. Something. Anything to keep him from discerning just how much he affected her. But her body seemed to act of its own accord. Her fingers touched his beard.

He lifted his mouth from her hand but cradled it. Still, his eyes had not left hers. And now there was a question in them.

How was she to answer?

He leaned toward her, lifting his other hand to touch the side of her face as his nose brushed hers ever so lightly. "Tell me to stop, Hana."

When had he stopped calling her 'my lady' and started addressing her by name? She liked it.

Closing her eyes, she leaned her forehead onto his.

His breathing became ragged. "I need you to stop me. I find I cannot."

She sighed gently. "I find I don't want you to."

He turned his face and captured her lips. His kiss did not demand, or overpower, but invited, welcomed, tested.

She wanted more. Moving her hands to his shoulders, she attempted to draw him to herself.

He reached for her hands, taking them in his. Letting loose her lips for a moment, he said, "A wise man needs not behave as if there are no limits."

She didn't understand, but she trusted him. He had not led her astray. So, she surrendered her lips to his once more and let him keep space between their bodies.

Then she lost herself in him.

Pavel sat beside Karin. He could not keep his gaze off her. How long had it been since they'd been able to be together? This war had all but consumed him. Only...not here. Not when he was with her.

Duke Novak had let them be for the last several days. It was as if they were newly married once more. They had been left to themselves without disturbance, save the nooning and evening meals.

And it had been glorious.

Still, Pavel sensed that the duke wished to speak with him. With them. There was the issue of Pavel's father. He had gotten only pieces of the story from Karin, and that had been somewhat blurred.

His father had brought Karin here as he sought out the Baroness Krejikova. Upon arrival, they had discovered her recent departure into Tabor. And so, Pavel's father had gone to collect her, leaving Karin in Duke Novak's capable care. No one had heard from Pavel's father since.

If this were so, why did Pavel not intercept his father on the journey here? What *had* happened to the man?

Duke Novak caught Pavel's eyes at the high table during the evening meal.

Pavel nodded in his direction.

"I believe, Lord Krejik, it is time we deal with the matter of your father."

"I agree." He gave the man more of his attention. "But I wonder what is to be done? By these accounts I have heard, I should have crossed paths with my father during my time in Tabor."

The duke nodded.

"I saw neither a sign of him nor any hint of anything amiss."

"Perhaps your sire simply went by another way?"

"Even so, I would think him to have arrived in Tabor before I left."

"'Tis a reasonable assumption." Duke Novak steepled his fingers and nodded. His features were grim.

"What do you suspect?" Pavel's voice dropped. His breath caught, but he worked to keep his own face neutral.

The duke glanced at Karin. "My lady, I apologize. But it may be best these things be discussed in private."

Pavel reached for Karin's hand. "My lady wife has been through much. I trust you will find her strong of spirit and able to hear what you have to say."

"Something...or rather some*one* stirs trouble in western Bohemia."

"Yes, I have heard of the civil unrest."

"That is not of what I speak. It is the deliberate acts—the burning of Baron Krejik's castle, the taking of innocent men... Nefarious acts. Troublesome things."

Pavel's brows rose. "Do you know of such men who would rise up and commit such atrocities?"

"*A* man...who would oppose General Zizka. A man who would dare show support for Sigismund and fight for that man's cause within the boundaries of a Hussite-controlled Bohemia."

"Who?" A thickness filled Pavel's chest. He fought it down, this heat, this anger rising in him. What a daring man indeed—to light fire to a man's home in the night—a home where the man's wife, daughter, and servants slept. And then to ambush a man on an errand to reunite with his family...such were acts of cowardice.

His fingers curled until his hands were fists.

"Ulrich of Rosenberg." The words were out of Duke Novak's mouth, and they could not be unsaid.

Pavel looked down as he flattened his hands on the table. Yes, he had heard this name...from Zizka's own mouth. This man had captured a group of priests and executed them all. A man who had well earned the title 'enemy.'

"I will find this man. And he will be punished." The words came through clenched teeth.

Duke Novak nodded. "As well he should."

A small sound came from the other side of Pavel, and he turned.

There sat his beloved, pale and wide-eyed. Had his anger and tone scared her?

He must seem a monster to her! Forcing his anger to dissipate with each breath, he then reached for her.

She resisted his touch at first, but soon let him take her hand after a moment.

"My lady wife, do not worry. I am a soldier. And I am trained for such things."

"That is exactly what I am afraid of," she whispered.

Eva took her seat beside Zdenek and prepared for yet another long dinner. She had not seen much of her husband this day. He and his father had been riding and even visited the neighboring barony.

Something had passed over Zdenek's face when he mentioned it, but he would not say anything further.

It stung that there may be something he kept from her. When did they start keeping secrets from one another? And more, a secret to do with his father?

No, she didn't like this at all.

As she took her seat, she rubbed his forearm and offered him a gentle smile.

He returned her smile, but briefly. Then he shifted his focus to the meal. How could it be that a man could be so different with her in private, and then someone else when in the company of his parents? But it was so.

As the meal commenced, Zdenek and his father conversed lightly about their visit.

Eva soon became bored with the whole affair. She looked to Zdenek's mother. But the woman remained quiet, focused only on her trencher.

"And wasn't Lady Lucia even lovelier than you remember?"

Zdenek drew back just enough for her notice and shot a look in her direction.

*Lucia?* He hadn't mentioned this lady before. Why wouldn't he? She met his eyes, but he wouldn't hold her gaze. Her heart stopped.

What was going on here? Her stomach turned, and she became nauseated. She had to get out of there. Now.

"My lord, if you will ex—"

A servant approached the table, a letter in hand.

"What is it?" Zdenek's father's voice boomed.

"A missive. For your lordship's son."

Zdenek's father indicated to whom the servant should deliver it.

Reaching for the letter, Zdenek took hold of the paper with shaking hands.

Why might he be nervous? Was it not she who should be off put?

As he looked at the writing, Eva fought between staying and going. Which was best? Perhaps she could excuse herself. She felt less and less like his wife in this place.

"Will you not read it?" his father all but shouted.

"My lord, you might excuse me. I am not well." Eva glanced at the man who hadn't looked at her but to find displeasure.

He didn't bother to look now. Only waved a hand in her direction.

This must be some kind of nightmare.

A hand caught her arm. She peered down.

Zdenek.

Her eyes met his. She shook her head and pulled free. And, without looking back, she walked out of the Great Hall and to her chambers. There she fell onto the bed and let her tears overwhelm her.

How long she lost herself in that state, she did not know. But a knock on the door jerked her out of her reverie.

Had Zdenek's mother come? Of her own volition? Or by compulsion of her husband or son?

She sat up and wiped her tears. But she could do nothing to clear the effects of crying from her face. For certain, her eyes and cheeks were red and puffy.

"Come," she called.

The door opened, and Zdenek entered.

She looked at her lap. "I do not wish to speak with you."

"Eva, don't let my father tear us apart." His words seemed half-hearted.

"You are doing well enough on your own." She stared at him. "Why did you not tell me about the noble lady you saw today?"

He pushed a hand through his hair. "I don't know."

"Because you enjoyed her presence? Because she was beautiful? Because you wished for a wife more refined as she?"

"No!" his reply was sharp. Then he softened. "Of course not."

She fixed her gaze on her lap again.

"I didn't tell you because it was meaningless, and I didn't wish to have this conversation."

Should she believe him? He had been secretive of late. Why?

"Don't let my father win."

She pushed out a breath. "Me? What about you?"

"Fair enough. But there is more to this than you may think."

What could he mean? Why wouldn't he just tell her?

"I...hoped to share this missive with you." He stepped farther into the room. "It's from General Zizka's camp."

She looked at him then. "General Zizka? What does it say?"

"It talks about the civil unrest in Bohemia. And tells that Zizka's army is to search out Ulrich of Rosenberg in Tabor. He is calling us back to war."

Eva stood. "He needs us. We must go." She crossed the room and began gathering her few things.

"It is not so simple."

She stopped and turned to look at him. "What are you saying?" Why did she fear she knew the answer?

"My father does not wish me to go."

"What of you? Of me? Do we get a say in what *we* do?"

"Yes, of course." He stepped to her and laid his hands on her shoulders.

The gesture that should have been natural between them felt somewhat awkward now.

"And we will go. I promise. But my father has some things to speak with me about."

Eva let out a deep sigh. "You promise?"

"Yes. We will leave one month from today."

She backed out of his reach and crossed her arms. "One month? But we have already lingered a fortni—"

"Yes, yes," Zdenek said, his eyes pleading. "That is what my father requested. How could I not give him that?"

"You have been a man of war, Zdenek. The tide of an entire war can change in one month. We *need* to be out there, doing what we can to preserve Bohemian freedom."

"I agree. And we will be."

She eyed him.

He took a step toward her, closing the distance. "I am trusting my father. Will you trust me?"

This was her husband, the man she spoke vows with. They had promised their lives to each other. She could grant him a month with his parents.

She nodded. "Of course, I trust you."

He opened his arms, and she leaned into his embrace.

A month...she could find some way to survive, couldn't she? Maybe Zdenek's father would even change his mind about her.

# CHAPTER 9

Radek assisted Hana's near-slide down the rocky hillside. As she no longer used the oversized stick, he had offered to let her hold to his arm. He considered it a compromise. Or perhaps, he simply enjoyed this connection to her as they walked.

What was this between them? Attraction? Heat? He might accept many words, but not love. He had no place in his heart for love.

Everything he had ever loved was gone—most certainly his closest friends. Would he see them again? With the ongoing conflict of war, where did he belong? He was neither Hussite nor Royalist. Where did others go? Must he pick a side?

Hana, it seemed, belonged in the Hussite camp. That would never be for him. Not again. And so, they would ever be at odds.

No, this was not love. Could not be.

Her hand slid down his forearm and into his. She intertwined their fingers.

He glanced toward her features.

Her eyes looked to him only briefly before turning away. Was that a tug of a smile upon her lips? What did she think this was?

Did she think him in love? If so, did he risk leading her astray? He must be careful to maintain proper boundaries and give her no encouragement, no thought about a deeper connection. More, he must let her know the ways that they could never be compatible.

Yes. That would work. Must work.

For she was intent on the Hussites. And God.

Neither of which would ever be right for him.

He turned back toward her to speak of the Hussite general and his misdirections, and he caught the widening of Hana's smile—a smile for him and only him.

Indeed, she trusted him. How could he take that away?

He but wished to ease her journey and see her home to safety...to care for her and make light her load.

For the rest of her days. A lump caught in his throat. Oh yes, he was in love.

Karin lay upon the thin mattress and slid under the covers. She bemoaned the emptiness of the space beside her once again. And so soon. Too soon.

Pavel had been summoned by Duke Novak. The man had wanted more of her husband's time. And while she did not appreciate it, perhaps it was best on this eve. She needed time with her thoughts.

Much had occurred these past days. Had the Krejiks' castle burned only two months prior? And then the waiting for Pavel, the babe, and Pavel's return followed in succession. Much indeed.

Still something was amiss...

The door opened, and her time of quiet came to a close. Her husband was both too soon and too long in coming.

The rustle of clothing behind her and a shift in the bed alerted that Pavel had joined her.

She faced away from him and made no attempt to move. How could she let him see the worry upon her features? The evening meal had been a couple of hours past, but she had not yet been able to bring her expression under control. It told more than it should.

Pavel scooted until his body was just behind her, fitted to hers. He rubbed a gentle hand down her arm and kissed her shoulder. "Are you well?"

How could she answer when her emotions were so uncertain? She found she did not know. So, she refrained.

"Karin?" His voice bore in it the strain of concern. And confusion.

"I am...well." She couldn't keep her voice from shaking.

"You don't seem well." He drew her shoulder across and down until she lay on her back, looking up at him. As his gaze took in her face, the nuances of the fine movements of her body, his features contorted all the more. "Why so worried?"

Her chest shook. Tears spilled. But she bit her lip to prevent any sound, so they came in silence. "You are not the same."

He lay a hand to the side of her face. "I don't understand. I am who I say—the man you married. One and the same. How can you not know me? What can I do to prove it?" There was deep pain in the depths of his blue eyes, darkened by emotion.

She shook her head, cutting off another cry that threatened to slip out. Taking in a ragged breath, she calmed her voice as much as she could. "No, I know you are, in person, in truth, my Pavel. It's just..."

"What?" he prompted when she didn't finish, his eyebrows pressing downward.

"I fear this war has changed you." She pressed her lips together then to keep her sorrow in check.

His mouth became a thin line. Was he angry?

"And I don't know what to do." Her wavering voice betrayed what she fought so hard to keep hidden.

He shifted onto his side and pulled her into his embrace.

She wanted to resist, but she needed his arms more. The steady beat of his heart reassured her. And there she pressed the side of her face, listening to its steady rhythm.

"There are...rough edges you had not encountered. And they may be more evident now. Especially as we are faced with a villain who wishes to..." He was silent for a moment. His skin seemed to warm. "...*has* hurt those I love dearest in the world. I do not relish that it bothers you. I am not perfect. But I am human all the same."

She released a muffled cry and, turning her head, pressed her face into his chest. His words at the evening meal and the force of them had frightened her. Was there a monster growing within her beloved? Would it come out at some unexpected time? Even be directed at her? Or their child?

"But this is a thing of war. Of hating evil."

She nodded against him. Was it true? Or something said to make her feel at ease? Perhaps he did believe it. That didn't make it true either.

Pavel let out a long breath. "Let us pray together. And ask God to show us, to show *me* how to tame it."

She looked into his eyes. *There*...that was her Pavel.

He wiped at her tears with the pads of his thumbs. "Shall I start?"

"Yes." She shifted to rest her head beside his, laying her hands over his heart as he began to pray. Yes, this was best—for God, more than anyone, would know what to do.

His words to the Lord were heartfelt and true. She also lifted her own honest concerns. And after they prayed, she was more at peace.

"You are tired?" He kissed her, the contact more brief than she would have wanted.

"Such is the way, I'm told." She smiled.

"The way?"

She pressed a hand to her belly.

"Ah...of course."

He placed a hand on top of hers and smiled. These moments were treasures.

"I do have something I would speak with you about." The corners of his mouth, which had creased, fell.

Fear gripped her, but only just. *I will trust Pavel. I will trust God.* She worked to keep her face neutral. "What is it?"

"I received word from General Zizka."

"Oh?" Dread threatened to overtake her again. She continued to fight it, swallowing...hard.

"There has been much civil unrest, as you well know. And he comes to Tabor to root out this man...this Ulrich of Rosenberg."

"What will you do?" She spoke before thinking.

"I must join him when he arrives. I have given the man my sword."

"What of your father? Your plans here?" Again, her words fell from her lips without a thought.

Pavel frowned. "Likely, this Ulrich is the very same who has taken my father." He searched her eyes. Did he suspect there was more to her words than concern for his father? That she spoke more for herself than she revealed?

Though, while she did have thoughts for Baron Krejik, her concerns were more after Pavel and the possibility of his going back to battle. She didn't like it.

Meeting his gaze, she became desperate for some way, for words, for something that might keep him with her.

"But what of..." She stopped herself and held her tongue. How could she speak for herself in such a way? Dare she be so selfish? Would she go so far as to remind him of their lost child to keep him with her and thus quiet her fears of losing this one?

"What of...?" Pavel prompted, his voice soft. Did he know of the thoughts in her mind? His hands caressed her arms. Did he seek to soothe her? "What is it, my love?"

"It is nothing." She turned away.

"Look at me," he entreated her with gentle words.

She did not wish to. For he would then see the hot tears spilling anew.

"See me, Karin." There was more force in his tone. But the back of his hand traced lightly along the side of her face.

He had been through much. How could she deny him her regard? Even her tears? Could she not now trust him?

She turned.

His eyes felt a caress upon her features as he took every part of her in with his gaze. "If you wish me to stay. You need only speak it."

She closed her eyes. "I fear I ask too much."

"Then let it be for me to say." He cupped the right side of her face, letting his thumb trace her lips. "I will stay."

She sealed her lids tighter against tears of joy as she grasped his hand, moving it that she might plant kisses against his palm.

"I will write the general in the morning. He is a reasonable man." His words were warm on her face and a pleasant rumble against her chest.

She drew closer into him again. There was no denying the relief that washed over her.

As his arms held her tight and secure, she gave into her emotions. How could she thank God for this gift? For this man who understood her unspoken request and would honor her in such a way? She had never and would never know such love as this if ever he were taken.

And that terrified her to her core.

Zdenek awoke, his wife in his arms. Everything was well. He tugged her closer, pressing a kiss to her hair.

She stirred, leaning into his kisses, then turning to face him. Still, her eyes remained closed.

He scanned her features. What was this? Was she playing at some manner of coyness with him?

Angling his head, he placed a gentle kiss to each lid. Then trailed kisses down her cheeks, her nose, until his lips claimed her mouth.

At last, she shifted and came to life. Raising her arms, she then ran her hands across and around his shoulders.

Zdenek pulled at her waist, a familiar hunger sparked within. He needed her. Now. From what he could discern, she was more than willing to oblige.

A knock sounded on the door.

Eva jerked the covers up and shot a look at him, her cheeks coloring a bright red.

He shrugged, wishing he could do more to ease her discomfort. "I cannot answer," he whispered. "I'm not supposed to be here."

She rolled her eyes. "Who is it?"

"Bianca, my lady. The baroness asked I assist you in your preparations this morning."

Eva's eyebrows drew together.

Zdenek wondered at her confusion. Was this not normal? His mother always had a lady aid her.

"A moment...please," Eva said, her voice louder than necessary. She glanced at Zdenek and whispered, "What are we to do?"

"I care not if a lady's maid knows I am here."

As soon as the words left his mouth, he regretted them.

"Not a lady's maid? Who then should not know? Would you be put off if your father knew that you lay with your wife? I? An embarrassment?" She slid from the bed.

He wanted to reach for her. Or explain. But neither seemed appropriate. Would they only anger her more?

"Let me help you, then, my lord. You won't have to risk your father's ire again, as you will not be permitted in my chambers." She crossed her arms over her chest and looked away.

"Eva, you must know I didn't intend to—"

"I wish you to go." She glared at him. "Now."

He picked up his tunic. And, jerking it on, passed in front of her. But he halted just before her for a moment. What did he have to lose?

Placing a hand on the side of her face, he caressed her cheek with a thumb. "You are everything to me. More than all of this. That's why I married you. This thing with my father...is a complication. You are my ever after."

Her mouth moved as if she chewed at the inside as she closed her eyes. Did she fight tears? That he could not bear. He walked to the door and opened it.

The servant girl stood just beyond.

She feigned shock upon seeing him, but there was a tell in her eyes. For sooth, she must have heard him through the door. Stepping to the side, the younger woman revealed that Zdenek's father stood behind her at the top of the stairs.

He stared at Zdenek through narrowed slits, his face reddened.

Zdenek's heart dropped.

"Were your chambers not sufficient?" Father seethed.

*No, my lord, for they lacked my wife,* Zdenek wanted to say, longed to say, drew in breath to say... But what came out was much simpler. And more the lie. "Yes, my lord."

"And yet, I find you here." It was not a question.

Zdenek hung his head as if a boy, caught cheating on a test. Or worse—an adolescent, found to have defiled a maiden. But this was his wife. Why should he feel such shame?

Raising his eyes to meet his father's, he forced the words out that he had to put confidence in. "My wife had need of me."

"Is that so?" Father took a step closer.

Zdenek lost any further words and stared at the man.

The man glanced beyond Zdenek and the lady's maid toward Eva. Then he fixed his gaze on Zdenek, his eyes again narrowing. "If you must know, and I think it best you hear it from me, the Catholic Church will not recognize your marriage. It is an abomination. As far as I am concerned, you are soiling that maiden and risking a pregnancy that could ruin you both."

Zdenek had no words. Even his very breath had rushed from him.

His father continued, pressing into the room. He moved past Zdenek, and past Eva. "What I did, I did to protect you. And now I see it is for naught. That you have no qualms in dishonoring me and going behind my back?"

Zdenek's jaw had slackened. He sputtered for a moment before finding words. Any words. "The Catholic Church...ruining?"

"Yes." Father's words were resolute as he stood at the window, looking to the hills beyond.

"B-but the Catholic Church is no longer the rule in the land. Do you not see that?" Surely his father could not be serious. Could not expect him to cast his bride to the side.

Father's head turned, and the hard gaze landed on Zdenek once more. "Not in this moment, but it will prevail. It has always prevailed. Know this."

Zdenek did not have adequate words for the man before him, who had insulted his wife, declared his marriage a sham, and insinuated that he was consorting with a harlot.

Zdenek's father moved toward him, his eyes set on Zdenek's, his gaze intense. "Heed my words, *son*. If you continue and get that Hussite girl pregnant, it will be to your detriment and her undoing."

His father then brushed past him and walked out of the room and toward the stairs.

Zdenek followed him for several paces but only watched as he stormed down the stairway. Then Zdenek set his head in his hand. How was he to repair this? At least...

He turned.

By the bed stood Eva, tears flowing freely down her face.

"Eva, I don't believe—"

She slammed the door so hard the sound echoed in the hall.

Was it his imagination, or did he hear faint laughter coming up the stairs as well?

Hana tired of the journey. Should they not have reached Prague long ago? After all, they were not such a far distance away. Only across the Vlatava River.

When Radek did not lead them over the river initially, she assumed it was to throw off anyone who might pursue them, but they had traveled now for several days. Should they not now cross? Dare she question him? How might he receive it?

She glanced at him, walking not three feet's distance from her.

His jaw was set. And his eyes scanned the horizon. Were they lost?

Reaching for his hand, she made contact and halted.

He stopped his forward motion, turning toward her. In his eyes, she saw the questions she did not wish to answer—why had she paused? Did she have something to say?

She looked down to see his hand drawing back.

Licking her lips, she did not relish the conversation forthcoming. For it may draw them farther apart. But it must be had.

"Radek," she began. Her eyes focused somewhere on the ground. She should meet his gaze. He deserved that. But she found she could not.

"Yes?"

She sensed more than saw him lower his head. Did he attempt to catch her eyes? How she wanted to peer up and meet those eyes, that gaze. But fear kept her head bowed. "I...um...only thought...that is, I considered...how long we have been...traveling."

There was silence. Thick silence. After long moments, she looked up.

Radek considered the landforms around them, eyes narrowing slightly.

She fought to keep her arms by her sides. The desire to touch his face almost overcame her.

"Radek?" she whispered at last.

He exhaled and dropped his regard to the ground, shifting weight from one leg to the other. "I should have told you. Long before now. I had thought perhaps I would, but could not bring myself to speak of it."

She touched his arm without a thought. "You can tell me."

His gaze met hers. There was doubt in the soft brown. And regret.

Did he feel so judged by her? "I am not so certain where we are. Or how to get back to Prague."

Biting at her lip, she forced herself to swallow. It wasn't as difficult as it could have been had she not already considered as much.

He continued to watch her. Did he seek absolution? Anger? What *did* he expect?

More—what *did* she feel? As she checked herself, she could not discern the anger she had anticipated within her person. Only understanding. Their flight from the Royalist camp had been in the dead of night. Too, it had been harried. If Radek had mistook their way, it could be forgiven. For how could she hold this against the man who had risked all to save her?

"Say something." He pushed out another breath and jerked his head to the side. "For I know you are conflicted."

What had he seen in her eyes that she did not find in herself? She took another moment to consider herself.

Radek's breathing was ragged and heavy, his emotions nearer the surface than perhaps ever she had known of him. He stood before her vulnerable, perhaps even prepared to be shamed.

She inched forward. Now, only half an arm's length separated their bodies.

He fidgeted. His head dropped as he closed his eyes.

Lifting a hand to the side of his face, she spoke. "If I am conflicted, it is the war of my regard for you, not of some anger borne of a choice you made in effort to save us."

He lifted his head, his eyes meeting hers. Was it her imagination or were they glazed? It could not be.

"And of your regard for me?" His voice was firm, yet a softness caressed the words he spoke.

She pressed her free hand against the other side of his face, and she set her forehead to his. "I find myself more and more unable to... fight...my heart and its desires."

His eyes closed.

"For it seeks you, Radek, above all else. And I can no longer hide it. Will you be kind and tell me there is a hope?"

His hands moved and fingertips grazed her face. Then his lips were upon hers. Soft and gentle, then searching, as if a question were being asked.

She responded in kind, wrapping arms around his shoulders as he pressed her ever more to himself. Their kiss soon became more fevered; a passion awakened that she had not known.

And he pulled back.

She whimpered. Why had he—?

He gathered her into his embrace. "My lady, we dare only push so far. There are limits to a man's restraint."

She longed to press farther into his shoulder, to nuzzle his neck, and urge him back into their intimate kisses. But she heeded his wisdom. Still, his arms were bliss. So, she remained silent and relished them.

After some moments, the rumble of his voice against her drew her attention. "Don't you wish to know how we will find a way?"

"I care not," she said on a sigh.

A throaty laugh escaped him. "The truth remains the same. We must get you home."

"Must we?" She did not wish to be parted from him. If only they could stay in this blissful ignorance of the world around them—of the war, of the realities that people with their differences were not well-suited for—

"Do you wish to walk the rest of your days? Live off the land?" His levity lightened her mood. But only just.

"Perhaps not." Her lips lifted.

Radek pulled back, leaving her with an ache. He indicated the direction they had been walking. "We make our way northeast. This I know."

But the river would have turned northward after passing Prague. She pulled back farther to look at him better. "Not north?"

"No." His brows lowered.

"I should think we might try north by northwest."

"That may lead us over some ground we've covered."

She furrowed her brows. Was that something to cause concern? "And you fear we are still being pursued?"

He shook his head. "No longer."

"Then?"

Radek looked northward and back over his shoulder in the westerly direction. "We shall do as you suggest."

He pressed her to himself once more. And she felt a weight not previously levied upon her settle—the heaviness of their survival. She bore a part of that responsibility now.

And she wasn't certain she liked that feeling.

# CHAPTER 10

Pavel considered the landscape before him. He let out a long breath. Had he chosen well?

For certain, it was good that he honor his wife's needs. Zizka was more than capable without him. In fact, it was rather arrogant to assume the man needed Pavel's sword. As if the general's tactical skills were not enough. Or that Pavel's abilities outmeasured those of any number of Hussites among the fighting men.

Pavel shook his head. There was more to it. Images of Karin—stricken, pained, in the depths of sorrow after the loss of their first child. He wasn't certain he could understand the full toll it took on her body. How safe was it for her to carry another child so soon? Should he be more concerned?

He could not deny that he was. And that drove his decision to stay. Not Karin's pleas. Or what he saw in her eyes. Not that those things didn't move him. They had cut him to his very soul.

But it had been more. Much more.

*God...*

*Where are you? My heart aches to the point it fairly bleeds. Can you offer me some assurance? Some peace? Will my child live? Will my wife? What will be?*

*Do I stay? Or would you have me serve my people at war? Ask anything of me, Lord, and I will do it. Just tell me that my wife and child will be well.*

The sun beat down upon him, its rays warming him. But something had changed. It seemed as if he were being heated from within.

What was this? What could it mean? Perhaps it was the hand of God upon him.

He bowed his head and knelt. *Speak, Lord, your servant is listening.*

The silence around him became thick. Not even the birds dared to break it. Still, Pavel embraced it. And sought the Lord in that stillness.

How long he remained, he did not know. It could have been mere moments, it may have been hours. His heart inclined toward God Almighty as he waited for some sign, some word that would guide him, let him know what he was to do.

The moment broke when a presence approached from behind, breaking the solitude that had captured him.

He turned, a hand on his sword.

Duke Novak stood some distance away. He nodded at Pavel.

Releasing his hold on the hilt, Pavel stood and faced his host.

"I did not intend to disturb you." The duke's words were delivered without emotion.

"You did not, my lord." Pavel looked to the horizon once more. Why had God not answered?

Duke Novak took several steps closer. "I must speak with you."

"Of course." Pavel tilted his head.

The duke's gaze narrowed as he watched Pavel. What was in his mind? Did he still harbor some disbelief about Pavel? "I understand that General Zizka has returned to Tabor."

"Aye, my lord. My understanding is the same. I believe he seeks to end the cruelty of Ulrich of Rosenberg." Pavel's hands curled into fists as he remembered the grievances numbered against the man.

"And we are in agreement on this: that it is likely Ulrich has taken your father."

"Aye," Pavel ground out, as he looked to the side. Would the duke venture where Pavel preferred left alone? To his reasons for remaining? Was Pavel ready to defend his decision?

"Yet, you have given me no word, no indication that you shall make ready to take your leave." The man's features hardened. "An oversight, perhaps?"

"No, my lord. I do not intend to do so at this time." Pavel met the duke's gaze. It became difficult to maintain a neutral expression, torn as he was. And put off at the man's reaching into areas best left alone.

The duke frowned, and his brows furrowed. "I do not understand. Will you not join Zizka in his efforts? You care not to seek out your father?"

Pavel let his eyes close for a moment and let loose an extended breath. Why must the Duke push into matters that were not for him to determine? "It is not that I do not wish those things."

"Then what could keep you?" The duke's voice rose slightly.

"Because you have been good to my family, I will speak true." Pavel found the courage to catch the man's eyes once more. "It is of concern for my wife."

"Your wife? Do you not think her safe within these walls?" Duke Novak became more agitated. His face colored, and his eyes widened.

"That is not so. I do not question your ability to protect my lady wife. It is more to do with her...condition."

"Condition?"

"We have not yet spoken of it, but she carries my child—"

The duke's demeanor melted into an openness Pavel had not before seen. His smile broadened and his features warmed. "That is wonderful news!"

"Yes." Pavel hoped to quell the congratulatory spirit before the duke made a scene. "But all is not as it seems."

The duke halted his open-armed advance toward Pavel. "Not as it seems?"

"This is the second time the lady has carried a child. The first time, it came to naught." Something hard hit the bottom of Pavel's stomach. Something he couldn't describe. His insides became unsteady.

The duke remained quiet. Perhaps a bit too quiet. He stared at the ground, but as if he saw through it. At length, he spoke. "I know this pain."

Pavel opened his mouth to ask further. But a glance at the man, lost in a world of sorrow, prevented anything further. Would there ever be a time it didn't hurt?

Seconds bled into minutes. But as quickly as it started, it was over and the duke spoke again, "Alas, Lady Karin is strong. She will prove herself able. I know she will."

Duke Novak laid a hand on Pavel's shoulder and offered him a somewhat forced smile. A moment later, his hand dropped and he turned back toward the donjon, a slowness to his step. It seemed the matter of Ulrich and Zizka had been forgotten altogether.

And for all Pavel's seeking and beseeching, he found he wasn't any closer to an answer than he had been before.

Radek gathered food for his and Hana's evening meal...if it could be called that. He tired of living off berries and nuts. Did she? How he wished to provide her with meat alongside the simple things he could find in the forest. If only he had a bolt and crossbow. Perhaps he might use his sword? An awkward hunting tool, yet he was becoming desperate. When they drew near the river, they would at least have the fish he could spear.

For now, it would be whatever the forest could provide from its bushes and limbs. At least it would sustain them.

He returned to where he had left her.

She sat, her knees gathered to her, her eyes scanning the area surrounding her as the sounds of dusk falling upon the wood came to life. The animals that awoke for nighttime made their presence known. Was she so uneasy?

He could not suppress the smile that pulled at his lips. Perhaps that was not so unlike the many ladies of his acquaintance. The secrets held in the depths beyond the tree line were foreign to them. Still, no harm would come to her. Not while he could keep her.

Even if the sword were not the most ideal hunting implement, it would provide sufficient protection from much of what lurked beyond.

The noises did not disturb him. There was the call of the owl, the screech of a bat, a rustling of the small creatures on the forest floor... all preparing to take their meals. Not so different from him and Hana.

Her head jerked in his direction, and she met his eyes. The blue orbs were wide and concerned. But the fear there melted in his presence.

Warmth stirred anew in his chest. She trusted him so deeply...put her life, even, in his hands. Was he so capable?

Her chin dipped, and her cheeks colored. Had he made her blush? And he realized he stared. How could he not? The light brown hair surrounding fine features shimmered with golden touches in the moonlight. And the gentle beams served to highlight her complexion. It seemed as smooth as porcelain. Would it be as cool to the touch?

Drawn to her, he stepped forward and dropped to his knees. After setting the foodstuffs between them, he wished to raise a hand to the side of her face and find the alabaster as he remembered it— soft and warm with life.

As he looked closer, he saw that the ivory skin had been marred by dirt from the journey. It seemed wrong somehow.

She lifted her eyes to meet his. Did his gaze require such intensity from hers?

He tore his focus from her and looked toward the gathered items. "I have brought our meal."

She glanced at the ground but soon met his gaze again. "I see." Licking her lips, she seemed to be asking for more from him.

Was he prepared to oblige? Dare he?

His heart thundered in his chest. It took everything in him to resist pulling her into his embrace. But the perhaps wiser part of him warned against it. Night had fallen. Things became more dangerous. Yes, it would be best if he...if they...did not become overly affectionate.

He leaned back and soon settled, sitting where he was, still a good two arms' lengths away.

Something passed over her features. Disappointment?

That was not his wish. But if it must be, it must.

She pulled her legs to the side, granting her access to the items he had set between them.

"You have not told me," she began, popping a berry in her mouth. "What will you do now?"

He could not help but stare, almost losing hold on the handful of nuts he held, as the red berry passed her lips, nearly the same shade. How had the evening become so heated? Shouldn't it be cooling?

"Radek?" Her brow creased.

Had she asked him something? He shifted his gaze to her eyes. "Yes?"

She appeared concerned. "Are you well?"

He coughed. "Quite." Shoving the few morsels from his hand into his mouth, he reached for the berries. But he thought better of it and grabbed a few more nuts.

"I asked you what you would do now?"

"Now?" What could she mean?

"Yes. Will you return to the Hussite effort? Or...go elsewhere?"

She turned her attention to the foodstuffs. Did she not wish to mention the Royalists? After what they had done to her?

He swallowed. What prompted such a thought to begin with? "It is...complicated."

How could he answer her when he had not come to a conclusion himself? Where *did* he belong? He could not follow Zizka, nor could he abide by the practices of the Royalists.

They continued to eat in silence for a few moments.

Then she spoke, her voice quiet, timid almost. "You might allow God to show you."

Ah, this was the heart of it—God. Why must she push this point?

"As I said, God has never been more than a story to me," he pressed out, trying to communicate his displeasure with the very idea.

Her eyes did not leave his. And her face was unreadable. Had he stunned her? Injured her? Still, he found he could not hold her gaze for more than a few seconds.

She spoke into the moment with gentleness and a strength that surprised him. "But He *is* more than that. I could—"

"What is your goal?" His voice came out harsher than he'd intended. "What do you hope to gain?"

The twisting of her features reflected the effect of his abruptness.

She looked at her hands in her lap. "I only wish that you not lose your soul."

"My soul? I..." What did he have to say to that? For certain, she cared for him. Was this some misguided way she showed it? He took in a breath and measured his voice. Leaning forward, he lifted her hand. "I appreciate your concern for me. I do. But I think you must let me care take my soul."

"But—" Her voice was pained.

He shook his head. "Let *me* wrestle with it."

She nodded as she dropped her head. His words did not set her at peace. But he became confident she would let it go. And perhaps, at last, they could be as they were.

He offered her a smile.

She did not return it, but she did press his hand with her fingers.

He noted the slump in her shoulders, the way her whole being sighed, the weariness that seemed to pervade her being. "You must be tired."

She nodded.

Wishing once again he had something to soften the ground for her, he watched her lie down. Her eyes set on him.

"I will sleep soon," he said, moving the food farther. "But after I visit the nearby stream."

A small smile graced her lips.

"I will return soon." He scooted closer and laid the back of his hand to the side of her face. It was every bit as smooth and fine as he remembered from earlier touches.

She took his hand in hers and pressed it to her lips.

His eyes widened. Should he pull away? Dare he not? *Could* he?

But after the contact that set his blood afire, she released his hand and shifted, turning away from him.

He watched her for a moment before pulling back. What had happened here? How had he let this happen? Was there any way to stop it? Did he want to?

At length, he stood and traversed the wood the short distance to the small stream nearby.

He crouched and splashed cool water on his face, his hair, and, removing his tunic, refreshed his body as well. All the while, he wondered after what he had ever heard or known of this almighty God—a God who had never done anything for him. The God his father claimed to know.

It had made the man meek—the weakest among his warriors. And his house was not well-kept. Father was too kind, too generous, too forgiving, and too understanding. He showed mercy instead of strength, grace instead of correction. It didn't work. His army thought him soft, and they were right. The man barely maintained a hold. If it weren't for Father's man-at-arms, he would have been overtaken by now.

This God left a bad taste in Radek's mouth. Not only did it make his father weak, this deity divided Radek's homeland, drove Zizka to do things that were vile, and tore friendships apart. God indeed.

The water had long since dripped off him and dried. Radek stood and pulled on his tunic. Picking up his sword and belt, he carried them as he turned back to the makeshift camp.

He tried to push the issue of God to the back of his mind. It would do no good to continue to struggle with it. As much as Hana, or even he, might wish it, nothing she or anyone said could change his mind.

Soon enough, he neared the place he had left her. But Radek paused a few paces away. Something was not right. He could sense it. Pulling his belt in front of him, he placed a hand on the hilt of his sword.

Before he stepped farther, he strained to the limits of his ability to hear. The sounds of animals at the hunt continued to echo through the trees, but nothing else...

*Wait*...there was something.

He inclined his head, tilting it to discern what he had heard. Faint as the sound was, but most certain—a scream.

*Hana?*

He rushed forward and into the clearing where she had lain. Nothing.

She was gone.

Eva looked in the mirror as the servant sent by Zdenek's mother laced her dress. She'd never had anyone assist with her preparations, save the few times Patricie managed her hair. But a sister's touch was much different than that of a stranger's. And a servant at that!

Still, she did not pay the woman much heed. Her thoughts were too tangled.

Zdenek...his father...and the things that had been said only two days past. They were horrendous. Just the memory of the words turned her stomach. She lay a hand across her midsection.

"Is it too tight, my lady?" The woman paused.

"No." Eva shook her head and looked down.

The servant went back to her work.

Eva stole a glance at herself in the mirror. Why did she stay? Why bother? Zdenek's father did not wish her to remain. And Zdenek did not care enough to stand against his father's wishes. How long would it be before their marriage was declared void and the man had Zdenek remarried?

A small whimper left her lips. She raised a hand to stop any further noises.

The servant paused once more. But remained silent. What was she doing?

"It isn't right."

Eva kept her hand clamped over her mouth. Had the older woman truly spoken such?

"I shouldn't say it, my lady. But I've been with her ladyship for many years. It isn't right—the way that man treats her...and the way he is treating you."

Eva's vision blurred. And moisture baptized her features. Dare she face the woman who would be so brave as to speak out against her master?

With a brush of skirts, the woman moved a few steps to the right.

Eva could no longer watch herself fall apart, so she let her gaze follow the sound.

The servant gathered the things needed to make Eva's hair presentable.

Presentable.

Why would she think such a word? As if she weren't acceptable as she was. Wasn't she?

Not in this house.

She stepped to the waiting stool and allowed the woman to pull at her hair, this way and that. Her tears dried as the minutes passed.

Eva stole glimpses at the servant's face—kind. Or at least she seemed so. Could she be as understanding as Eva wished? What she needed so badly was an ally. One she could trust.

But what was there to say? Eva feared if she opened her mouth, all that warred within her would pour out—her frustration with her husband, her sadness, her fears, her doubts, her pitiful conclusions. But she had to start somewhere.

However, when she did permit herself to speak, she whispered only two words. "Thank you."

The woman stopped and met Eva's eyes in the mirror. A smile so slight it would almost be missed and the tiniest nod was passed to her before the woman continued her work.

It wasn't necessarily an alliance, but it was a start.

*Knock, knock, knock.*

The older woman's eyes caught Eva's.

How could Eva know who it would be? Would Zdenek's father dare speak with her alone? Or did Zdenek have the courage to face her so soon?

She shook her head, trying to communicate to the servant.

The woman, thin lipped, nodded, and moved to the door. "Who is calling?"

"It is the lady's husband."

He did sound sad. And lost. It almost broke Eva's resolve. But the sting of his earlier actions—his unwillingness to defend her—gave her strength. She gripped the seat until her fingers ached.

"Her ladyship is not receiving at the time, my lord."

Silence.

Would he force his position? Or honor her request?

A light *thunk* gave her to think he thrust his forehead against the door.

"Aye," came his muffled reply through the thick oak. "I shall speak with her in the Great Hall."

Eva held up a hand as the maidservant turned.

She halted.

Listening, Eva kept the lady in waiting at a pause. For some moments, there was no sense of movement beyond the door. But at some length, the faint sound of footsteps in the corridor gave her confidence that he had walked away.

She dropped her hand and released her breath, nearly falling over. Had she held it so long?

"My lady!" The woman rushed to her side and gripped Eva's shoulders should she indeed lose consciousness.

Eva offered a small smile. "I am well."

Nodding, the generous woman came back around to Eva's hair.

Eva squared her shoulders, sitting straighter, and focused more intently on how the woman wove her long tresses into a tamer, more contained design.

If only the emotions raging within her were as easy to put right.

Karin awoke with a start. What had disrupted her sleep? She stretched an arm out for Pavel, and her hand landed on his pillow.

He was not there.

She sat up, prepared to call out for him. But his form was silhouetted in candlelight as he sat on the edge of the bed.

Scooting closer to him, she placed her hands on his bare shoulders and leaned against his back. "What troubles you?"

He turned, his features in profile betraying his turmoil.

"Pavel?" What could it be? Was he so disturbed?

"It is nothing to concern yourself with, my love." He raised an arm to press her head to his shoulder. "I did not wish to waken you."

"Nor do I wish that you lose sleep." She pushed against his hand, turning so she sat beside him. "Tell me. What keeps you from your rest?"

He dropped his head.

What could be so terrible that he did not wish to share it with her? Her heart beat faster. Was something amiss between them? Was he hiding something?

"Pavel, please..." She drew her hands to herself, clasping the front of her chemise. "I must know."

He shifted to face her and placed hands over hers. "It's nothing that should cause you fear."

Her breathing calmed. "Then what?"

His eyes glistened in the flickering flame. They were serious. She could no longer see any hint of laughter.

It drew her back to that first meeting. When his eyes so captivated her. And the way his smile lit the intense blue such that she lost herself in his gaze. Now those orbs were darkened. Like the sky when a storm was coming...muted, near gray. One more thing that had been lost to this war?

"What is it?" His brows furrowed.

She shook her head. "Just...caught in a memory."

One side of his mouth lifted, but the half smile did not reach his eyes. "I pray it is a good one."

"Yes." But she could not admit that it made her ache for what had been.

He cupped her face, caressing her cheek with his thumb. And, leaning in, he brushed his lips against hers.

Was that all there was in him?

His forehead rested on hers.

She stole a glance at him, but his eyelids had closed.

His words came, breaking the moment. "I fear I have made the wrong choice."

She pulled back. "The wrong choice? Staying with me?" A sharp pang hit her heart.

He took her hands. "Yes, but hear me—"

Wriggling her hands free, she continued, "You...you said all I had to do was say it."

"I know." He dipped his head.

"And then *you* said it." A heat filled her chest. And it rose. "Now, it is as if I made you stay."

"Karin!" His voice was abrupt.

She widened her eyes and froze at his tone.

"You know that is not what I meant."

She blinked. He had never spoken to her thusly.

"Please," he said, reaching for one of her hands, enclosing it in both of his. "Listen. I only meant that I struggle with *my* decision to stay."

Licking her lips, she fought the urge to speak. Her mind screamed for her to listen. But the rising ire bade her prepare her defense.

"It seems as if I should be out...there." He motioned toward the window. "With the general. Looking for *my* father. Helping search out the man who took him and probably burned down my family's home."

Was it her turn to speak yet?

"Can you understand that?" His eyes met hers.

The turmoil naked in the stormy blue-gray melted her defenses. Her planned words were crushed. Because, in that moment, she wanted peace more than she wanted to be right. She wanted to understand her husband as he had sought to show her compassion on many occasions. More than she could count.

"Yes." Her eyes filled. "I can."

He continued to watch her, a softness in his regard.

After some moments, when she longed for him to speak so much that she prepared to ask for his thoughts, he opened his mouth.

"Thank you." The words were not much more than a whisper.

She moved to his chest, and he enveloped her in his embrace.

How long she remained in his arms, she was uncertain. But at length, she began to feel the whole of the day and the lack of sleep upon the night.

"I fear I must return to bed, ere you find me asleep upon your person." She tilted her head upward and smiled at her husband.

He kissed her full on the lips. A more meaningful kiss than before. "I shall oblige you, wife. But only if I may lie beside you."

"Ever you shall, my lord."

He let out a throaty laugh. That one she loved so. And from her position, she felt it vibrate as she was pressed against his chest. And as she continued to lean into him, he shifted her toward the bed.

Moments later, she lay upon her pillow, covered, and husband beside her, reaching to put out the candle.

*Knock, knock, knock.*

Pavel's eyes met hers.

Was it a dream? Had she become so sleepy?

But his alertness made her believe it was indeed someone at their door.

"Be still, my love. I will see to it."

How could she be still? Was it friend or foe?

He stepped to his discarded tunic and slid out his sword. "Who goes?"

"My lord, come quick! Your father has been recovered. They are bringing him forthwith!" The identity of the voice was neither discernable nor truly important.

Karin sat and moved to stand.

"No," Pavel commanded. "Stay. I will see to this news."

"But if your father—"

"If he needs help, there is naught you can do." Pavel pulled on his tunic. "He will require a healer."

"Still, I would like to be with you." How could he ask her to stay behind?

He crossed to the bed and placed a hand on her face. "I do not wish you to see him. He may have any manner of injury. Think of the babe. My father wouldn't wish it. If you must do something, speak prayers for him."

She nodded. "That I will." Why must he treat her as if she were so delicate? Because of the first loss? Or would he have been this way regardless? There was no way to know.

He dropped his head and claimed her lips once more. But only briefly. As he pulled away, he spoke in a gentle tone. "Please, rest. For me. For the babe."

She nodded and watched as he strapped his sword on and walked out the door.

Who would bring Pavel's father to the castle? Would they convince Pavel to join the fight?

Though she lay back, her thoughts raced. And her heart was worried.

# CHAPTER 11

How had he gotten into this?

Zdenek looked after Eva as she ascended the stairs.

She had not given him the slightest opportunity to speak to her. Or had he not taken it? Insisted upon it? Dare he follow her and force the issue? Would that make things better or worse?

"Zdenek," his father called from across the room.

He turned in that direction.

Father stood behind his place at the high table, the captain of his guard beside him. Had they been conversing?

Zdenek looked back toward the stairway.

Father cleared his throat.

And Zdenek didn't need to turn to know that his father glared at him. He could feel the searing of the heated gaze upon him. Still, his wife needed him. His marriage hung in the balance. Could he sit by and watch it teeter precariously? How much longer would it survive? But if he defied his father...

He shifted back to the Great Hall.

Father returned his attention to the man next to him.

As Zdenek moved farther into the Hall, his mother's eyes caught his. He saw a sorrow there he wasn't certain he had seen before...but yet, it was familiar. Somehow. Was he certain he had not seen this upon her countenance before? Or perhaps he had simply not taken notice?

Zdenek paused as he passed her, letting a hand graze hers.

She bowed her head, and her breath caught. And though no words were spoken, he sensed her support, her consideration for his plight.

He needed to go to his wife.

Pulling his shoulders back, he then pressed his chest forward. Maybe it would display a confidence he didn't quite feel. He looked to the high table and drew in a breath.

"Father," he began, forcing his gaze to remain steady. "I must speak with you."

The older man peered across the Hall, raising a brow. He continued his conversation, speaking a few more words to the captain before waving him on.

Was Zdenek just as easily dismissed? He might do well to see how his father prioritized him.

"Now." Father's gaze laid heavy on Zdenek. An air of condescension in his voice. As if Zdenek were a child who had interrupted two adults speaking. "As I would have words with you, my son."

Zdenek sucked in a breath. He would stand firm. If not for the salvation of what dignity he may have left. For *her*.

The larger man stepped down and came to Zdenek. His darkened eyes lifting. He pressed a hand to Zdenek's shoulder. "I have a surprise for you."

Zdenek widened his eyes. What was this? He had prepared himself for the man's harsh words berating him.

"Aye." Father dipped his head. "Let us speak privately." He looked over his shoulder as he slid an arm around Zdenek's, steering him from the room.

Wasn't there something Zdenek intended to say to his father? He couldn't remember. But he had. And it had been important. All seemed to have been swept away in his confusion.

What was this hold his father had on him? Why couldn't he break free of it? He wasn't the small child who once feared this man; who had been paralyzed by his ire and had no hope of freedom, no hope of a will of his own. What then, was this?

In a matter of moments, they had traversed the Great Hall and entered Father's solar.

Zdenek's thoughts returned to Eva. And he kicked himself for his thoughtlessness. What power did this man have over him? How had he managed to clear Zdenek's mind of all else yet again?

"Please," Father said, waving toward a couple of chairs. "Sit. Ease yourself."

Zdenek moved to the closest chair and sat, tension filling every muscle. Something within him fought his desire to speak, but his longing to protect Eva won. "Father, I have something that must be said."

Father held up a hand. "Do not trouble yourself. I understand."

"My lord?" Zdenek's brows came together.

"Yes, I...noticed your interaction with your mother."

A muscle in Zdenek's face twitched.

"You are concerned after her." Father's words were matter-of-fact. As usual, there was no room for opinion or argument.

Zdenek rubbed his hands on his thighs. What was he to say? How could he shift the subject? Could he just say what was in his heart? It would be a first.

Father continued, leveling a hard gaze on Zdenek. "I will speak on her behalf. She is only worried about your future." The man fairly glowered as he peered across his desk. "As am I."

Shaking his head, Zdenek's gut, heavy with emotion, pressed him to speak for himself. For his bride.

"And so, I have made arrangements." The words were a pronouncement. Not a suggestion. Not an opening for debate.

Zdenek's heart skipped a beat. "Arrangements? What arrangements?"

His father's gaze softened only slightly to become one of confusion. As if Zdenek were the hardheaded of the two. "For Lady Lucia and her parents to come, of course. How else are we to know if the match will take?"

Zdenek dropped his head. Lady Lucia? Here? What trouble would that bring? How dare he not speak against this? Against Father's treatment...and outright dismissal of Eva?

He lifted his gaze to meet his father's once again. "My lord, I appreciate your concern, but I must insist that—"

Jerking his hand, a harsh movement, Father spoke over his words. "Zdenek, do not make me repeat my sentiments from before. The matter is...unpleasant, and I truly do not wish to revisit them."

"But you don't understand, Father, I—"

"Don't..." Father's eyes flashed, and his voice filled the space. He was on his feet in a moment, his chair teetering and almost crashing to the floor with the force of his movement.

Zdenek drew his mouth into a tight, thin line. Why? Was he so afraid? Of what? What did he think his father would do?

The looming figure strolled to the window. "Such unpleasant things you have forced me to say." Father's voice was firm even as his attention drifted beyond the solar and into the distance. "To do."

Forced him? Rising, Zdenek found a measure of strength he didn't know he possessed. "Respectfully, my lord, I did not—"

Father spun on him then, his features hard. "Do *not* make me revisit them."

Zdenek stared at Father, his gaze matching the older man's for several long moments. But, at length, he remembered who the man was to him and all he had done.

The simple truth was that he and Eva were guests in the man's home, if nothing else. But there was certainly more to it than that. Much more. Was he not a beloved son? A son returned home seeking reconciliation...something he continued to fight for. But at what cost?

Dropping into the chair, Zdenek nodded even as his heart dropped, weighing heavier than ever. "I am...pleased for the opportunity to see Lady Lucia and her family again."

Father nodded. "As I knew you would be." Something that might be considered a smile spread on Father's face.

But Zdenek could not find even a small joy in that. For his entire chest ached. How was he to find a way through this?

Hana's hands were raw. And her nails had become torn at her struggling. The fight remaining in her after these days of travel surprised even her.

But her life hung in the balance. Of that, there was little doubt.

What deep-seated ire had possessed these men to leave their camp and pursue her and Radek for days? Such desire for vengeance was beyond her. And these men planned well, striking only when they had begun to let their guard down.

A mistake that had cost them. Had cost *her*. Dearly.

As she sat, propped and bound against a tree, bruised and worn, she wondered after Radek. What had he done when he discovered she was gone? Did he think she had walked away? Were things so tense between them? Or would he be in pursuit, even now? She could not be sure.

The things that had happened between them in the last days gave her pause...gave her hope. Although...maybe what he felt for her was only born of a man's desire. And no matter how much she had longed for more, it was for naught. Perhaps, in that, she had been the fool.

The stiff, rugged bark of the tall elm rubbed against her sore back. But the men refused to let her rest with any sense of comfort. Since they snatched her from her and Radek's makeshift camp, they had been always on the move or she had been tied as if her limbs would be wrenched from her body.

And there was a chill in the air now. Summer had begun to fade into autumn. The nights became more uncomfortable out in the elements without the benefit of better protection.

Nearby, the men snored. Even the one who was to be keeping watch.

She rolled her eyes.

Sleep would not come for her. Hadn't for so many nights now. Too much ladened her thoughts. What would become of her? What did they intend to do with her? Why had they not just killed her and rid themselves of the nuisance? For certain, she slowed their progress, as she had Radek's.

If only she had taken more heed to his words.

If only...

Hot tears burned her raw skin. Too many tears. It was enough. There was naught for it. At least she might find some comfort in that, for fear of their leader, the men left her be. For now. But how long would it be until they took their chance? How long until *he* did?

What a sight she must be! Her dress muddied and torn. She had made it through the Royalists camp and many days' journey with Radek—far too many nights upon the ground, without the proper care she was accustomed to.

*Enough!*

If her mind must be relieved of sleep, let it be lent of some manner of escape. But how? What chance had she?

A stirring nearer the men drew her attention.

She jerked her head in that direction.

The horses shifted and snorted.

She let out a breath.

Pulling against the bindings, she tested them for perhaps the hundredth time. A burning on her wrists was her only reward. She hung her head. Was there any hope? Decidedly no.

Dropping her head back against the tree, she let her eyelids slide closed and thought about the last moments with Radek. Why had she made the moments contentious? Those minutes should have been marked by something more—words spoken that could have meant more, could have unburdened her heart. But it was not possible to feel for him as she believed she did. It was too soon. For certain, this was nothing more than her own flesh.

*God, forgive me.*

She was weary. So very weary of fighting...her heart and her body. Perhaps she could let her mind surrender to the darkness.

A great commotion arose in the camp.

The man at watch made a noise. Did he attempt to sound an alarm? A gurgling was the only noise that came forth.

What had cut off his warning?

She scanned the area. There must be something...

There, in the trees, a movement.

No...there. To the right.

Now to the left.

The men were on their feet faster than she thought possible, swords in hand. They were three strong, but perhaps not able to fight off a foe that surrounded them. What army had been summoned to rescue her? Had Radek reached his friends with such speed?

Her captors backed toward each other. Did they find some measure of comfort in the security of having their hindquarters no longer vulnerable?

A swoop here and a swish there.

The zip of a dagger found its mark and one more fell. Dead before he could blink, his eyes stared forward, frozen in death.

Two remained, their eyes wide and searching. But it was for naught. The men surrounding them would not show themselves. Or give away their positions.

"Give yourselves up, and you may live," came a voice from the darkness.

"Death first!" the leader cried.

The second man gave him a sideways glance. Perhaps he was not as prepared to die for the cause.

Stillness fell over the area, and the air became thick. No sound could be heard within or without.

Hana did not see much in the dimness from her position. But the moonlight caught the glisten of moisture beading on the exposed skin of the second man. She became more certain that he was not ready to lose his life tonight.

She searched the trees for any sign of movement. Had her rescuers abandoned her? When would they make their move? The odds were in their favor. Only two soldiers remained between her and freedom.

The second man threw his sword down and ran into the night.

"Coward!" the leader called after him. Then he held his sword up and drew it around him, slicing the air. "Show yourselves! Fight like men! I shall take you all!"

Footfalls neared. Unhurried and measured, they came.

When but a silhouette was visible, her breath caught. It was unmistakable—Radek.

Then he stepped forward, moving from the cover of the trees until the moon lit him completely.

"You," the larger man rasped. "I will take great pleasure killing you." He gripped his sword, raising it in preparation to cross blades with Radek.

How could Radek fight such a man? The man's weight far outmatched her rescuer. Surely, the oaf would overcome Radek with brute force alone. Why would Radek sacrifice himself? Were there not others in the contingency that would join him and help surround and take this German?

Radek spread his legs, anchoring his stance, and prepared to take on the man.

Hana wanted to scream, to warn Radek not to do this crazy thing. But her voice caught in her throat. And she could do nothing but watch.

Their swords met and clashed. Blow for blow, swing for swing, Radek met his opponent. Radek's lightness on his feet seemed to make up for the fact that he lacked the mass of the man he faced.

Round and round they went, covering much of the open ground as they parried. Soon enough, their blades locked. The burly German used his weight to press down on Radek and force him to the ground. With a flick, Radek's sword skittered away.

Radek was now on his knees, looking up at the man who had bested him.

"No," Hana cried to herself. She could not bear to watch a death-blow delivered upon the man she cared for far too deeply. She shut her eyes against the reality of what would happen and cried into her shoulder.

The German gave a great battle cry.

Then all was silenced.

Dare she peer out? Could she contain herself if she were to view the remains of her last hope?

But what of the army? Why was Radek her last hope? Yet, he was. In the ways that truly mattered.

Hands were on her arms then. But they were not the massive, roughened hands of the German. No, tender fingers searched her out with the gentle touch she knew to be her Radek.

She opened her eyes, staring into the deep brown of Radek's.

"H-how?"

He opened his mouth. Would he tell her how he survived?

She cared not.

Stretching against the very limits of her binds, she claimed his mouth.

His lips opened for hers, and his hands came to the sides of her face.

When they parted, she cried openly. "What of your friends? Your army?"

His brows furrowed. "Army?"

"The soldiers with you?"

"Hana, 'tis but me."

"You?"

He nodded.

"You faced them alone?"

"I would do much more."

She held her breath.

"For you."

Her arms, somehow no longer bound, came around him.

And her shoulders ached. How? Her wrists hurt. She pulled them around to look at them. Unbound, but still, they were rubbing. What curse was this?

She looked to Radek, a question on her lips.

His mouth moved, but she couldn't hear his words.

She reached for him.

He faded as if but a ghost.

"No!" she cried. "Radek!"

She opened her eyes. And found herself still strapped to the tree. Still in the same camp.

The watchman, no longer dead somehow, stood over her. "Quiet, wench, or you'll wake the whole camp!"

She bit her lip as her eyes pricked.

Had it truly all been naught but a dream?

The corridor was dark. Pavel followed the shouts coming from below stairs. His feet were steadier than his heart, as it became compressed. Was he so fearful?

Voices that were once only a collection of sound began to separate and make sense as he reached the last stair.

Lights aplenty drew him to the small crowd, which even then passed into the recesses of the far hall. Did they intend to take his father elsewhere?

He opened his mouth to call after them, but a firm hand fell on his shoulder. As he spun, he all but forgot his words, losing them in a moment of shock.

General Zizka stood in the corridor, eyeing him.

Pavel caught his gaze for a moment. But only a moment, for he did not wish to be deterred from his father. He turned toward the retreating group once again.

"Let them go, Pavel." Zizka's words were spoken with more gentleness than he could recall having ever heard from the man.

It gave him pause.

Still, he stared after those he had seen.

"They will tend to Baron Krejik."

"How does he fare?" Pavel faced Zizka then, daring the man to speak false, knowing he would not.

Zizka's arm fell to his side. "We must pray." He turned. Did he intend to lead Pavel to the chapel?

"Do not put me off, General." The bite in Pavel's words surprised even him.

Zizka halted. His shoulders heaved with a great sigh.

Pavel, too, took in a breath, if only to prepare to entreat Zizka tell all he knew or Pavel would continue toward his previous destination, pressing his way to his father's side.

The great general made a half turn. Now in profile, he seemed no nearer satisfying Pavel's inquiry.

Pavel stretched his legs and moved across the Great Hall. "I shall determine if—"

"Enough!" The strength of Zizka's voice hinted at what may lie beneath the rather calm exterior.

Pavel stilled but did not turn.

"Ulrich has earned every strike my army makes against his. Every one of his men that is felled to a Hussite hand cannon or sword. Nothing will be punishment enough for the special evil he has inflicted upon the innocent." Zizka's tone was dark. Gruff.

Pavel's heart froze. "What is your meaning? What has he done to my father?"

"You need not know." Zizka's voice softened. Footfalls warned that he neared. "Trust me in this."

Glancing over his shoulder, Pavel noted that Zizka's gaze shone clear and true. The man of war did not wish to speak of the baron's state. What could that mean?

Pavel tried to swallow, but a hardness in his throat prevented him from fully doing so.

His father. Were his injuries such that he may not survive?

*Father.* Images of the man throughout Pavel's life passed before his eyes. So many things, so many memories...pressing in on him, filling him with emotion. All within a matter of a few seconds.

It was too much.

But Pavel did not wish to break in front of his general.

"Let us now to the chapel then?"

Pavel looked to the hall down which his father had been taken. "No."

The general sucked in a breath.

Turning to catch his eye, Pavel said, "I will remain here. I do not wish to be far when word of my father's wellbeing is forthcoming."

Zizka nodded. "Then I will wait with you."

Eva breathed in and out slowly. She had made it to the gardens without interference from Zdenek or his father. She took in the fresh air, somewhat cooler now. Had the seasons so shifted? When they came to this place the heat of the sun had born down upon them. But now...

How long had she consigned herself to her chambers? It seemed like an eternity. For certain, it had been too long.

But was she truly relieved to have avoided her husband? Or did her heart long for a glance, even if it were to be a hard exchange, with her beloved? Something...just so there would be acknowledgement that something remained between them?

She frowned. Could that be so? Did she a disservice to herself and him in her claim that she only wanted peace? A thick heaviness settled in her midsection.

It was true that she wanted her husband. Wanted to know he cared. And that there was hope.

For as of yet, she had none.

*God, is all lost to me?*

How she longed for Patricie! Surely, a few moments with her sister would give her the support and the strength to make it through. But for how long? For there was no discernable end in sight.

Long passed was their agreed upon time of departure. But that was before.

Before the things spoken by Zdenek's father that had...

Things said that should not have been. Things done that should not have been permitted.

She continued to move through the carefully laid out foliage without a thought about the life brought forth from the earth. Or where she wandered to.

A sigh stirred her to the present.

There, on the edge of the far half wall, sat a lone figure. A woman, finely dressed. Zdenek's mother?

Before Eva could retrace her steps and slip away, the woman turned and their eyes met.

"I ask your pardon, Countess." Eva dipped in her best curtsy. This, too, was likely not acceptable. Still, it was what she had to offer. "I did not mean to disturb. I will take my leave." She turned.

"Please," the woman's gentle voice called. "Do not trouble yourself on my account. I am not so disrupted."

Eva halted. Could she not then escape?

"The garden walk is big enough for the two of us." A smile graced the older woman's lovely features.

What was the lady's meaning? That the gardens could hold them both or that they could walk on the path together? Dare she ask? Should it be obvious?

The Countess did not rise, leaving Eva in quandary.

"My lady?" she ventured. Would the lady be kind in face of Eva's ignorance? Eva had not been much exposed to the woman.

The expression on the Countess's face did not change. Had she anticipated Eva's lack of understanding?

If only Eva could shrink back and retreat.

The Countess scooted on the bench and indicated the empty space beside herself. "Come, sit with me."

Eva's desire to disappear grew. But how could she now? There were no tricks she was aware of, no excuse she could conjure that would hope to alleviate her of furthering this encounter. And so, with tentative steps, she closed the distance that may well have been a league for how long it took Eva to cross it.

She could not keep her hands from shaking as she lowered herself next to her mother-in-law. How could God expect her to endure more chastisement? More shaming? *May it be quick!*

The Countess took a few easy breaths, turned toward Eva, but did not seem hurried to speak.

Eva prayed her own ragged breathing was not as loud as it seemed.

Zdenek's mother lifted a hand and moved it toward Eva's, clenched in her lap. But then perhaps changed her mind as she pulled it back into her own lap. What could that mean?

The Countess's eyes rose.

Eva hesitated, but, at length, lifted her eyes to meet the woman's gaze.

As the older woman examined her, Eva was overcome with the desire for this woman's approval. Why? Because her own mother had been gone so long? Because she was all that remained of Zdenek for Eva to hope to connect with? Whatever the reason, it mattered not. It was hopeless. Had she not already learned that this family's acceptance was not to be had?

"Lady Eva," the Countess began.

The words, spoken quietly, took Eva aback. She jerked free of her thoughts. Why would the Countess afford her a title? It didn't fit.

The woman's gaze caught Eva's again. She watched Eva with expectation. Had she said more? Asked Eva a question? This display of poor etiquette was the fault of no one but Eva. And she had to answer for it.

"I...apologize, Countess. My mind was elsewhere." Eva fought a grimace. *No weakness. Do not show weakness.*

The Countess's features did not alter. "You have much to think on."

Was the woman baiting her? The Countess seemed gentle enough. Was she a wolf in sheepskin?

"I have not been privy to what words have been spoken over you."

The names Zdenek's father thrust upon her deafened her ears for a moment.

"But I know the heart from whence they came."

Now, Eva was not so certain which words the woman spoke of. Was this a trap? Eva licked her lips. "Yes, Countess."

The woman looked from side to side, prompting Eva to do the same. She then leaned closer to her daughter-in-law. "My Zdenek loves you. Very much. I know he does. Trust that."

In one fluid motion, the Countess rose and began walking before Eva could respond.

"My lady," Eva called after her.

The Countess continued moving as if she hadn't heard Eva's entreaty.

Eva watched her go. What was she to think? What was she to believe? Dare she not grab hope when it presented itself?

She stood and followed after the Countess. But as she turned out of the garden, there was no longer any sign of the woman.

# CHAPTER 12

Radek could never have imagined what an aid his hunting skills would become. Even with the stealth and skill he possessed from his many hours stalking prey in the wood, still he was uncertain he would catch Hana's captors. And if he did, what then? How many were there? Many had followed the man who held her captive within the Royalist camp. Would he have been able to entice ten to accompany him? Fifteen?

For certain, Radek could not fight so many and survive. But try, he would. He must. For Hana.

Kneeling, he examined the markings on the ground. These men were either reckless or ignorant. They made little or no attempt to disguise their tracks.

If they but worked at it, they could hide their numbers. With no effort to have done so for their flight with Hana, he doubted they would bother with concealing their numbers either. He guessed no more than four to be in the group. Four seemed more manageable than fifteen certainly. But four trained mercenary soldiers with weapons against one man? Those were not odds he liked.

If only Zdenek were with him. And Pavel. The reasons for abandoning his friends seemed less and less clear.

But then, had he not, he would not have met Hana. She would have been utilized as those men desired, killed, and left in the dirt. The thought sickened him. For anyone to be left so. Much less an innocent. And all the more this woman, who had awakened his heart to things he never...

Pushing those thoughts to the side, he rebuked himself. He could not do what he had to if he let his heart rule. Yes, it was best if he let go of his emotions and focused his energy on the tracks and any other evidence of their direction. And home his senses on these things. As he did so, their path became clearer. All a bit too easy for a man whose pastime had included hunting.

Yes...it was. *Too* easy it seemed. Was it?

He paused and looked at the tracks again. *No* attempt to hide their foot markings or where they had slept. They might should have even left the ropes that bound their prisoner...

His heart skipped a beat.

They might should have even left the ropes that bound their prisoner for all the care they took covering their presence. In truth, it would not have taken a skilled eye to find their trail. Looking in the direction they traveled, uncertainty filled him.

An ambush awaited him. How far ahead, or when, he could not know. But it would come.

But what choice did he have? Abandon the chase? Abandon Hana? That was not an option.

Wariness must then be his constant companion and vigilance his only hope.

And so, Radek stood and continued into the depths of the forest.

This night proved once more that Karin desperately needed Pavel. Being so close, separated by nothing more than a series of walls, would not permit her to rest. She longed for the comfort of his arms, the assurance that all was well. But could he bring such?

He did not return to her in the night, nor as the darkness faded into the morning hours. It gave her pause to wonder it. Was all well? Or would she come to discover that the situation was dire? Perhaps that they would face a loss?

Even so, why would he not seek her? Did he not also find serenity in her presence? Was she not to him as she imagined? Or as she wished to be? Now was not the time for such thoughts.

She dressed and wrapped a cloak about her, then descended the stairs and moved into the Great Hall.

And there he was. Seated on a bench against the far wall. He had a companion—a larger man with one eye covered. Could this be the great General Zizka? She had heard tell that an injury in his adolescence left him with only one good eye.

The conversation between the two men was sparse in the few moments she watched, their voices kept low. But she could not help the uneasy feeling that came as she watched. Had this man's company brought her husband solace when she could not? As much as she wanted to deny the selfishness of the thought, a pang shot through the center of her chest. Perhaps she should go.

She turned. It would be best if she left them to their camaraderie.

"Karin?"

It was Pavel. What had drawn his attention? She could not have made enough noise in her movements to be heard across the room.

She looked over her shoulder.

Pavel had risen.

The general even then stood.

Her husband stepped toward her. Tentative steps.

Turning more fully to receive him, she fought the emotion warring within her.

He lengthened his stride, closing the distance between them. As he approached, he gathered her in his arms.

"Are you well?" he whispered into her hair.

"I am." She hoped her strangled words, hiding her tears, could be disguised as her breath being taken.

A hand moved into her hair, cradling her head. His lips found her forehead. "I did not wish to wake you. My father..."

Had he lost his words? Was he attempting to control his own emotion?

She reached a hand up to press against the side of his face.

"My father has been injured. The healer has been with him through the night."

Swallowing her own concerns, she pulled back to look into his eyes. "Have you seen him?"

Pavel shook his head. "His injuries are severe."

She gripped Pavel's shoulders, moving fingers upward to brush the hair from his forehead. "He is strong."

Pavel nodded. "The general has sent for my mother."

"That was good of him."

The blue depths that Karin oft fell into then glazed. "I suppose that is all we can do."

"Aye. And we can pray." Karin caught his gaze. "Our Lord is almighty God. He can work miracles."

Pavel nodded. But there was a hesitation to the movement. Born of doubt? Or of weariness? She had best not speculate.

The general waiting several paces behind Pavel, coughed.

Pavel looked in his direction. Then, taking a step to the side, he spoke. "General, I would like you to meet my wife, Lady Karin Krejikova."

"It is an honor, my lady." The man bent at the waist.

"It is I who am honored, General Zizka. Tales of your exploits have spread throughout Bohemia. It is a privilege to meet you."

The man blinked and straightened. "You are too kind, my lady. It is God who paves the way for any success that befalls the Hussite army."

She nodded. "And I shall thank Him in my prayers. As well that you have brought my husband home safely."

"He is a capable soldier who has God's very hand upon him. And we are in need of such men. All the more, as these lands continue to know conflict." The man's eye seemed to bore into her husband.

Would he guilt Pavel into returning to the fight? With his father perhaps on his deathbed?

Pavel shifted beside her. "But let us not speak of such things today."

"Of course." Zizka's shoulders relaxed. "My apologies."

Karin looked to her husband. She did not trust her eyes upon Zizka for too often her affect spoke of her inner thoughts too well.

"I must take my leave," Zizka said, drawing her eyes regardless.

His gaze swept over her. Did she perceive a slight frown? What did he see in her?

"My men have long since needed word from me."

Pavel nodded. "Thank you, General. For bringing my father back to us."

Zizka dipped in a slight bow and strode past them and out of the dining hall.

Pavel caught Karin's gaze once Zizka had left, raising a hand to graze her face. "I regret that worry has taken you from rest."

"What rest, my love? I could not find sleep after you had quit our chambers." As the words left her tongue, she wished them back. There was no need to weigh him so.

His eyes searched hers.

She pressed her hand to his on her face. "Forgive me. I do not mean to add to your burden."

He pulled her into his embrace once more. "Even so, I do not wish to neglect you, dearest wife. Not during such a time as this." Resting a hand on the swell of her abdomen, he continued, "*Your* burden is great indeed."

She let her head rest against him. Today may bring rejoicing for a life brought back from the brink. Or it may hearken a life come to its end. But one thing was certain—she would be by Pavel's side.

And they would get through it the same way they overcame so

many challenges in their lives since their paths had first crossed—
together.

Zdenek neared the stables to whence he had been summoned. Something had vexed the stable master and required his attention. It did give him pause. Why would the man call for his, not Father's, oversight?

Raised voices drew him nearer. One was that of the stable master; one was definitely feminine. Could it be? Eva?

Zdenek had not perchanced to engage her in days. Though now his heart beat quicker and he pushed his feet to hurry, the sooner to find what trouble was afoot.

Stepping through an opening into the stables, he then halted. There, just beyond the first set of stalls, stood his beloved. Though she was several hands shorter than the stable master, she squared off with him, addressing him with hands on hips as if she were deter-mined not to be the one to relent. Indeed, he believed she would not.

The man's face had become a shade of red Zdenek had not seen on the stable master before. Was she such a frustration to him?

It almost made Zdenek chuckle. Almost. He opened his mouth to make his presence known, but halted as he watched the stable master grasp Eva's upper arm.

She tried to jerk away. "Unhand me!"

He jerked her a bit closer, drawing his face down toward hers, teeth clenched. "You do not have the power to order me to do anything."

"You are hurting me." She again attempted to wriggle free.

Zdenek's chest tightened. And he marched forward before real-izing he did so. "How dare you treat my wife thusly!"

The man's large hand opened.

Eva stumbled but maintained her balance. Her eyes were wide on Zdenek.

For his part, he did not stop until he had inserted himself between the man and Eva. "What cause could you have for treating the lady in such a manner?"

"Forgive me, my lord, but the wen—the lady was arguing against your wishes. And she would not yield."

Eva's regard altered, and he sensed her eyes now bored into him.

"My wishes?" Zdenek's brows furrowed.

"That she not leave the manor unescorted."

Zdenek let out a breath. "Aye."

"You?" Eva sputtered. "You pronounced such a limit upon my behavior?"

Closing his eyes, Zdenek hoped to ward off the distant aching of his head that was certain to worsen. One thing was certain—he could not take on both challengers at once. He met the stable master's gaze. "You are dismissed. But we will speak on this again."

The man shook his head and moved off farther into the stables.

And then Zdenek turned toward his wife, but slowly.

Her eyes were hard on him. "You? You dare limit my movements?"

"For your protection." He softened his words. Would that dissipate some of her anger? It did not.

"My protection?" she scoffed. "What care you of my wellbeing? You do not seem to care for my thoughts, my feelings, or how I fare. Why should you bother after my wellbeing?"

"Eva, that's not—" He reached for her hand.

She jerked it away. "You care not." Moisture pooled in her eyes. "Of what I suffer."

He pulled his lips in and closed his eyes. Why must it be so difficult between them?

"What is it to you if some brigand attack me? All the better for you, methinks?"

His eyes flew open. "Eva!"

She turned her head and looked away, toward the manor house. "You cannot think that true."

No response was forthcoming, aside from her sniffling. He reached tentative hands toward her arms. She flinched as his fingers set upon her skin, but she did not pull back.

"I don't know what to think." She put a hand to her face, wiping at the tears.

He stepped closer. "Then *know* this."

Moving his hands up to cup her face, he gently turned her features toward his. Then, with some measure of hesitation, he lowered his lips upon hers. Once, he brushed the lips that had captivated him. Twice, and he lingered, moving over them.

A sigh escaped her as she opened herself to him.

As the kiss deepened, he slid his hands around her waist to her back as she wrapped her arms around his shoulders. Couldn't they remain this way?

When their kisses became hungrier, he began placing light kisses upon her nose and her eyelids before pulling her into his chest.

"How, Zdenek? How am I to endure? What am I to believe?"

"Trust *me*. I will find a way out of this and yet maintain a relationship with my father. I know I can. Just give me more time."

She nodded.

He pressed a kiss into her hair. "And I will not let him deal with you so ill."

Her hands gripped his tunic all the more firmly.

"We can get through this...together."

"Together." The word came from her, but it was not as assured as it had been from his lips.

Hana was weary. It was beyond the weariness that came solely from a lack of sleep. This was a bone-deep exhaustion. She was drained of all hope, all thought of a future, any prayers that might have remained on her lips. Truly depleted.

And cold. She could not remember being so cold. It was not

possible to arrange her limbs to preserve any amount of body heat. So, she shivered.

But had she lost all fight? Would she no longer do what she must to preserve herself? She was uncertain.

Her body shifted as the horse beneath her came to a halt. Was this where they would pause for the night?

The burly man behind handed her thinned frame to one of the other soldiers. Which? Did she care? She looked up. The one with the scar across the right side of his face.

A thud behind her warned that the leader, once astride with her, had landed solidly upon the ground. His footfalls brought him closer.

She dared not move. The most recent bruise above her left eye was enough to remind that she should not. Now, with the heat of his body warming her back, she forced herself not to step away.

As if he could sense her thoughts, the guard in front gripped her upper arm. Tightly.

"Tie her to that tree." The man's thick, branch-like arm stretched out, and he pointed toward a sturdy oak several feet ahead.

The guard stepped in that direction.

Hana held a hand out to the larger man. "Please, wait!"

While the soldier continued to pull at her, she dug her heels into the dirt.

"Please," she pled.

The leader, marked above the others by his size and intelligence, held up a hand. "What is it?"

Hana tried to jerk her arm free, but the soldier would not relent. "I must ask for a moment to...relieve myself."

"Did you not have opportunity enough on the journey?"

"Yes, of course. But I find myself in need once more."

His eyes narrowed and lips thinned. Might he doubt the veracity of her request?

She prayed not, for her need was truly great. But there was more. Perhaps this time...she might gain an advantage. Mayhap not. But what would be the cost? A beating? Death? She no longer feared either. These were acceptable risks. If only she had a chance for freedom.

If only...

"Take her to the river over yon," the leader directed the man holding her.

A stream flowed nearby? Which direction had they been traveling? Was it the Vlatava River? Had they come so much closer to Prague? Would that she had been more mindful on their travels instead of bemoaning her plight. But there was less use in pitying herself now. She must seize this chance if it were to be had.

Though she liked little the way the scar-faced guard tugged at her, she did not fight as he pulled her farther into the wood. Sounds of rushing water told that they approached the stream; and she held her breath. Would she do it? The opportunity had presented itself before, and she had not taken hold of it. Too fearful of what might befall her if caught. Too uncertain if she were prepared to face the journey home on her own.

However, that had changed. If not now, when? If not she, who? She tired of waiting for a one-time savior who may not come...for a rescue that seemed but a dream.

The guard fairly flung her toward the water's edge as he halted.

She stumbled but righted herself quickly. Scanning the scene before her, she hunted for something, anything that might aid in her escape. Several rocks lay near the stream. Could she brandish such a weapon? Strike at the man?

"What bothers, my *lady*?" The man spoke the word as if a curse.

When she looked at him, the leer on his face unsettled her stomach.

"I only wait for you to turn your head." She motioned with her hands for him to look away.

He folded his arms across his chest. Unmoved.

"Turn away," she pressed, allowing a sternness to touch her voice.

He laughed. "You think me a fool?"

Her gaze cut to the larger of the rocks. Might she close the distance, free a stone, and inflict some amount of damage to the man before he overtook her?

He stepped closer, and her chance was lost. "Do you require assistance?"

She backed away. The narrowing of his eyes made him appear almost predatory.

The stream slowed her retreat as the man's quickened pace and long stride prevented her from side stepping him.

His rough hands gripped her forearms even as she raised them to defend herself.

"Mayhap I shall assist you?" He grinned. His hands slid over her torso, discovering laces and loosening their ties.

"Do not!" she pled as she squirmed. Could she wriggle free of his grip? Her arms, though pushing at him with all she had, seemed useless. She drew a hand back and struck the side of his face with all the strength she could muster.

He halted his movements, pulling his head back such that he looked down at her. A thin line of blood was visible on the side of his mouth. Had she caused this?

He wiped at it. And spotted the discoloration on his hand. His lips spread across his face. "Is that all you've got?"

Her eyes widened, and she shoved against him with both palms, pressing against his chest with all her might.

Fingers dug into her hips. Painfully. Laughter filled her senses. Laughter? Did her struggle amuse?

He jerked her tight to himself. "Now it's my turn."

His hands were on the fabric of her dress again, pulling at the laces. Thank heaven, they would not give! The man cursed. And set his hands across a seam. Would he now rip the dress apart?

She twisted her torso, formed a unified fist with both hands and dug her elbow into his stomach. Air rushed out of him, and he gripped for his midsection, grasping for her arm at the same time. She maneuvered it away from his reach. No longer in his clutches, she gathered her limp skirt and ran. Only steps away, her legs came out from underneath her, and she slammed into the ground. Hard.

She fought for breath. Would it not come? At last, air rushed into her lungs. And then she was on her back, her limbs pinned, the menacing half-grin of the soldier looking down upon her.

"Enough!" he said, his own breathing labored. He licked his lips and eyed her features, letting his gaze wander as he willed.

She turned away.

Lowering his head, his lips pressed to the side of her face.

She bucked against his frame and let out a scream.

He grabbed her chin in his hand and jerked her face toward him. Would he kiss her lips? His face lowered. It seemed that was his very intention.

With a blur, his weight lifted from her.

Dare she sit up?

She shook as she rose to a sitting position.

Off to the right, nearer the stream, a scuffle of bodies. The soldier intending to...violate her had lost his balance and the upper hand to a man with dark hair and dark clothes.

Who would come to her rescue? Was it another of the Royalist soldiers protecting her virtue? That seemed unlikely.

But dare she not take this chance to run? No. It was now or never. She pulled herself to her feet, pressing a hand to her head as the world spun. Stumbling away, she hoped to create adequate distance and lose herself in the wood.

"You!" the soldier said.

She paused, but forced herself to keep going. Her progress impossibly slow.

The sounds of bodies shuffling and fists connecting were all she heard. How could she leave when someone risked his life for her? She turned back.

"Go!" the man yelled, looking up from the kerfuffle.

Could it be? It seemed so. Radek!

Was this but another dream? Had she drifted into a daydream to escape? This couldn't be real. What was the use in escape? She would only wake to be devastated.

Dropping to her knees, she let frustrated tears flow as she watched on. It was no use.

As she knew he would, the dream-Radek got the upper hand, secured a branch and knocked the soldier over the head. And he was out. The wearied dream-Radek then turned toward her, taking steps to close the distance.

"Hana," he entreated as he held out a hand to her. "We must away."

She dropped her chin to her chest. If only it could be real.

"Hana?" dream-Radek said as he dropped in front of her. His hands were on her shoulders. "Are you well? Did he hurt you?"

She looked up. "No. Not truly."

A hand touched her face tentatively before cupping her cheek. "Please, tell me. We must get as far away as possible."

She lifted her hands to cover his on her face. "How I wish you were real."

"I assure you, I am. My cuts and bruises most real."

Fresh tears filled her eyes as she shook her head. "You don't understand."

"Perhaps. But one thing I do know is how much I need to get you out of here."

He rose and, reaching down for her hands, lifted her to her feet.

"It will only make it worse..."

"What?" He spoke softly even as he scanned the area.

"The more I give in to this delusion." Tears made trails down her features.

"Delusion?" He pulled her closer and set her hand to his heart. "Is this not real enough?"

Her eyes widened.

"And this?"

His fingers grazed the side of her face.

"Or this?"

He lowered his head and pressed his lips to hers.

She fought the urge to give in, but as his mouth moved over hers, she relented and shifted to yield to him.

His arms surrounded her.

She gripped his upper arms. Could she garner some of that strength for herself?

When he pulled back, he whispered, "I am real enough, aye?"

"Aye," she breathed.

"Let us make our way out of here, then." He gripped her hand and led her off to follow the river to the north.

She paused. Would not her captors predict such a move? What would they not think?

*The river.*

"What if we crossed?"

Radek looked at her dress. "I fear your safety."

"I think it's the only way." She met his gaze.

He seemed to consider her for a moment before glancing toward the river. Did he weigh their options? Then he reached for her hands, gripping them with a firmness that offered a strength she needed more than she realized.

Holding onto him, she allowed Radek to lead her into the water's chilling depths. And, as the current strengthened and she could no longer touch the bottom, she began to second-guess her decision.

# CHAPTER 13

Silence filled the Great Hall. A thick silence. It pervaded everything within the space, pressing until it nearly choked Pavel. Was there nothing more to be done? Nothing he might do but live out these horrid moments in dreadful anticipation?

His hands ached for action—to swing a sword, to work against the enemy, to do *something* more than sit in this...silence. It seeped into his very soul and pushed out all that might offer respite.

He sat, then he stood, then he paced, then he sat once more. How could one remain still? How should one endure keeping such a vigil?

Pavel stood yet again. There was nothing for it. He could wait no longer. Impossible!

A hand touched his arm.

He turned and looked into bright green eyes. Loving eyes. Curious eyes.

Lifting a hand to her cheek, he caressed her. "I do not mean to disturb you."

She nodded.

"But this is intolerable." He looked off toward the corridor where they had taken his father. "How much longer must I wait?"

She stood, setting both hands on his shoulders. "We must trust the physician. He does what he thinks is best."

"I will never forgive myself if my father dies without that I am able to speak to him. To tell him..." A thickness in Pavel's throat prevented him from continuing.

"I know. We must hope that will not be the way of it."

He glanced toward the floor.

"Please," she said, as she lowered to the bench by the fire once more. "Sit with me."

He caught her eyes. They did not plead but shone of sincerity. Still, he could not tarry.

Instead, he turned opposite and moved in that direction, allowing his gaze to shift to the door that barred his vision from a hall, a room, or wherever they had taken the baron. How much longer? What was required? What had happened to his father? Did the physician have hope? Or did he work with futility, knowing he must do whatever he could regardless?

Crossing his arms, Pavel walked the length of the Great Hall. Pacing, back and forth. Would his legs even permit him to stop? Or would he come out of his skin if he did so?

He glanced at his wife.

She leaned forward on her knees, eyes closed, hands folded, and lips moving. Did she beseech the Lord on his father's behalf? Or his?

How could he forget himself and not do the same? That was the only power he truly had—to intercede through prayer. He gazed toward the ceiling, wanting to look beyond it and see into the heavens.

*Oh, God.*

Silence.

*I don't know what I ought pray.*

He continued to pace.

*I am not ready for this.*

His eyes burned. And his chest tightened.

*I can't.*

That was the honest truth. Though he had come to learn that many things were possible that had not been before, he just... couldn't. He stilled.

*Father, I know You see all things and can do all things. I ask that You—*

A door opened into the Great Hall, pulling Pavel from his divine petition.

An older man stepped into the large area, wiping his blood-covered hands with a white cloth. The baron's blood? For certain.

Pavel was upon the man in a moment. "Baron Krejik...how is he? Is he...?" He could not make himself speak the words.

The older man held up a hand. Did he wish to silence Pavel? "The baron is alive."

Pavel let out a breath.

The physician's demeanor did not relent; tension continued to fill his body. "There is no other way but to be forthright, my lord. The outcome is uncertain. Baron Krejik's injuries are dire. I have attended to them and done what I can."

"I must see him." Pavel moved, intending to go around the man.

The physician sidestepped into Pavel's path once more. "He sleeps."

Pavel halted. "What has that to do with my ability to see him?"

The healer's eyes hardened, and his mouth thinned. "I must insist upon the baron's rest."

"And I would rather you answer me this: Is he well enough to receive his son?" Pavel's response was sharper than he'd intended. But he could do little to restrain himself.

A gentle hand pressed Pavel's shoulder and he almost turned, but there was no need. Karin had drawn near. He sensed it as easily as he could his own emotions.

"My lord," she addressed him for sake of the healer. "Perhaps we might leave Baron Krejik to his slumber...for now."

Pavel counted his breaths, only then realizing that they were labored. After a few moments, he drew in air more deeply and pushed it out. "I *will* see my father. Unless I can be satisfied there is reason enough I should not."

The healer's shoulders relaxed.

Would he concede?

The man shrugged and stepped to the side. "Down the corridor and to the left, my lord."

Pavel brushed past the man who deserved only his gratitude. But the heat within kept him from expressing those softer emotions. He would have to trust that Karin could ease any tension from his brashness.

He lengthened his stride as he moved down the hall that he had stared at these long hours past. Not three paces past the doorway, a chamber appeared on the left.

Nearly passing it in his hurry, he turned, bracing himself on the doorframe.

Two servants busied themselves within, gathering bloodied cloths and other things he did not look too closely upon. But his eyes soon set upon his father, lying on a pallet at the far side of the room. *A pallet?*

Ah, but then this was a but a space in the lower level. Not a functioning bedchamber.

Clearing the room and constructing a pallet was the best their hosts could manage. Were they fearful of his injuries in carrying him above stairs?

It mattered not. The baron slept. He seemed comfortable enough.

Pavel stepped into the room and closer to his father.

And his opinion of his father's comfort changed.

For certain, the bandages hid the severity of injuries imparted, but they did not disguise the number of them. They were everywhere —over his stomach, his chest, his right shoulder. Did they extend to his back? Blood leeching through the thin sheet covering him to his waist belied that he was marred on his legs as well.

Who was this villain that had set upon Father? Why had he done this?

Instead of calming Pavel's concerns, seeing his father brought on a new wave of anger that soon overcame him. It began as a burning in his midsection that moved upward as if flaming pith had taken over and grown within him, filling every available space. As he stood looking upon the figure of his father, it spread to his extremities. And he doubted his ability to control it.

His features contorted of their own accord, nostrils flaring. "Father, I will make sure this...man...pays for what he has done."

Then Pavel spun and marched out of the room.

Radek fought against the current. It pulled at him, threatening to toss him farther downstream and away from...

*Hana.*

Their once-joined hands tore apart. Was she still near? How did she fare?

Jerking his head around, he searched for her. There. Not two feet away—hair made darker by the water pulsed with the small waves. Her skin shone pale against the river, blackened by its depths.

She gasped for air, and the angry stream overtook her head, but only briefly. She re-emerged to draw in another desperate breath but was swept below once more. How long could she continue thusly? Was it possible for them to make progress to the other side despite their struggle?

Dare he risk himself in an attempt to assist her? Would she survive if he did not? Would either of them survive if he did?

It mattered not. As she fought for breath over and over, Radek's one purpose became clear: she needed him.

But how would he help her?

Without pausing to ponder it, he pressed his arms forward into the waves and was at her side in a few strong strokes. He wrapped an arm around her torso. It proved difficult to maintain his grip as she struggled, fighting even against him for her next lungful of air.

"Cease!" he commanded.

She continued to pull against him. Was she so caught in her rhythm of life-sustaining movements?

"Hana, stop! You will take us both down!"

She went limp. Had the desperation in his voice penetrated her instincts? Her smaller hands clung to his arm.

Sucking in a breath, he reached deep within, searching for a strength he had never called upon, a strength he prayed he possessed. And, thrusting his free arm into the water and bringing it around, he kicked his legs furiously, hoping against hope for forward momentum.

Hana's grip on his arm tightened, but she neither fought nor assisted. With her skirts about her legs, she feared any movement would only further entangle them.

He continued his efforts, working, giving each stroke all that he had. It wasn't long before his lungs burned and his muscles ached. His whole being, it seemed, longed for the promise of release from the pain. It would be so easy to just stop and surrender.

*But Hana...*

Even if he had nothing to live for, she had to make it. She deserved to live.

And so, he pushed forth again and once more kicked, knowing his, and her, life depended on it. Pain radiated from his toes. Had his foot struck something? What? An animal? His heart raced. No, it had been too solid. A branch or rock? Was it possible? Could he touch the riverbed? He straightened his body and felt the solid surface below.

They were saved! Thank...

Who? God?

He shook his head and shifted his attention to Hana. Turning her in his arms, she now faced him.

Her eyes were shut, but not in gentle sleep, they were clenched, as if to avoid all that surrounded. Even her fate. And though he moved her, she still clung to him, nails digging into his skin.

"Hana!"

Her mouth jerked, but did not open. Nor did her eyes.

He set a hand against her cheek. "Hana, we are safe!"

Her eyes fluttered open. The blue orbs set upon him for a moment. And then flickered around. "Truly?"

"Aye." His voice was soft, his thumb stroking the side of her face. "Put down your feet."

The twist of her features wrought skepticism, but she did, in some moments, lower herself to set her feet upon the river bottom. Her eyes widened and her lips parted.

Radek nodded.

She flung herself against him, wrapping her arms around his shoulders. Her whole body shook. With emotion or from the added chill of being soaked through?

He embraced her, pressing his face into her shoulder. The danger was over and nothing could keep him from relishing in their survival.

Eva stared at the likeness of Zdenek on the wall. He was several years younger, posed with his parents. No smile touched his mouth, but it was there in his eyes.

How? How was that possible? How did it happen that her husband of such good humor would now be bereft of all pleasantness in the mere presence of his father? Had something happened? If so, what? Dare she ask him? If she did, would he share?

It bothered her that she doubted him. Was it so long ago that he and she had lived openly? Or was it only in her mind that it was so? For it was clear he had kept a part of himself from her.

Closing her eyes, she hoped for a day when all would be well between them... when his word would be kept and all trust could be returned. And they would be whole again. Such a thought warmed her, soothing the ache in the center of her chest—the pain that never seemed to go away.

She folded her hands before her hips and continued down the hall.

Raised voices bounced off the stark walls, drawing her attention up the far stairs. Was that Zdenek's father? Who incurred his wrath now? Zdenek? If so, should she intervene? What good would that do?

Her heart beat wildly at the hatred in his tone. Could a man so despise his own? No matter how her pulse may thunder, she would not abandon her husband.

She took the steps as quickly as the hem of her gown permitted. At the landing, a great door stood ajar. It became apparent that the thunderous sounds came from what must be the master's solar.

Whomever the large man berated did not protest, nor speak up. Was Zdenek so weak? Who was this man? How could he be so different from the man she believed him to be on their wedding day? The man who had fought so fiercely at her side in the bunker on Vitkov Hill? Reduced to *this*?

Eva swallowed, fear threading through her body as easily as her blood flowed. To every part of her. Her knees became weak. Would they hold? She closed her eyes, *Dearest Father, What is this? Give me strength!*

Taking slow, tentative steps toward the door, she paused and peered through the crack afforded by the slightly open door. And her breath caught.

Zdenek was not within.

The monster of a man stood over his wife, who cowered on her hands and knees before him, head tucked to her chest.

The wild pounding of her own heart muffled the words spoken in anger. What offense had the woman committed? As she watched, breathless, the terrifying, looming man's face continued to deepen in color, and he lifted an arm across his chest and flung it toward the defenseless woman.

Zdenek's mother pitched to the side. Marks on her face reveled that this was not the first blow dealt. This must not continue!

Eva reached for the door.

And hands jerked her back.

She opened her mouth to scream, but a hand clamped over her lips, cutting off all hope of salvation.

Her body, now jerked tightly against a man's chest, was dragged across the landing and down the stairs she had not long ago ascended. Who would attempt to take her? What manner of injury might they intend her?

She worked an arm free as the man pulled her toward a closed door. Pressing her elbow back with all the force she could muster, she relished the howl when her strike found its target among ribs.

The man gripped her all the more tightly; it hurt.

Twisting against his grasp, she fought in futility as he fumbled with the door's latch and they fell inside.

Only then did he release her.

She stepped away and turned, prepared to fight with all she had for her freedom. Though it was not as she feared. Zdenek slouched against the door, arms set to his side.

"Zdenek?"

He peered up at her. "You fight well, my lady wife."

She rushed to his side. "Oh no! Have I injured you?"

"Perhaps a bruised rib. Nothing that will not heal." He managed a half-smile.

Where was the humor in this? Why had he snatched her from intervening on his mother's behalf? Did he know what transpired in that room? And now, he would think her attack on his person to be such a diversion?

His features fell as he met her eyes again.

Did hers betray her thoughts? She made no effort to disguise them.

"Do not worry so. All is not lost." His words were simple.

She refused to give in to his attempt to make light of the situation. "Why did you stop me?"

His lips twitched. And his gaze seemed to hollow.

"Zdenek?"

He looked to the side.

She closed the distance between them in a couple of steps. What was this? What was being concealed from her? "Tell me."

His head dropped, hanging as if he were being scolded.

Reaching forth, she pressed a hand to the side of his face. "I am your wife. Your Eva. You can tell me anything."

Lifting his face to hers, something flashed across his eyes. Something she couldn't make sense of. Something she didn't like.

"Don't press me for answers which you will not like." The words were ground out.

"Zdenek, I simply..."

"Do *not*..." He stood straight then, causing her to step back.

She caught the hem of her gown underfoot and stumbled. Her arms circled as she attempted to right her balance, but to no avail. Landing solidly on her backside, she crumpled on the floor.

When she gathered her bearings, she sought out his face. How had this happened?

There was a hardness in his regard for her. But soon enough it was replaced by the tenderness she expected.

"Eva!" He crouched beside her. "I didn't mean to... I shouldn't have... Will you ever forgive me?"

She turned away, her gaze on the floor. Had it been the accident she believed it to be?

His words were pleading, but the soreness in her body and the sting in her heart were not assuaged. A motion to the side drew her attention. Fingers reached for her, tentatively, near but not touching.

"Eva?"

The choice was hers. Would she believe it an accident? Or blame him for the injury incurred upon her person? Searching her memory of the quickly unfolding happenings, she knew it to be unintentional.

Grasping for his proffered hand, she spoke. "Forgiveness is not necessary. For you did not strike me, nor push me. It was by happenstance."

He nodded slightly. "I would never..." The remainder of his sentence was choked out.

She gripped his hands.

His eyes glazed. Did he fight tears? Fear? What monsters scrambled within him?

Would he ever let her in?

Karin leaned over her lap in prayer. How long would Pavel linger with his father? Should she go after him? He may not receive her well.

Must he treat her so delicately? While she appreciated his care and consideration, she was not made of glass.

Still, the truth remained that the most use she could be for Baron Krejik and Pavel would be in supplication. She dipped her head once more.

Sounds came from the hall beyond. Pavel?

Rising, she leaned forward to better catch a glimpse of the source of the disturbance.

The clomping of boots, rapid in their momentum, neared. What could have happened to cause such haste? Soon enough, Pavel emerged into the lights of the Great Hall.

She moved toward him, but something in his demeanor gave her pause.

He did not afford her more than a glance.

"Pavel?" she questioned.

He did not slow, marching through the Great Hall and out the other side.

Where had he gone? Would he return? Why had he passed her by without a word? Should she stay? Return to their chambers? Try to follow him?

She sat, pondering what she might do next. There was nothing for her but to return to their chambers. Perhaps recapture what sleep she could. If she were to trust God with Pavel and their future, she must do so completely.

As she stood and stepped toward the stairs, a rustle of clothing drew her attention. Pavel came through the same opening where he had previously disappeared.

She quirked a brow.

His eyes set on her and he closed the distance between them, stopping only an arm's length from her. "Do you return to bed?"

"Aye."

He nodded. "As well you should. It is best for you and the child." His gaze flitted to her abdomen.

She set a hand there on the swell of their child.

"We will speak again in the morning."

"Will you not come to bed with me?" What could keep him from her? From their bed?

"I have much to do. All will be known when you wake."

She moved closer. "Will you not speak to me now?"

He touched her cheek. "I do not wish to burden your sleep."

Pushing out a breath, she said, "You already have."

"Pray, do not ask me to burden it further." His eyes searched her face. The blue pools were deep. There was much unsaid. Dare she press further? Dare she not?

Trust. Or not. Did she trust him? Or did she not? She must choose.

"Goodnight, my love." She leaned into him and kissed him well.

"Sleep well," he said as their lips parted.

She started up the stairs. Then turned. "And should you find yourself in need of respite, please join me abed. It will not disturb me. Rather it will give me comfort to find you next to me."

"I thank you. But do not concern yourself so. I have much to attend to."

She opened her mouth to speak, stung as she was by his words.

But, remembering her commitment to trust him, she closed it. And, nodding, resumed her journey up the stairs.

While she trusted, she could not suppress her worry.

# CHAPTER 14

Zdenek did not know how he had found himself in the dim recesses of the castle's chapel, but he did. And he was thankful he was alone. He did not think even Eva's presence would be welcomed in that moment. No, he needed the space... to think, to ponder, perhaps, yes...even to pray.

Though his faith was still young, he had found it to be true. God had proved Himself in a mighty way at Vitkov Hill, and no one could convince Zdenek that He did not exist or did not care for those with whom He sided. Was it Zdenek?

He had thought he followed God's path when he continued his pursuit of Eva. And married her. Hadn't he?

But everything had become so confused. Shouldn't he honor his father? Seek to heal the rift between them? Was that not something God would want for him?

Nothing was certain, it seemed.

Zdenek moved farther into the room that held an added chill, more so than the rest of the vast structure. How was that possible? Was it the location of this room? Did it not get ample afternoon sunlight?

Or was it something more? Something beyond the physical?

He pushed all other thoughts to the side and pressed on to where he might kneel at the altar. There he did so, falling not only upon his knees, but leaning his upper body on the raised wooden fixture meant for such supplication.

Would that he had adequate words to pour out his heart! How might he express just what churned within? He was new to prayer. New to this whole idea of communicating with an Almighty Being. Even new to the thought that God might care to hear from him.

*Lord...*

What to say? Dare he speak of his own needs? Was that selfish?

*I...ask you to be with my wife. Show me how best to...*

To what? Treat her? Manage his position? Because he wasn't doing a fine job of it at the present. Just yesterday, when she had spoken in opposition, it had sparked an anger in him. Worse, he had unleashed it upon her. Only with words, but even that was too far. Was the lashing of a tongue such a far cry from that of a fist? Or something even more...damaging to the body?

What had he been thinking? But then...that was the problem. He hadn't been thinking. Hadn't the opportunity and hadn't needed to. Not to rise to the moment of speaking thusly. It came so easily. Far too easily.

There was more of his father in him, he feared.

*Oh, God, help me...*

He was no longer that child that once cowered in fear. But wasn't he? He had not acted so differently these last several days. And he had not taken the opportunity to defend his mother. Then again, history had taught him better. *That* would only lead to pain. Immense pain.

He saw his father's hand, moving to strike him as if the memory were fresher than the five and ten years it had been. Could he not still feel the blows? Though the greater injury came not from the strikes to his physical body, but from the words levied upon him on that day and the ones following. Those he could not erase. Those he heard when all was silent. Those chipped away at any confidence he had. And they tore at the core of who he was, goading him to rise up and fight against anyone who would try to belittle him again. Only...

That would take him down a road he did not wish to follow.

His head fell to his arms once more. All the tension slackened from his body, and he lay on the altar. And he would throw himself upon the mercy of God Almighty if there were but a hope he could be rescued and his path altered from that of his father.

For he would not become that. He would not.

Hana sat at the edge of the river. And waited. How long had it been since she was in her father's care? Since she had left the safety that the strong walls of his fortified home afforded her?

Perhaps too long.

She had traded it. For the hope of aiding the Hussite army and the glory that might be forthcoming.

Did she still believe it worth the sacrifice? She was not certain. For she had sacrificed much. Risked much. Nearly lost all.

And for what? Had she contributed? Made any measurable change in the resistance to the Catholic Church? Where did her efforts land her? Other than in the Royalist Camp...and subsequently wandering the wilderness, fighting for her life?

No, it was for naught. She had to accept that.

It was time to go home. Time to give up girlish notions and return to her father's protection.

But what of Radek? What of these new feelings he stirred in her?

Even then, she looked over her shoulder and to the right. He worked to gather branches and other things from the forest to build a fire and construct a makeshift shelter in which they might warm themselves and pass the night. She longed for the heat of the fire. The wet garment and chill evening air had a rather freezing quality.

But she would not complain. She was thankful to be alive. Thanks to Radek.

He had been strong, brave, and capable. And he seemed to have a care for her. How deep did it go? Would he seek her hand? If so, where would they belong? By his own words, he was not interested in returning to the Hussite army. Nor did it seem he would go back to the Royalist Camp. Heavens, no! Thank the Lord, no.

But where did that leave him?

She closed her eyes, weary of thinking. Of all of it.

Home. She wanted to go home.

He would get her there. If nothing else, she knew that to be true.

Opening her eyes, her gaze flitted across the river once more, the waters that tried to claim her life—only the most recent of the threats to her continued existence. But for the hand of God...working through Radek. Even if he was an unwitting vessel.

The grass crunched behind her. Radek drew near. His footfalls halted. He couldn't be more than an arm's length away. Why did he pause?

He drew in a deep breath and pressed it out. "I think we will be in Prague soon."

She nodded. Numbed more than she thought she would be. Because of her earlier thoughts? Or because of his words?

"Perhaps one more day."

His tone seemed to betray nothing. As if he only reported the weather. Did he, then, not care more than this? She looked to the ground.

The silence became thick.

He spoke again, his voice softer. "It will be dark soon. We must eat and settle in for the evening."

As he said, it *would* be dark soon. And, indeed, they should. She shifted to stand.

His hands were on her arms in a moment, assisting her to her feet. Then their bodies were closer than they should be. His breath on her neck. Is this what he intended? Or had it taken him by surprise as well?

She turned to the side, the warmth of his exhales now on the side of her face. "Radek," she breathed. "I..."

His thumbs caressed her arms where they made contact.

The movement stilled and thrilled at once.

She turned.

His hands slid down her arms and connected with her hands. He looked into her eyes and swallowed.

How did they find themselves in these moments? Locked in such contact?

His eyes drew her in. She leaned into him.

But he closed his eyes and turned his head, pulling back. His disengagement was abrupt enough to leave her stung.

"You are shivering," he said plainly, still avoiding her gaze.

She looked down at her dress, clinging to her in places, but in no way offering her protection from the coolness of the late day.

"We must get you to the fire." He turned and walked up the gentle slope.

And all she could do was stare after him. What was she going to do?

Pavel rode hard into the darkness. Would that he had not allowed General Zizka to leave! He had known in his gut that it was the wrong thing to do. That he needed to go with the man of war. To pursue this evil that reigned within their lands, not so far from his home...even that it might terrorize those he loved and threaten their lives.

Why? Why did this man show such a special hatred for his family? For his father? Had they wronged the man in some way?

What did that have to do with it? Did evil even have reason? Or was it just as it was?

The first strains of morning broke against the horizon. Dawn would be forthcoming soon. And he wished to return to Karin. He needn't cause unnecessary worry. Nor be away too long should his father regain consciousness.

He turned the horse away from Tabor and to the south. He must be close.

Moments more and he spotted the edges of the camp. Memory of other camps, not unlike this one, filled his mind. And the things that had happened—acts he regretted and those he did not. But all were for the cause. For the betterment of his people, his brethren. It would all be well. He would have to trust.

Pavel slowed his mount as he neared the somewhat concealed collection of Hussite soldiers. Where would the general be? He must speak with him. And quickly.

He scanned the area, taking in as much as possible. The number of troops had diminished. Drastically. But then it was harvest time. They had not the benefit that the Germans did. The Hussites were not truly soldiers. Or even noblemen, who could lend their sword at their leave. No, these were farmers, simple men of the villages. As such, they must return to attend to home and field regardless of the army's need of them.

How could Pavel have neglected this truth? Zizka sought his aid, not only because he wished it, but rather because he was in great need of Pavel's sword arm. As he gazed over the men, it became apparent that the man must be desperate for each and every warrior he could muster.

Now bringing his horse to a halt, he shifted as the destrier sputtered. The animal would need to be refreshed. Could he see to that first? No, his errand was of utmost importance.

"Who goes?" He heard a deep bark from farther off to the right.

He turned.

The general had been moving among his men. Even then, he had a cluster of five around him—all of the simple sort. Where were

Zizka's men-at-arms? Still, Pavel could not disguise his relief. There was one problem solved.

"It is I, Pavel Krejik."

"Lord Krejik?" Zizka seemed rather disbelieving. Had Pavel left him with the thought that he cared so little for the Hussite army and efforts?

"Aye, General." Pavel dismounted and strode through the men gathering with interest toward the bulky man.

Zizka stepped forward as well and clapped Pavel's shoulder before gripping his arm. The hold was firmer than need be.

"Come. There is much to speak of."

Pavel remembered the labor of the beast that bore him there and paused for a moment. "General," he began. "If I may, I would see to my horse."

Zizka shifted to the side, waving to one of the boys beside him.

The lad, who could be no more than seven and ten, reached for the reins. "My lord, allow me."

Pavel nodded.

Zizka offered a crooked smile before turning toward the west side of the camp where the trees thickened. As he led, Pavel took in the state of the camp and the men. They were worn, to be certain, but in good spirits. Did Zizka's efforts find success despite their smaller numbers then?

Soon enough, they stopped before the larger of the tents. Zizka bade the others leave, and he then faced Pavel.

"How does Baron Krejik fare?"

Pavel faced the approaching day, not wishing for his general to see any of his weaker emotions. "He...lives."

Zizka waited.

But Pavel had nothing further to say, so the silence hung between them.

"I did hope for better tidings."

Pavel's eyes leveled on Zizka. The man's face was unmarred by grooves—sincerity the only emotion discernable.

"I must ask, Lord Krejik, why have you come? Have you...considered my words?"

Why *had* he come? Did he plan to offer his services to General Zizka? In that moment, he was not certain. How could he leave his vulnerable wife and his father who may, even now, be expending his last breaths?

How could he not?

This man...the one Zizka pursued...must be stopped. He could not be left to bring injury to Pavel's family any longer. Pavel would do what he must to that end.

"Yes, General, I have. My sword is yours." Why did it seem something solid filled his gut at that pronouncement? His vision wavered, and Karin's face flashed before him. He pushed those thoughts to the side. He did this *for* her. For their child. For their future. She would have to understand.

"And you are certain?" One of Zizka's brows rose. Did he doubt Pavel's commitment? His loyalty?

"You question my word, General?"

"Of course not." Zizka's gaze deepened, somehow knowing. He studied Pavel.

The scrutiny seared through Pavel. And fell heavy upon him. Did he lie to himself? For certain he either lied to Karin or to Zizka. The question was...whom?

How long Eva had been in the small garden, she did not know. She had sat for much of her time, watching the various birds and butterflies about the buds and chasing her thoughts.

Try as she might to find their end, she could not. Thus, she was in the same place now as when she started—no closer to an answer or a sense of peace about any of it. Not Zdenek's reaction, not the way he had behaved since they came here, not to what she saw of his father, standing over his mother...

She shivered. And she knew it was not solely because of the ever cooling weeks pressing in on them. But more due to these thoughts, this memory.

It was horrid. The man was a beast. Her own father had cherished her mother. Treated her with tenderness and kindness until sickness took her from them. That's what love was to her. What marriage was.

She was not ignorant to the fact that this kind of abuse happened, but she had never witnessed such. It shook her to her very core. And the images plagued her. At first, only when she closed her eyes. But now, they were before her constantly.

*Father in heaven, How am I to endure this? Would you banish these thoughts from my mind?*

All was silence for a moment.

Then there was the drawn backhand, the cowering lady, and the sound... It all remained firm in her memory.

A rustling of clothing came from the corner of the enclosed area.

Eva drew her limbs tighter to herself even as she glanced toward the sound.

The swish of skirts and the movement of brown hair belied that Zdenek's mother had entered the gardens.

Dare Eva go to her? Did she have the courage for such awkward conversation? But could she abide not? How could Eva not offer the woman what little comfort she could?

"My lady!" she called as she rose. Grabbing at her skirt, she rushed after the woman.

It was no easy task to catch up to her, though she did find her just within the inner bailey.

"Lady Ambrozova," Eva said, reaching to touch the woman's elbow and sucking in a deep breath. Would that these dresses and underthings allowed for more breath.

The lady turned, but her eyes were downcast. She would not meet Eva's gaze. Did she know? What Eva had seen?

There was a slight swelling to one side of her face, though her features were much paled with powder. How much had been neces-sary to cover the bruises?

"My lady," Eva said on a whisper, ducking to seek out the woman's gaze.

The woman avoided Eva's eyes at every move. Was she shamed? Embarrassed?

Why should her husband's actions shame her? Eva could under-stand, she supposed, but she didn't truly fathom why that would be.

"He doesn't have the right—" Eva's voice was not much more than a whisper.

Lady Ambrozova's chin lifted, and her eyes sparked. "What would you know? How could you possibly understand?" Her voice had a bite to it.

Eva stepped back, stung. Even her body, though stiffened, seemed to shake. Had she overstepped so far?

The woman whirled away from her and moved off once more.

Eva watched her go. Her whole body paralyzed. Her thoughts would not shake loose either to command her to move. Or to deter-mine where she would go or what she would do.

And so she stood, long after the woman had vanished from sight.

# CHAPTER 15

Radek watched as Hana settled near him in front of the fire. It would be good. They would be able to dry completely. And it would warm Hana. He feared for her wellbeing. When he touched her body earlier, the complete lack of heat had surprised him. How had he so neglected her? She needed to be near the flames. For her own benefit. And for his peace of mind.

But must she sit so close to him? That made it difficult to think. Then again, would it not be the same no matter where she sat—be it beside him or across the fire? The flames would catch the lightness in her eyes, tinge the blond in her hair until it was golden, and highlight her fine features.

What was in his head? He could not allow his thoughts to continue in this direction. She belonged with her father. And with the Hussites. Her father would keep her safe, as would her allegiance to the cause.

He could not rejoin that effort. Though the desire to do so *for her* was great. Perhaps too great. But he had been through this. It wasn't possible for him to deny his better judgment, or his very conscience, and fight with General Zizka.

He poked a stick at the base of the fire. Embers rose and flames lapped higher. And he laid the small branch to the ground.

But he sensed her gaze on him. Dare he return it? Or perhaps it would be best for him to be direct? "Might I ask for your thoughts?"

He heard her shift. Still, he kept his focus on the glowing limbs.

"I..." Did she, too, struggle to find words? To move forward in this...situation between them? With the knowledge of what weighed against them?

Unable to resist any longer, he turned and let his gaze take her in. And that he did—drink in her visage as if he were a parched man. Did he regret so much that they would soon be parted forever?

Her eyes widened slightly as they met his. Could this connection affect her so? Her lips remained parted as if to speak, but no sound came forth. Though they tempted. Oh, how they tempted.

She did, at length, find words. "I just...I wish..."

"For what?" Was that his voice? It seemed far away. And far too quiet.

She swallowed and her lips seamed. Was he so fixated on her mouth? But, try as he might, he could not tear his gaze away. Every part of him was alive. And all too...aware.

"I wish..." She spoke, but her words, too, became soft and distant.

"Yes?" He was in a trance. She filled every thought, every sense.

"I don't know that I..." She didn't seem sure of herself, or of her words. Was her struggle the same as his? Did she long for something that could not be?

His mind screamed at him. Beseeched him. How to close this gap between them? To take her in his arms, let the feel of her and the movement of her lips banish all other thoughts.

He wanted to. But was there wisdom in that? Then again, he wasn't sure he cared for what was wise. Not in that moment. With his eyes caught on her, he leaned forward, toward her. And in doing so, for that brief second, broke eye contact. Reality rushed in.

It gave him pause. And he settled back onto the ground. Yes, this separation, small though it was...was best. He drew back into himself.

The breath she released was ragged and sputtered.

He regretted his retreat. Yet, he would do it again. For deepening whatever this was between them would not help.

Silence filled the space between them for several moments.

They should prepare to bed down for the night. Yes, that would be best.

He shifted to rise.

"Tell me, Radek," she spoke into the emptiness.

He paused.

She looked at him. "What will you do?"

Furrowing his brows, he attempted to make sense of her question. "What will I do?"

Her hazel eyes, wide and glassy, did not move from his face. "When we return. Will you..." She swallowed.

What lay unspoken in her fading words? Did she fear he might rejoin the Royalist camp? He looked away. How could he answer her when he had not come to a satisfactory response for himself?

"Radek?"

How long had he left her question unanswered? It mattered not, he decided as he sighed. There was little hope of anything forthcoming that would assuage her mind.

He set his gaze upon her. The desire to touch her face was almost unbearable. Still, he restrained himself. He refused to continue to push into something that could not be. "It is late."

She dropped her regard to her hands in her lap.

And his heart dropped. If there were any remedy to be found for her ache, he would provide it. Any, that is, that would not lead to deeper wounds. As it was, he could not...*would* not make overtures or promises he could not keep.

Not even to staunch this terrible tearing pain in his own heart.

Karin watched the coming dawn. But not from her bed. She sat by the window, the coverlet about her shoulders. Not truly for a chill in the air, however. Heat from the fire suffused the space quite completely. What was it then that found her clinging to the cloth, as if it sheltered her from her surroundings? Perhaps therein lay her answer—she perceived a need of protection. Of her person or of her heart? Where had Pavel gone? When would he return? Why had he been abrupt in his parting?

She sighed and sank into the chair she had managed to pull to the window. There would be little she might do to persuade anything from him he did not wish to give.

He was much grieved by the state of his father. And of the happenings of the weeks past. Could she blame him?

She wanted him to long to be with her, to crave her presence...but that desire was nonsense. Nothing more than a girl's dream of marriage.

*This* was real. The raw truth of suffering had been visited upon her enough for her to know better. And yet, she did not.

She still thought in fanciful daydreams...the stuff of fairytales.

Selfish. That's what she was.

Wishing her husband to cleave to her side when there was much unrest within these borders. And the need of him elsewhere so great.

*Lord, forgive my stubbornness. And my inability to look beyond my needs. He is Your vassal, Your weapon. Show me how best to support him as You...*

The creaking of the door drew her attention in that direction.

Pavel's lengthy stride carried him into the room. His gaze first on the disheveled bed. Though his eyes soon found her figure not far away.

"Karin, are you well?" The clear blue of his eyes darkened. He did care so deeply for her welfare. And that of their child.

She pressed a hand over her abdomen as she rose. "Yes, I...could not sleep." There was little to be gained in lying.

He frowned. "It was not my intention to rob you of your rest."

She stepped to him, closing the distance between them.

He watched her every move with such intensity.

"I know that well enough. But is it not right for a wife to await her beloved husband when he is on an errand in the middling of night? Not knowing when he shall return? Or...?" Catching herself, she halted her words. She had promised herself she would not betray those feelings to him. He did not deserve her selfish delusions.

"Or...what, my love?" His voice was low and quiet but firm.

She looked away. "It is nothing. I have spoken out of turn."

He took her chin between his thumb and forefinger. "No. I daresay not. Your gaze is clouded. Your face is lined. There is much you do not say."

Why must he push? He could not want to hear the whole of it.

"I...only meant to say that I worried for your safety." There. That was true enough.

He pulled her into his embrace. There she found comfort...and reluctance. From him? Or from within herself? Perhaps both?

Even as she laid her head to his shoulder, she found she could not release herself fully into him. What was this hesitation? And there was something in him holding back as well. She sensed it.

He pressed a hand to her hair, stroking the length of the tresses down her back. At length, he exhaled. Still, he did not relax his stance.

She pulled back. "What is it?"

His brows furrowed as he looked down at her. Not so much that she thought him perplexed. But more concerned. Did he hide something from her?

As she released him to step away farther, his hands caught her upper arms, holding her within his grasp. His grip was gentle. Was it meant to remind her she need remain until he dismissed her?

Such a notion! This was not the Pavel she knew. And she would not press such accusations on him, not even in her mind.

Settling her hands on his chest, she looked into his eyes. They were still more gray than blue. His heart must be troubled.

"I will be gone within the hour."

She would have jerked away had he not secured her with his hold. "Gone?"

His mouth thinned.

Looking down at the small space between them, her mind raced. What could she ask? What would he answer? How far might she push?

Then she met his gaze once more.

This was Pavel.

Pavel.

Her beloved. She had no need to fear him or think he would not be reasonable with her.

"Where..." Her voice caught as the words came forth. "Where will you go?"

The muscles in his jaw twitched. But he did not turn away from her. In a fluid motion, he released his hold on her and let his hands fall to his sides. "I have given my sword arm in the hunt for the man responsible for..."

His jaw clenched.

He didn't need to continue. She knew. The man who had done injury to his father.

Would he, then, leave with his father's life in the balance?

"Will you not stay until more is to be known of the baron's chances?"

Pavel turned, stepping to the window and, leaning forward on hands set upon the ledge, gazed out.

The silence between them stretched.

She watched him. How could such a joyous reunion not a week past become this moment of uncertainty between them?

It became unbearable.

"Pavel?" Though she tried to keep her voice strong, still the tremble was evident even to her.

"I have to do this."

Had to do this? Leave her and their unborn child? Leave his

father with his fate yet unknown? Leave on this mission of revenge that may lead to very dark places?

She sealed her lips against the words that wanted to pour forth. And instead sent up a prayer. *Father, help me. Lead me. Guide me.*

Pavel spun back toward her. His eyes full of emotion. So much so, it was difficult to name one apart from the others. "Can you not see? I must stop this man."

The force of his conviction overpowered everything else in his regard. And in her response. So, she remained silent.

"I couldn't live with myself if I let others go in my stead and this murderer slipped through. And then came back to..." His gaze on her in that moment made the rest unnecessary.

He feared for her. This was the crux of it. The reason he would abandon his father in this desperate hour. For her.

Did she have the faith to let him go? Did she have a choice?

Zdenek neared Eva's room. His heart a weight within his chest, pulling at him as he trudged forward. How was it that he would wish to put this off?

What had become of him? Of them?

Was she not his wife? His beloved?

Then what should prevent him from baring himself to her? Why did he not trust her to handle his heart well? Had they not made such promises to one another?

To delay the encounter or not...mattered little. For he stood outside her chamber, staring at the oak separating him from her.

Could he take the last steps? Did he have the strength?

He closed his eyes and pictured his Eva on the day they wed. Her dark eyes bright, shining with adoration. Yes, she had been hopeful and eager for their future. How was she to know that he...

What?

Was a coward? Was a mirror of his father?

Everything within bade him turn and retreat. Yet that part of him, the piece that maintained that same hope as she, kept his feet firmly planted.

Drawing strength from that place, he closed the distance to the door and knocked before he could think more on it.

Moments later, the door opened and Eva stared up at him. Her eyes betrayed her confusion. Had she, then, lost all faith in him?

"My lady, I..."

She looked down. Did she find herself so undeserving of such an address?

Something entirely different sparked in him. She was his *wife*. As such, that title belonged to her. Regardless what his father may think.

"Eva," he said, more softly. Still, his voice bore more confidence. "I would speak with you."

She nodded.

"May I...?" He motioned forward. Would she not invite him into her bedchamber? Had they become such strangers to one another?

Her gaze met his for a moment. And she gave a quick nod, stepping back and allowing him to pass. Something in her manner remained more formal than he liked.

As he stepped around her, he indeed felt the intruder. His eyes fell to the bed. They had lain there together so many nights ago. How many? Too many.

"My lord," she broke into the expanding silence. "Did you...need to speak with me?" Her words were even.

Must everything be so difficult? He crossed his arms and let his head drop back.

She remained as she was. Waiting.

He dropped his eyes to her. She seemed so timid, so unsure of herself in the middle of the stark room. How had it never seemed so sparse before? Perhaps her smile and laughter had warmed the space.

One of them must have boldness. He pulled in a breath, drawing on the strength he knew to be in his love for her.

"I would, wife."

Her brows furrowed.

He stepped closer to her. "There are things that must be set right between us."

Her features remained set as if she did not understand. "What do you—?"

"Much has been said that should not have been said. More has transpired that should have been stopped."

"My lord?" She sucked in a quick breath. At his words or his closeness? For now, he stood less than an arm's length away.

"Yes." His words were not much more than a whisper. "I have failed you, my love."

Her regard fell to the floor with a catch in her breath.

He tugged her gaze to his with a finger under her chin.

Dark eyes glimmered with moisture. Had he so injured her? It sliced at his heart. So much that he fought the urge to clutch at his chest.

Sliding his hand forward, he cupped the side of her face. "I have wronged you, dearest wife."

A whimper escaped her.

"Betrayed you."

With each confession, the ache within deepened. And the cords that bound him loosened a bit more.

"And there is much more to confess."

Her eyes widened. It was as if she knew. But, how could she? Pulling away, she moved to sit on the edge of the bed. Now settled, she patted the space next to her.

He took in a breath, steeling himself for what was to come. Closing the distance, he lowered himself to sit beside her.

She offered a small smile, simple and encouraging.

He ran his hands over his thighs. How would he manage this? It had seemed so easy to think to proceed. Now, his courage waned.

A hand covered his. Her slender fingers pressing upon his. But she said nothing, only waited.

"My...relationship with my father, as you know, has always been rather...complicated."

She nodded, but remained silent.

Did he wish her to speak? Would that make it easier?

He licked his lips and continued. "And you have seen that he can be a...harsh man. Even...violent." His voice broke on that last word.

A gentle squeeze on his hand drew his gaze to hers. Her eyes shone as if moisture already collected there.

He blew out a breath. He couldn't stop now. "My mother was always the focus of his anger. She took the brunt of his...attention." The guilt still cut deeply. "I thought her weak...not to stand up to him, to speak for herself."

Glancing at Eva once more, he wondered at her thoughts.

She looked to their clasped hands. And did not give him her eyes.

Perhaps it was for the best. "But I learned it was a strength within and her love for me that sustained her and stayed her hand through the horror of it all."

He let his attention drift out the window. How many times had he sought solace in those trees just beyond the walls of the castle? How often had he pretended to be anywhere but here?

"What happened, Zdenek?" Eva's voice was soft, without pressuring. Only prompting him to return to his memories. The very place he wished to run from.

"I decided that it had to end. If she wouldn't stand for herself, it was up to me to make it stop."

There was a slight tremble in Eva's hand. He almost missed it. But it was there and then it was gone.

"What happened?" she asked.

"He turned on me."

"Zdenek," she breathed as she lifted her other hand toward his face.

But he pulled back. He needed to finish. He needed to say all of it. If he stopped now, he would never return to this place.

"That was only part of it. It was the beginning of a berating that would last the remainder of my childhood years. No matter how I tried to endear myself to him and prove I was *his* son, he pierced me with his words until I was sent away."

His gaze had not left her face. She seemed confused. He could imagine it. There was still the heart of it to reveal. The thing that might injure her, too.

"There is something I have not told you before. My mother's parents were a rather uncommon match. My grandfather had fallen in love with a peasant girl. And I am not privy to the details of their joining, but they were permitted to marry."

Eva's features betrayed her interest. But that was another tale, for another time. Though the remaining details he had were few. He needed to get the rest of *his* story out.

"My father believed it was a tryst that had resulted in pregnancy, of course."

Eva's eyes widened. And the hurt beneath the surprise was evident. He could feel it in the space between them.

"And so, that day, when I stepped between him and my mother, he declared that I had too much of that common blood in me...that I was a peasant's son, that I would never be more, and that he was ashamed to have sired me."

She pressed a hand to the side of his face.

He allowed the supportive touch, but refused to lean into it. Would she now tell him how it wasn't true? That he was so much more? Words that meant well but rang as hollow as they had when his mother had spoken them so many times?

"I can't begin to imagine the pain that you endured. Sitting under such vile words."

He looked down. That was not quite what he'd expected.

"And I don't know about your past. But I know who you have become. And I have seen glimpses of who God is crafting you to be."

He peered up at her.

"And it is magnificent."

The ache within dulled. Dare he hope that there was truth to her words? Could he go on if he believed otherwise?

"I would that—"

A man cleared his throat nearby.

Zdenek jerked toward the sound, rising in a second.

The man stood just beyond the doorway, making every attempt to appear as if he were not watching.

Zdenek did what he could to tamp down his ire. "What is this intrusion?"

Though he turned from her, his hands still rested near her features. Enough that her flinch was evident. Failed...again...to protect her from this anger.

"Forgive me, my lord, I did not intend to trespass. A message came for you."

Zdenek crossed the room, jerked the door wider, and held out his hand for the missive.

The man pressed it forward, bowed, and stepped back.

Turning to the interior where Eva stood, Zdenek tore at the seal, all but dismissing the man. Who would have sent tidings? Radek? He had not heard from him since Vitkov Hill when his friend...when Radek chose to abandon their cause.

He paused. Dare he go on? Did he wish to know what had become of his once dear friend? As if Radek's choices had not affected him...wounded him.

Then again, perhaps it was Pavel. Zdenek had been given to understand the man was near Tabor searching out his family. Urgency drove him into the letter all the more rapidly.

The seal was that of a family friend—a man he fought beside in the conflicts of the last months. But why? What could warrant sending word?

"Zdenek?" Eva's voice was laced with concern.

He spread open the letter and took in what he could as quickly as possible.

"Who is it from? What does it say?" The strain under Eva's words bade him respond. And soon.

"It speaks of the army still in battle."

"Oh?"

Zdenek looked at his wife. She could not disguise her interest. Her heart was with their people. Fighting. For their freedom. For their beliefs. Was not his?

"How do they fare?"

He turned his attention back to the writing. "Hynek Krustna of Lichtenburg seeks to take the Vysehrad."

Eva's eyes widened. "A fortified castle? May God be with him!"

Their gazes collided for a moment.

Eva broke the silence. "Does the...writer...only seek to let you know of these plans?"

Zdenek let his hand and the letter fall to his side. "My brother at arms writes for my aid. He shares that there is great unrest in Prague and in many places. All are being called to action."

"Of course." Eva came to life. "We must go. At once." She stepped closer to Zdenek.

He swallowed, knowing full well that she was right. Though it was also true that his father would not take this news kindly.

His test would come sooner than he thought.

Hana opened her eyes to a new day. But nothing about it felt new, refreshed, or hopeful. They were closer to Prague. To safety. Yet that realization only brought another wave of regret.

What had she done? Why had she opened her heart to this man?

She did not blame him for his withdrawal. This had put him in an impossible position. It was likely that her pain mirrored his.

If only they might find solace in each other. But that would only deepen the problem.

How had she not foreseen this? How thoughtless, how senseless...

And so, the interchange of her thoughts had continued throughout much of the night. Had she slept at all? She could not remember releasing her hold on consciousness once.

Dawn approached and they would be on their way soon enough. Would they reach Prague today? Tomorrow? She was not certain, but it would be within the next few days.

She turned her head, shifting to look where Radek had bedded down for the night.

He was not there. How had he risen without her knowing? Perhaps she had slipped into a brief sleep after all.

She moved to her back, giving her shoulder relief and a chance to return blood flow to her arm. Even as she gazed at the twilight sky, her heart was heavy. How could she have wrapped so much into this man? It could not be. Would not be. This must stop.

Determined anew, she rose to a sitting position.

"Sleep well?"

The sound came from off to the side, opposite where Radek was expected.

She turned.

He sat, gazing over the rolling hills. Had he even looked at her? What did he seek? Was he gauging the direction they must go? Did he, too, wonder at how much longer they would be together?

"Yes." She stretched her arms in front of her. There was no sense in worrying him with her fatigue. "Perhaps escaping death does good for one's rest."

He scoffed. "You do not lie well."

She paused. "Lie?" Even as she said the word, her face heated.

Only then did he turn toward her. "You forget yourself, Hana. I fought my own demons most of the night as well."

Dropping her head, she let out a breath. And guilt swept over her. Not for her lie, but that she had been so caught up in her own emotions she had not even noticed that he...

"I think we will reach Prague by nightfall if we can make the most of our journey today." His gaze scanned the horizon once more. "Then you will be rid of me."

Her head jerked up, her eyes on the back of his head. Did he truly think that was in her mind?

"How can you say that I would want to be rid of you?" Though she pressed out the words, her ire stirred, her voice held a slight tremble.

His shoulders drooped, and his regard fell to the ground.

"How?" Her eyes pricked. Was this so upsetting?

"I..." he started, but the word hung in the air.

She rose with as much grace as she could muster, her ankle stiffening. In her flustered state, she found herself tangled in her skirt and struggling to balance. But she maintained her footing even as she grimaced at putting weight on her right leg. The pain was not as sharp as it once was, more a dull ache from the constant use of the last days. The splints Radek continued to supply were much to thank for that. But it did not mean all was forgiven.

When she raised her chin to glare at him, she found his gaze on her, studying her.

She crossed her arms. More in an effort to protect herself. Though she hoped it appeared defiant.

He stood in one quick movement. How did he do that?

She stomped to him. Well, what would have to pass for stomping as she favored her right foot. "What have I done to deserve such words from you?"

He searched her features. What was he looking for? After several seconds, he let out a breath and shame settled over him like a shroud. "Nothing."

"Then why do you do it? To push me away?" Was that what was in his thoughts? To create distance between them with their journey's end in sight? Did he think to put her off this way? That she would be thwarted so easily?

And why should she push? Did she truly care so much?

He glanced up at her.

That was all the answer she needed. In his eyes, she saw his regret. And felt her own. She *did* feel for him. Deeply. And so, it may well be up to her. How to reason with him?

She softened her voice. "I don't understand. There are challenges, yes. But we have come so far, faced so much. How can it be so hard to—"

"You are right, Hana. You *don't* understand."

His words stung. She jerked back a step.

"We are not the same. You believe in some invisible, all-knowing God who is behind this war. Even fighting alongside the Hussites. All I know of this God is that belief in Him made my father weak. And that General Zizka made compromises and questionable decisions in His name."

She tried to process Radek's words. His father? General Zizka? Was this the whole of Radek's experience of God? Had he not seen more of God in her then?

Radek held a hand out as if to touch her, but paused. "I want to believe. For you. If only you knew how much."

Her breath caught.

His hand fell. "But I can't."

The silence between them gave her precious moments to think. "I do not wish that you would make yourself believe anything for me. Least of all this. Belief...faith in God has to be something that comes from here." She put a hand over his heart.

The contact stole her thoughts, and her words.

He looked down at her hand on his chest. His hand covered hers. "You don't understand. I would give anything...everything...if only..."

She licked her lips. "I know. But faith isn't like that."

He dipped his head. "And I can't trust a God like this."

She swallowed. "I only wish you would let me tell you about Him. Tell you the truth."

His brows furrowed, creating creases on his forehead. "Dare I not trust what I know, what I have seen?"

Taking in a full, deep breath, she sent up a silent prayer and continued. "Perhaps, I want for the chance to tell you what I know, what I have seen."

He regarded her closely with narrowed eyes. Would he give her the chance? Or was he so burned that his decision had been set for all eternity?

She prayed not. Oh, how she prayed not.

His eyes softened.

And she knew...he would listen.

# CHAPTER 16

Pavel watched his father's chest rise and fall. Slowly. Too slowly.

Though it may be unnecessary, he found himself praying for each breath forthcoming to follow its predecessor. But could he pray it, could he will his father to continue living?

The great baron had not regained consciousness since he was brought to the castle. Should Pavel wait for at least that much? Or would that be an exercise in futility? Was his father set for eternity?

Scanning his father's form, still but for the shallow breaths, he beseeched the Lord once more. He begged for the man's life. Not just a continued existence in this state.

As his eyes fell on the bound wounds, his anger flamed anew. He must find this evil where it lurked and snuff it out.

"Forgive me, Father. I wish that I might remain. But idleness is not in me."

There was no response. Would be no response.

Standing and stepping closer to the man's side, he wished for something...some manner of closure with the man that was so dear to him. But there would be none.

A thickness filled his throat. The time had come to remove himself.

"I will not let this go unpunished, Father. I will not." Pavel's words could not have been more than a whisper.

*Vengeance is Mine.*

The words brushed across his mind. He pushed them to the side. It could not be that the Lord would ask him to stand aside in this. No, that would not be fitting.

Turning, he slipped from the space and his father's presence. But the thoughts of vengeance continued to trail him. What would he have said to Stepan had he the chance to intervene in the man's thirst for violence?

*Vengeance is the Lord's.*

He paused, dragging in a breath.

Could he? Submit his anger to God and let Him…trust Him to…

*No.* Pavel would not yield. He must see this threat ended. This was different—he sought to end a threat, not seek retribution.

He picked up step once more. Though the heaviness in his stomach told of the lie he fed himself.

Stepping out to the donjon, he found his horse waiting. The stable hand had seen to the animal's nourishment and refreshment. And his final preparations had been made. All that remained were his final words to Karin.

But she was not there among those poised for his departure.

He furrowed his brow. What delayed her? Surely, she had not decided to be absent in protest.

The thought settled into his mind. He wanted to dismiss it, but it found root. It was true that while she spoke of understanding, there had been more in her regard.

Would she now make her true feelings known? Like this? Before the whole of the castle?

The stirring in his chest became hard. And unpleasant. As much as he did not wish to think such of his Karin, what was left?

He glanced at the men around him. They found other places for their gazes.

"I had hoped to see you off," a loud voice called as it neared. But masculine.

Pavel peered around the horse. Duke Novak. He closed his eyes as his ire grew, expanding in his chest, pushing out every other emotion. "Yes, Duke. I will depart soon enough."

The man neared and clapped Pavel on the shoulder. "God speed and bless your search. May He double your efforts. And make swift your return."

"From your lips to God's ears." Pavel spoke with calm words, but the muscles in his jaw were hard.

"And..." The duke halted as he looked around. "The Lady Karin? Is she ill?"

"I know not," Pavel said through clenched teeth.

Confusion filled the duke's features. "She will not see you off?"

"Aye, she will." Pavel's anger had reached a boiling point. How could Karin dishonor him so? She may not agree with his actions, but he'd thought they might at least be able to stand together. He would not let her hide from him. If she wouldn't come to send him off, he would have her answer for it.

Pavel brushed past the duke with no further word and into the castle. He moved through the great hall and corridors, his vision focused only on his destination. Everything else blurred. As he came upon the stairs to the upper chambers, he found a small cluster of maidservants huddled at the base. They blocked the way.

"If you will excuse me," he pushed through.

The women gasped as they moved away.

As they did so, they revealed another woman, on the ground, her red-blonde hair splayed haphazardly and her limbs askew. Was it...?

He fell to his knees beside her, brushing hair from her face. *Karin!*

His hands hovered over her body while his heart stuttered within him. What had happened? Had she fallen on the stairs?

"Karin!" He found his voice at last.

The women around him shifted. And he remembered that they were there.

"The physician," he commanded. "Now!"

He gathered Karin into his arms. Her form was limp. So lifeless.

Collecting himself, he felt about her for breath and the pulse of life. They were present, if faint.

*God, help me.*

Reaching under her to lift her into his lap, he then pulled his hand back around to touch her face. And saw blood upon it.

His gaze jerked to the floor.

She was bleeding.

The baby!

*Dear God in heaven, no!*

Radek drew in as much air as possible. Prague was in sight.

Relief washed over him. Hana was safe. No more would she be at risk from a Royalist party finding them, sneaking upon them, taking her, hurting her. If only he could have prevented them from...

He shook his head. There was naught he could do now but learn to live with the guilt, with the fact that he had failed her. But she was whole and well, and promised she was none the worse for it.

Dare he take solace in that? Take her at her word?

What of the other things she had told him this day? Of God? Now, that had seemed rather fanciful and grand indeed. Simply the ideals of a woman wanting a fairytale come true.

She shifted as she leaned against a large rock nearby, drawing his attention.

"It is not far." Was that regret in his voice? He looked over his shoulder at her, hoping she would not be able to discern it.

Her gaze was set off in the distance. "Aye. I can see Vitkov Hill."

He refocused on where she looked. There the mound stood, proud and firm, strangely unassuming. Despite what had occurred there not so long ago. The images flashed in his mind—the attack, the fear, his friend in great peril.

Radek's heart ached. His friend. Once more, he wondered what Zdenek, or even Pavel, must think of him—a defector to their cause. An enemy to everything they stood for.

"What troubles you?"

The voice, so incredibly soft, was near. Too near.

He jerked at the sound.

Hana. She had drawn closer, only inches from touching him.

Though she flinched, her features settled into concern. Had she such a care after him? After all he had said to dissuade her? Even as he continued to reject the beliefs she held dear?

Yet there was no such judgment in her. Not that he could discern.

"Radek?"

He looked to the ground and shook his head.

"I will not remember that day well, either."

When he sought her gaze again, he found her staring into the distance once more. Had she her own terrors of that day? Of course, she did! It would have been the day she was taken captive.

Without a second thought, he took her hand, interlacing their fingers. "All of that is over now. It is behind us."

She nodded.

"And we have nothing but to move forward."

Her eyes found his. There was something odd in the way she regarded him. What was that?

And his words struck him. Did she think he spoke for himself as well? That wasn't possible. He couldn't just pretend that nothing had happened. There wasn't the opportunity for him to start anew. Life wasn't so kind...

Or was it?

He let his thoughts quiet as he dove into her eyes for a long moment. But only that. Then he pulled away and tore his gaze from hers. "Let us finish this."

Then he picked up step once more and continued toward the large city before them.

Zdenek moved toward the Great Hall. Now, as the nooning meal approached, it was the most likely place he'd find his father. He sent up prayer without ceasing that the interaction to come would be brief and peaceful. But, were he honest, there was much doubt in his heart.

If possible, Eva and he needed to extricate themselves from this place as quickly as they could and be on their way. Reconciliation with his father would happen or would have to wait. Perhaps the man was, indeed, too set against Eva. But Zdenek feared the pattern of his youth—giving over to his fear of his father, of trying to ingratiate himself to the man—was a habit too set in place. Lingering any longer would be unwise.

He entered the large room to find many still setting the benches and tables for the large gathering. Was he so early? It did not seem so. Perhaps the meal had been delayed?

Where, then, might he find Father? If, in fact, he wished to seek the man out? Uneasiness coursed throughout his body, pumping through his veins. Or was it something else? Something he dared not admit to himself?

Pushing the thought to the side as he took in a deep breath, he pressed out an exhale and a determined prayer. He would do this. He could.

The solar.

Aye, his father may be in his solar, at his desk for any number of reasons.

Zdenek turned, his extremities more solid now with a purpose in mind. As he stepped toward the stairs, however, a young man moved into his path.

"My lord," the uncertain words of the youth spilled. Had he reason to be ill at ease?

Zdenek nodded. Even as he did so, a hardness thickened in his midsection. Should *he* be concerned?

"The baron requests your presence at once." As the young man remained tipped forward, a slight tremor in his voice betrayed him. Was he on an errand for a baron so vexed it disturbed the lad just yet aged enough to take on the duties of a household servant?

Zdenek frowned. "I was myself seeking him out. If you will take me to him, I will do as he wishes."

The boy let loose a lungful of air and then caught himself. Had he been fearful enough that he held back his breath?

Zdenek could not help the smile that tugged at one side of his mouth. But only for a moment. For his own predicament did not permit such levity. The pressing of it upon his shoulders snuffed out all traces of the would-be smile.

The young man turned and moved through the castle and out into the gardens. Such a strange place for his father to venture. This was his mother's sanctuary. Had he ever known his father to set foot here? Or show the slightest interest to do so?

As the lad before him stepped through the archway, Zdenek was able to discern that there were several voices within. Had his father invited guests for the day? Was Zdenek supposed to have known?

He searched his memory. But nothing came to the surface. Perhaps the recent happenings between he and Eva had snuffed any traces of it.

The baron's jovial, booming voice seemed all the more so as Zdenek neared. And he prayed once more.

Stepping through and into the main section of the gardens himself, he startled at the sight before him. As he knew, his father was within. And on his arm, Zdenek's mother stood by, placid and quiet. Though unpleasant, that did not bother as much as the others who had joined the party.

It was the Viscount and Viscountess from beyond the wooded ridge, along with their daughter, the Lady Lucia.

Every head turned as he became as visible to them, and they to him.

"Ah, Zdenek! Back from your hunt, I see."

Hunt? Is that where his father suspected him to be? Furrowing his brows, he opened his mouth to correct his father.

But the baron cut off his response. "It is no matter. We have decided to forgive you as long as you provide a tale of your great adventures to engage us as we eat."

Zdenek wasn't certain yet that he understood what his father was doing. For whatever reason, his father insisted he was hunting. Did he think it necessary to explain Zdenek's absence?

"Of course." The words rang hollow. Why did he allow the man to control him so?

Eva's face appeared in his mind and once again, he felt the urge to be direct with his father.

"Father," he began, attempting to keep his gaze from connecting with the lady's. Though it was not easy. She bored a hole into him with her stare. If only he didn't feel the prey to the daggers of her eyes. "I would speak with you. Alone."

"Come now, Zdenek," his father's tone slipped only just. A shade of hard under the brightness warned. "Let us not be so eager to turn aside our guests."

The baron lifted an eyebrow and indicated the Lady Lucia.

Zdenek swallowed. And could not stop the path his eyes traveled.

The lady had settled into her position somewhat, head tilted downward, such that she now peered at him through her dark lashes. Her gaze met his and then she looked down, drawing his eyes with hers. Must they? She was fine of figure. He would be blind not to notice. And he did not wish to.

Tearing his regard from her, he met his father's intense glare once more.

"Father, I—"

"Yes, I see." The green of his eyes danced and revealed more than perhaps they should.

Zdenek swallowed. This, he did not like.

"Let us, then, to the Great Hall." The baron looked toward the Viscount's all too interested features. "We have...much...to discuss."

Zdenek wished to protest. Indeed, opened his mouth to do so.

But the group turned and moved off, leaving Lady Lucia lingering behind, still taking in the whole of Zdenek with her eyes.

He forced his gaze to the ground. *Flee from temptation.* And brought up only images of his Eva. There was where his mind should dwell. There was where it belonged.

When he looked up, the lady had picked up step to rejoin the others.

Zdenek moved to follow, lengthening his step as he went.

Soon enough, they were in the Great Hall. Lady Lucia was given a seat beside Zdenek. Would they share a trencher?

As she was seated, she brushed a hand against his arm.

"My lord, I must say, I am so...honored to become reacquainted with you as you have returned home."

"Lady Lucia, there is something I must tell you—"

"I had always feared my father would marry me off to someone older. Someone pudgy. Balding. But *you*..." She put her hand to his arm and leaned toward him, pressing her shoulder to his.

He attempted to lean away, but could not do so without making more obvious the overture she made. "My lady, I..." His throat dried, and his words emptied. There was something...something of great import he was meant to say.

"My father was delighted to have received the invitation from the baron." Lucia seemed to take advantage of his momentary lapse to insert herself again. "In fact, I don't think my father would mind at all if it became a more...regular acquaintance." She fluttered her lashes.

"I fear you have been misinformed," he pressed out, averting his gaze and making every effort to be firm.

A servant girl set a trencher between them. It appeared he and Lucia, indeed, were to share. It should not bother as it did. Or should it? Such was not uncommon. Except...that it was for husband and wife in such cases.

"Why do you not eat? Is the food not to your satisfaction?" Lucia leaned even closer and whispered as if it were a great secret.

He pulled away. "It is not that. It is just that I..."

"What is this?" the baron's voice thundered.

Zdenek jerked his head around. Eva stood at the edge of the Great Hall, eyes wide, gaze locked on Zdenek and Lucia.

"Who is that woman?" Lucia asked, wrapping a hand around Zdenek's upper arm.

"Have this imposter removed at once," the baron continued.

A man-at-arms came to Eva's side, grabbing at her arm.

How dare the man! Zdenek shifted to stand, but Lucia's hold on him was firm. He pushed at her hand on him.

Eva resisted the guard, pulling against his hold. Her eyes glistened.

The man-at-arms spoke to Eva, too quietly for Zdenek to hear. Eva shook her head and continued to try to free her arm.

Zdenek saw his father motion to another guard.

*No!*

Everyone's attention was on her struggle. The baron had not succeeded in the least in eliminating the problem.

And she was a fighter. His Eva.

Zdenek couldn't stand by and watch. No matter the cost.

As the other guard gripped Eva, Zdenek untangled himself from Lucia and stood. "Unhand my wife!"

"Wife?" Lucia shrieked.

The Viscount jerked toward Father. "What?"

But Zdenek gave them little notice. The momentary surprise of the guards gave him the opportunity he needed to cross the Great Hall and press himself between Eva and one guard. Then glare at the other, setting an arm across Eva's body, blocking the guard's access to her.

"Loose her, I say."

The guard looked to his lord baron. Zdenek gave his father his regard. The man's face had reddened.

"Zdenek, what do you?"

"What I should have done many weeks ago."

Eva gripped Zdenek's shirt. Because she was faint? Or because she wished to give him strength?

Father narrowed his eyes. "I warn you, Zdenek, if you insist upon this abomination of a marriage. If you do this, you will leave this place never to look upon it again. You will no longer have a father."

Zdenek sucked in a breath, ragged though it was. "If that is what you must do, Father. Then you must."

Gasps and murmurs filled the room.

"I will do as I must." Zdenek stood straighter, squaring his shoulders. "For my wife. And for my brethren."

Eva leaned into his back, laying her forehead to his shoulder. This was right. His wife beside him, supporting him. If his father could not understand, perhaps the man did not need to be part of his future. But *she* was his future.

"Out of my sight." The baron's words were more growl than anything.

No more words were forthcoming. None were needed.

Zdenek turned, wrapping his arms about his wife, and led her from his father's presence and into freedom.

Karin's mind swirled through darkness toward a surface she wasn't certain she wanted to breech. She opened her eyes. Brightness forced them closed again. As she blinked them to awareness, fighting the urge to plunge back to the soothing depths she had come from, she embraced the pain. It meant she was alive.

Everything seemed hazy. The shapes around her moved. Was nothing stable? Had she not one thing she might latch onto?

A voice shouted, but it was far away. And muffled. What words were spoken? Words of concern? Or of danger?

She attempted to shift her limbs. Was she at risk? What had happened?

A blurred face hovered above her.

Pavel. It had to be.

Of course, her beloved would come to her.

She reached for him, but her arms were too heavy.

"Don't...worry...lady..." The words echoed and stretched thin. How was this possible?

"Pavel," she pressed out.

The figure moved away. Why would he leave her?

Pain coursed through her. Her whole being throbbed.

"No..." She tried to call for her beloved. But he continued to move away.

The presence was again over her. "My lady..."

Not Pavel. This was a woman, unknown to her. As the nuances of her senses became clearer, so did the sharpness of the pain. Could she bear it?

She cried out.

Raised voices beyond and to the left drew the attention of the woman over her. She barked orders in that direction.

Fingers touched her face. "Karin."

And at last—Pavel had come. Most certainly. His tender, protective love surrounded and fell over her like a blanket.

"What—?"

"Don't try to talk." His words were strained. He connected his hands with hers, intertwining their fingers. The clear blue of his eyes pierced through what remained of the fog between them.

She clenched her teeth as another wave of pain slammed into her.

"Can you do nothing for the pain?" His ragged voice assaulted the woman who continued to move her hands over Karin.

What did this woman do? Why had she been called?

"No, my lord." The woman's words were plain.

"God be near!" Pavel turned back to Karin. "I am here, beloved." He kissed her forehead.

She nodded even as she bit her lip and swallowed a whimper. Gripping Pavel's hands, she clung to him for what strength she could take from him. For hers was much depleted.

After some long moments that perhaps blended into hours, the woman eased away and wiped at her hands. "The babe is not lost."

The babe? Had her baby been at risk? From what?

Had she hurt her baby?

How?

"Praise be to God!" The tension released from the muscles in Pavel's arms. And in his features.

Even as she looked to him for further explanation, his eyes remained on the healer. "All is well, then?"

The woman offered Pavel an odd look. "That...is difficult to say."

He frowned.

What had happened? The last thing she remembered was leaving her chambers to bid Pavel farewell. Yet, here he was. Had he not, then, gone to General Zizka's aid? Because of her?

"Pavel, I—"

His gaze set on her, and he leaned closer. "Shh. Please, don't trouble yourself. You are well. Our babe yet thrives."

She furrowed her brows. "But, I—"

He cupped the side of her face. "There is no need."

Why would he be so frustrating? She needed to know...*wanted* to understand.

He pressed kisses to her forehead, her hands, the side of her face. "I am so sorry, I..."

There was movement farther away. Perhaps those that cared for her? Did they leave? Or prepare to do more?

"I shouldn't have thought to leave you," he forced out at last.

What was he saying? Did he think what happened somehow his fault? Was it?

"And I won't, Karin. I will stay, with you...to keep you, protect you...and our child."

She wanted to protest but knew not what to say. A thick weariness fell over her, weighing her down, pulling at her. Could she insist on the whole truth of it right now? Or dispute his insistent pleas?

There wasn't even the strength for more than a muttering of his name before unconsciousness claimed her again.

# CHAPTER 17

What had just transpired? Eva looked to her husband as he led her farther from the Great Hall. To...where?

His features were set, determined. Was he so certain of his actions? After all this time of giving way to the overbearing man?

She couldn't deny that it had been too long in coming, yet...

"Do you have need of anything in your chambers?"

What did he speak of? Her chambers? After a moment, her mind cleared. Ah, yes, the chambers his father had accommodated her with.

"No." She had come with little; she would not delay them with the few things that were of no consequence to her.

He afforded her a glance as his steps slowed. Then he turned to face her. "Eva...I..."

She watched as emotions played across his face and in the depths of his eyes. Though she might have feared regret would be one of them, it was not.

She lifted a hand to the side of his face, bringing his eyes to hers. "Let us away, husband."

He pulled her to his chest and nodded into her shoulder. "There is nothing for us here."

Her heart sank. Was all truly lost? Was she selfish to push forward? To not allow for any attempt to put pieces back together? Or was he right—that there was no hope? What might become of Zdenek's mother?

Zdenek pulled back, pressing a kiss to her lips as he did so. "There is much to say to you. Much I would ask of you in pardon for egregious sins—"

His words touched the wall erected around her heart, mayhap not too hardened yet. "I know. But now is not the time."

He nodded again. "Yes, dearest wife. We must leave this place. Now."

She sensed the words he did not speak. For she feared the same—that he might be caught once again in the web of manipulation should he not depart forthwith. "Then we shall make haste."

Clasping her hand in his, he picked up step once more with such determination she had to rush to keep up. He did not slow until they were in the stables.

The man minding the horses worked to disguise his shock at their sudden appearance. "My lord! How might I—"

"Our horses. They must be readied. Quickly."

Though taken aback, the man put his legs under him and moved after his charge.

Zdenek squeezed her hand. "We will sooner be away if two sets of hands are at work."

She nodded and watched her husband follow after the younger man. They disappeared deeper within the structure. And all was still.

A breeze blew through, chilling her. How was that possible? Autumn had not yet taken full hold of the world. Still, she rubbed her upper arms.

Her gaze settled in the direction they would ride. The sky dimmed and the way darkened. How safe would they be?

It mattered not. They had battled trained men. For certain, they could manage in the wilderness for a night. Or had the weeks playing the part of a lady changed her so?

She shook her head. The sooner she could put this place, this heartache behind her, the better it would be. For her. And for Zdenek. Wouldn't it?

Or might he come to regret that which he did not presently? That he had abandoned his birthright, his father, his lands...for her? Would it not come to matter? Had she been the manipulator more than the victim?

No, this was the lie. She had only been true to her husband. And herself.

"As I feared." The voice, simple and measured, came from behind her.

She spun.

In the fading glow of the sun's light stood the baroness.

Eva clutched her arms more tightly. "My lady, I—"

The woman waved a hand in the air. "I am not here to cast blame. It belongs not on your shoulders, but on mine. I have allowed much to pass in these walls. Much I could have stopped. Should have stopped."

Eva's heart pinched. The woman took on more than her share. How might she have ended the abuse? What recourse had she?

The baroness looked to the ground. "How could I not have protected my son? Not even when his father..."

Eva ached for the woman before her, the mother who hurt for the injury done her son's body and heart.

"Zdenek had only tried to intervene...for my sake. He..." Emotion cut off her words.

Eva took a step toward the baroness, a woman who loved her Zdenek so very much. "He has shared it all. And he loves you. He bears no ill will toward you. When he looks back, he sees a strength in you beyond what others may see."

The baroness sniffled. Then, gathering herself, she spoke again.

"There is little I can do to spare my son now. But I can give him hope." She signaled into the shadows.

A servant came forth. They had been watched? Eva drew back a step.

The man did not seem to notice. He bore two bags. Taking the steps necessary to close the distance to Eva, he set them at her feet.

"Be well," the baroness said as she turned.

Eva lifted her gaze from the bags. "Will you not see your son?" She glanced toward the inner section of the stables where he had gone.

The older woman shook her head. "It is best this way."

Eva furrowed her brows. She was not so certain.

As the woman retreated toward the castle, she paused. "You have lightened a mother's heart. I know my son has love. And that his lady wife is of fine character. He will be well with you."

Eva swallowed and looked to the ground. Did she deserve such fine words? Was she good for Zdenek? Wasn't she? Or were they just good for each other?

She opened her mouth to put better truth to what had been spoken, but the baroness was gone.

It took some moments for Eva to rein in her warring emotions. Only then did she remember the bags at her feet. Bending, she opened one. It had been filled with gems, jewelry, and gold coin.

What had the baroness done? And how would they ever thank her?

Hana struggled to remain in the saddle. The knight behind her took hold of her to halt her body as it began to slide from the horse.

She stirred and nodded a simple thanks to the man.

And she was grateful. The leader of this contingency, the one who bore her upon his horse, had volunteered he and his men to see her to her father's home. She wasn't certain what she had expected when she and Radek had marched into Prague. But it wasn't this.

The commander of the army gathered and holding the city had not been able to spare men, only to allow those who wished to take on the mission to leave their posts. There had been many moments that passed in which she worried none would. Now, due to the danger, it was doubtful she and Radek would be permitted to travel unaccompanied any farther.

Not that her reputation would be unscathed as it was. Only the direness of their circumstances had kept her unaware of this fact. The glances between the men as Radek revealed their tale and the looks cast in her direction betrayed that there were questions left unasked. But questions all the same.

She scanned the small group for Radek. And could not help but wish that it were his chest she rested against, his arms around her. But he had made every effort to distance himself all the more since their departure from Prague.

There he was. On the edge of the group. He had dismounted and joined those gathered at the entrance to the inn.

As she watched, her heart begging for him to look at her, he did not so much as glance in her direction. And the heaviness in her chest became unbearable.

Why must it be so? Had he not cared for her as she believed?

"Lady Hana?" A voice called to her from the right.

She peered down at the face beyond the hands reaching up to receive her—Sir Ivan. He led these men. And he had treated her with a detached kindness she had come to appreciate as much for its distance as for its sympathy.

Dropping into the waiting arms, she allowed herself to be assisted from the horse and to the inn. The securing of accommodations and food proceeded as if a blur. Her thoughts were only on Radek. On the words spoken between them. And how he had so quickly created distance between them upon their reception in Prague.

What could his attention harm? For if these men thought her ruined in her days and nights alone with Radek, all efforts to place himself at odds with her now would not change their minds.

It only stung her. How could he not see that?

"My lady?" Sir Ivan stood nearby. How long had he been there, attempting to gain her attention?

"Yes, sir knight?"

"Your room is this way."

She sighed. Though she was weary, she preferred to linger. There was little chance of speaking with Radek once Sir Ivan secured her in her room.

As he had the previous evening, he would perhaps insist she take her meal in her room, away from what he called 'the unseemly behavior of the men of the town, drinking and leering at any woman in their vicinity.' Was it even true?

"I thank you." She lifted her chin, hoping she appeared more confident than she felt in that moment. "But I wish to partake of my evening meal before retiring."

"My lady? I would prefer to see you to your room. These village men can be—"

"I have such brave men to surround me and discourage any unbecoming behavior." She let her gaze rest on his. Her insides trembled. Could she hide it from him?

His eyes narrowed. "It is not that I doubt my men, my lady. I do not wish to tempt an uprising."

"It has been decided." She pushed the words out and stepped forward, set on moving past him.

He caught her arm. "I will warn you, Lady Hana. You make light where you should not. I fear you are too reckless...as history may indicate."

She shrugged, attempting to shake his hold.

His grip was firm.

She widened her eyes on him. "I thank you for your concern, sir knight. Your counsel is noted but not required nor requested."

"Lady Hana." The voice, softer and with gentleness, also held a depth and strength that poured relief through her. "At last, I find where you have gone."

She turned toward Radek as he came from the stables, making no effort to disguise the gratitude in her eyes.

He glared at Sir Ivan's hand, still clamped on her upper arm. Then, with hardened features, he looked closer upon the knight. "I trust that all is well here?"

She glanced back at the man, making more of an effort to shake him off.

Sir Ivan did not resist, but released her, only removing his regard from Radek to let his gaze slip to Hana and back again. His expression darkened, and something about it made her feel exposed.

What did that look imply? What was behind it? For certain, he couldn't think that she and Radek...

But she would be fool indeed if she continued to play this lie to herself. After what he had heard, and had known to be—that she and Radek were alone in the forest for so many days, without chaperone. Certainly, the man's thoughts ran in this vein. As must the thoughts of all these men.

What of her father? Her mother? Would they think the same?

With one last look at her, Sir Ivan spoke. "I will collect you after the meal to escort you above stairs." His eyes flicked to Radek. "And a guard will be placed at your door."

She could do nothing but nod. There was no other thought but that.

With that, he took his leave, stepping into the inn.

Radek's gaze followed the man's retreat.

What could Radek be thinking? Had she just made things worse for him? She dropped her regard to the ground. "I am sorry."

"What have you to apologize for?" His words had a tenderness that made her ache. Was it evidence of his feelings for her? Or of nothing more than his character?

"I do not intend to besmirch your good name." She peered up without raising her face.

He lifted his brow. Then let it fall again. "I do not wish you to worry about such."

Moisture blurred her vision. How was it that after all they had come through, she would find herself now so worried over her reputation? Why could she not just press into him? Take comfort from him as she had in the...?

It could not be. They had their places. And there were things that simply were not done.

When she met his gaze, there was sadness in his eyes. But only for a moment. Then it vanished.

And her heart hurt all the more for it.

"I believe it is time for the evening meal." His words had lost their emotion. All that remained was the simpleness of fact.

She nodded. But as she turned toward the inn and moved within, all too aware that Radek made no move to touch or direct her, she wondered if she would ever know what it would be to truly live again.

Zdenek assisted Eva's dismount. They had pushed their steeds long and hard. Perhaps too hard. But it was to their gain. For this evening, they found themselves in Tabor. Zizka could not be far from reach.

"Surely, the general will not have taken a room here." Eva's concerned statement drew Zdenek's attention back to her.

"Of course not," he assured her, letting his hand linger on her arm. He did not wish to relinquish that contact. So long had he allowed his father to keep them apart. How foolish he had been! How blind! How thoughtless!

Eva's brows furrowed.

Could she discern his thoughts?

"Are we not to seek out General Zizka forthwith?"

Ah, there was her meaning. Her heart was with the army already. Was she so prepared to join the fight?

His Eva. Steadfast and true.

He traced the outline of her face. "I admire your determination, wife. But I insist we find rest and refreshment."

Her features softened.

Because of his touch? Or his consideration for her well-being?

She closed her eyes and tilted her head toward his ministrations.

An ache grew in his chest. Did he indeed love her so much? Yes. And the hurt he had caused her, and had allowed to be visited upon her, crashed on him. His guilt became clear and heavy...the weight of it great.

Would he ever deserve her forgiveness? Earn her favor once more?

"Zdenek?"

The word—his name—from her lips, sounded bittersweet as he was lost in his self-loathing. But it brought him back to the present, and to her.

She watched him, seeking some answer...to what? Her trust seemed implicit. But his actions of the past weeks did not merit such. Still...

His other hand sought hers, intertwining their fingers. "Aye, it is best we take the evening for respite."

She nodded and pressed his hand.

Though he longed to tug her closer, to touch her lips with his, he did not think it fitting. For all he truly deserved was shame. He must prove himself not the scoundrel he had been before taking such liberties.

"Shall we?" He pulled back. It was the only way to save himself from doing those things he wished to.

Her eyes shimmered in the fading light of the setting sun. He did not want to consider that this may be the hint of tears forthcoming. Did she dwell on his sins of the past months? He could not begrudge her these things. But he did not relish them either.

Turning toward the entrance to the inn, he led her within.

All was well-kept. Zdenek somewhat expected to encounter all manner of travelers in all states of being—and levels of inebriation. But that was not the way of things.

The tables and chairs were filled with guards, well-mannered and on alert.

As Zdenek and Eva entered, the three closest the door rose, hands on the hilts of their swords.

Zdenek pulled Eva behind him, out of harm's way.

"What do you seek?" one of the men spoke, plainly.

"A meal and lodging for ourselves and refreshment and rest for our horses." Zdenek held his ground. What had he to fear? What had he done to earn such suspicion? Were they not in Hussite lands?

The men exchanged glances. Then another spoke. "This inn is full."

Was something foul afoot? Zdenek narrowed his eyes. "Might I trouble the keeper of the inn?"

The man-at-arms that had engaged Zdenek frowned. It was clear he wished to turn them away with nothing further.

"It won't change the answer," the man said, his words short.

"Still, I insist."

Eva clung to Zdenek, tugging at him. Would she prefer they take their leave? Perhaps that would be best. But their horses needed the rest. It would not be safe to search out other options with the animals so pressed already.

The guard released the sword hilt and indicated that Zdenek should move farther in, past the rows of tables.

Gripping Eva's hand to keep her close, he did so, knowing that their every move was watched. From every angle.

As they neared the kitchen, a woman appeared. And she seemed as surprised by them as they she.

"Heaven's above, what are you about?" The woman clutched at her chest while trying not to drop the platter of bread she bore.

"My apologies," Zdenek offered. "We meant no harm. But my lady wife and I are in need of accommodations for the night."

The woman continued to move about the room, dropping off bread at different points along the table. "I am terrible sorry, my lord, but I cannot offer ye lodging."

"You would turn away a lady?" His voice rose. "These men would not be displaced for the sake of a noblewoman?"

The woman turned on him then. "It isn't that, sir. I would give up me own bed for your wife if it possible. But her ladyship wouldn't—"

"Ladyship?" Zdenek puzzled.

The woman's hand flew to her mouth.

"There is a woman of status already within?"

"I cannot say any more than I have. I've said too much." She turned.

Zdenek caught her arm. "Who?"

The woman's eyes widened. "I cannot!" Her words were all but hissed in her attempt to keep quiet.

"As you can see, my wife and I have traveled far. We will not be put aside unless we are satisfied you speak true."

The woman stuffed the side of her fist into her mouth and glared at the guards.

A couple of the men glanced her way. Their conversations became more lively. Did they suspect she had given away details she had best not?

"Let me speak with your husband, then."

"It is just me and my children."

Zdenek paused. She alone kept these men at bay. And catered to a noblewoman. And here he was pressing her to speak where she'd best not.

He turned to Eva.

Her look was sympathetic. Did she know what a difficult position they were in?

Eva glanced around him and to the innkeeper. "Might *I* seek an audience with the lady?"

The woman chewed on her lower lip.

A handful of men came around them.

"What goes here?" one of them said.

Zdenek turned to face them, again placing himself between Eva and the threat as best he could.

"N-nothing," the innkeeper said. "These kind folks were just leaving."

The man in the front leveled his gaze on Zdenek. "That so?"

Zdenek swallowed and opened his mouth to speak.

"Is this how you conduct your men when I am not looking?" a woman's voice carried across the room.

A rather regal-looking lady stood near the stairs. How long had she been there? Something about her was familiar.

"My lady, these encroachers are not willing to take a simple 'no' from our kind host." The man, who just seconds ago threatened Zdenek now faced the noblewoman, his entire demeanor changed.

"Is that so?" She moved across the room.

As she neared, her practiced gaze moved over Zdenek and Eva. But it was Zdenek that she seemed the most captivated by.

"We are travelers, my lady. Much in need of rest and respite. I am not certain that our horses will be able to take us elsewhere."

The lady nodded. Then looked to the innkeeper. "Can we make room for this man and his wife?"

"Aye, Baroness, that we can. If..." The woman indicated the guards near Zdenek.

"Yes, if my guards must, they can make...other arrangements for bedding down."

The guard glowered at Zdenek.

"I thank you, Lady..."

"Krejikova."

*Krejikova?*

"Baroness Krejikova?" Zdenek's mind whirled. "Your son is Pavel Krejik?"

The lady's eyes flashed as they settled on him again. "Why do you ask?"

How much longer could he endure? Radek kept his horse at a steady pace, maintaining just enough space from Hana to prevent further speculation. And only that.

For he would not—could not—remove himself any farther. Not one moment sooner than he had to.

And that moment was fast approaching. More so than he dared think on. His mission neared its end. They would soon reunite her with her father.

Only...

After that, he would be required to remove himself and may never see her again.

That opened a pit within him large enough to swallow all else. But it did not leave him void of emotion, rather it reduced him to great pain.

How was he to endure it?

Even now, as he watched her without watching, he longed for the feel of her in his arms and the taste of the lips that were now forbidden him. How could he have permitted himself to believe the dream possible? To allow his heart to claim hold of something that would never be?

He was a fool.

She turned.

He jerked away, making great effort to examine the tree line. And though he felt her gaze upon him, he refused to return it. No good would come of that.

There was the intensity of her attention and then it was gone. Was she too, then, coming to the realization that he had? Why did that not bring relief? It only doubled the ache within.

Sir Ivan spoke, pointing something out with a raised arm. His voice was low and rumbling. Radek could not discern his words even from this short distance.

Hana did not lean away.

Radek did not like it. His hands tightened on the leather straps in his grasp. Why should it bother him so?

Hana nodded. Though she didn't move away, neither did she make any move that could be interpreted as encouragement.

Radek let out a breath. She was not his to grate over. Hadn't he decided to release her?

Hana's tone that at one time raked on Radek's nerves, filled his senses. But, like Sir Ivan, she spoke too quietly for Radek to pick up anything beyond her voice.

The knight shook his head and indicated the clearing ahead. He moved in front of her and three of the other men came around and behind him as they approached the wider space.

What was this about? Were they in danger? Was Hana at risk?

Radek put a hand to his sword and urged his horse forward, closer to Hana's. His concern for remaining distant became less important.

Their horses carried them out of the cover of the trees and into the opening. Where they found themselves surrounded.

Some fifteen men-at-arms hovered about, their weapons drawn and prepared to end the perceived threat.

Sir Ivan did not flinch under the scrutiny of the band of men that outnumbered his three to one. "We come seeking Duke Novak. We wish only to see the safe return of his daughter, the Lady Hana Novakova."

Radek's heart flipped. It would be now. Would the men hand her over here? He pressed his horse the steps required to move alongside Hana's mount.

She jerked her head to face him, a question in her eyes.

He shook his head, hoping to quiet her. And his hand covered hers on the pommel of her saddle. How was he to communicate what was in his heart? Why did he dare? It was not fair to him or to her.

"If this is true, we would see the lady," the larger of the other guards said.

Their leader turned. When his gaze fell upon Radek beside Hana, he frowned. But his surprise was short-lived. He lifted a hand and bade Hana come to him.

"No," Radek said under his breath. It wasn't safe.

She pulled her hand away and urged her horse forward.

Radek's heart dropped. Had he lost her so completely? That was nonsense. She never belonged to him. Not truly.

He could do nothing but watch as the men conversed, with Hana playing the part of a pawn.

Their fates decided, Hana was maneuvered between the two leaders and the two companies followed.

It was not long before they reached Duke Novak's castle, situated on the side of a hill...as if he might be able to spy out any and all dangers that may come.

How had he let his daughter leave and become a prisoner in a Royalist camp? Was he not more vigilant?

Radek pushed such thoughts to the side; they would only incite him to greater anger.

After they entered the fortified structure, Hana was whisked away with several of the guards.

But he remained. It happened so swiftly he'd not had the opportunity to speak words with her or even protest. Now, he stood stunned.

"Where...?" Was all he managed.

"To her father, I suppose," one of the other men offered with a sly grin. "Guess Ivan's tricked you out of whatever reward you hoped for."

Had he? Radek's heart cried for something entirely different.

The remaining men tended to the horses. But Radek struggled to put his attention there. His thoughts were on Hana, on what she faced, what she must be feeling. And how he had abandoned her these last few days.

"Lord Miklas."

Every head turned.

The larger guard stood in the stables.

"I am he." Radek responded after a long pause had settled in the space.

"Duke Novak demands an audience with you."

Every eye fell on him. Radek felt more than saw the heat of their stares. He cared not. His heart, his mind, all his awareness...was focused on Hana's situation.

He gave a quick nod and followed the man.

The journey through the castle and to the lord's solar was hastened by the man's pace. Was he in such a hurry? Or had he been summoned with haste?

Just outside the solar, the guard halted at last.

Radek took a long breath.

The man looked at him for the first time before opening the door and holding up an arm for him to enter.

Radek passed.

A man several years his senior sat at a desk to one side of the room. A man in priestly attire behind him. Hana sat in a chair near the desk but to the other side. The guard that had traveled with them stood beside Hana, as if *he* were there to protect her.

Radek didn't like it.

He stepped farther into the space, acknowledging the master of the castle with a bow.

"Lord Miklas?"

"Yes, Duke, I have come as bid."

"And am I to understand that it was you who rescued my daughter from the dangers of the Royalist camp?"

Radek resisted the urge to look at Hana. It would not speak well of him.

"Yes, my lord. Myself and my brother at arms."

The duke's eyes lit up. "And, where is he?"

"We had to leave him behind in our efforts to escape."

The man's features darkened. "I see."

All became quiet once more. An uncomfortable quiet.

"Father, I didn't—" Hana started.

Duke Novak held up a hand to halt her words.

She was silenced and dropped her gaze to her lap. What had transpired here in the preceding moments? Was there trouble?

Radek squared his shoulders. There was nothing he couldn't… wouldn't take on for her sake.

"And, Lord Miklas, am I to understand that you and my daughter were alone for many days in the forest as you escaped from that camp?"

Radek's throat became thick. So, this was the whole of it. His concern about his daughter's virtue? Or the appearance of impropriety?

"My lord duke, I assure you, I am a man of honor. I hold your daughter in the utmost—"

The duke held up a hand. "I respect that. But there are things that cannot be undone."

Radek worked to maintain his stance and neutral expression.

The duke watched him. "Are you telling me, Lord Miklas, that you would refuse to marry my daughter in light of these circumstances?"

Radek swallowed. His heart flipped again. Its desire well-felt. He wanted Hana. So much. But he could not consign her to a life with him, a life at odds with the things she held so deeply.

"If I might, I would explain that—" As he spoke, Radek glanced but briefly at Hana. Her features betrayed deep pain at his words.

"No?" the duke countered, rising. "You would turn away the Lady Hana?"

"I did not mean to say that—"

"But such was evident in your response." The man narrowed his gaze.

"You must see," the priest said, stepping from around the desk, "as a man of honor, that you must save the lady from the ruin that will follow if you do not."

How could this be happening? This was impossible! He didn't want Hana to think him forced to love her. To want her. She must know that wasn't true. That he only resisted for her sake.

"I do not wish to trap any man." Hana jumped up and inserted herself between Radek and her father.

The duke's eyes became wide at her intrusion.

"If I may," Sir Ivan said, stepping forward and alongside Hana. "The Lady Hana is not without other options."

Radek felt sick. He couldn't be saying...

"What other option might present itself?" Duke Novak turned from Radek, giving the knight his full attention.

"Perhaps, my lord, you might consider myself a suitable match for the lady."

# CHAPTER 18

Karin stirred. And opened her eyes. Awareness of pain filled her. She seemed to hurt everywhere.

As she attempted to take in her surroundings, she decided that it was not truly night—only that the thick curtains had been drawn. Was she alone? It appeared so.

She shifted to sit.

Sharp pain jerked all breath from her, and she halted her movements. As she could, she eased all muscles to rest once more. No, she would not make that mistake again.

What had happened to her? She searched her memory. Her thoughts of the past few days were hazy, but they slowly returned.

Pavel had determined to leave. She was to see him off. Only...

On the stairs, she lost her footing. She had fallen! What of the baby?

Her hands flew to her midsection. The great swell there gave her some comfort. She was amazed again how much the babe had grown in the last months as they had lingered in Duke Novak's castle, waiting for answers, waiting for Pavel's father to...

She prayed he still lived.

And she paused, waiting for the movement of her child.

In time, it came.

*Praise You, Lord!* Her gratitude came with tears of joy. For she did not think she would be able to endure more loss. Not now.

Had Pavel gone as she slumbered? Or had he remained as he said? Yes, his words came back to her. As did the woman working over her. And the woman's words.

*"All is well, then?"* Pavel had asked, seeking assurance.

*"That…is difficult to say."* The woman had not been willing to give him anything more.

Was there danger lingering?

Karin rubbed her hands over her protruding stomach, wishing against the things that had happened. And wanting to keep her child safe. It wouldn't be long now, after all.

How long she lay in silence before the door creaked, announcing another's presence, she did not know. But it came.

Who would enter, unannounced?

The healer? Or had the woman been a midwife? A servant coming to tend to her? Or would it perhaps be Pavel?

Heavy footfalls gave her reason to hope for the latter. As the presence neared the bed, her husband's silhouette became discernable even in the dimness.

"Karin?" His voice soothed over her worn senses. Was there a hitch in his words? "You are awake?"

"Yes, my love. I am." Her own words came with more trembling than she wished to betray.

He sat on the edge of the bed. Perhaps too close. The shifting of the bed moved her more than she'd have liked, bringing more pain.

Try as she might to bite back the evidence, the sharp inhale was audible.

"Karin?" He jerked upright. The movement again bringing great ache throughout her body.

"It is all right." She spoke through clenched teeth.

He moved to the window and parted the curtains just enough to bring the smallest amount of light in.

Karin blinked, hoping her eyes would adjust quickly.

Pavel was by her side again the moment they did. His features etched with concern.

"I am well enough," she lied. Perhaps not a complete lie. She was better than she feared possible. "Only sore."

His gaze scanned her, resting where her hands did, on their babe. "And our child?"

"He moves."

Pavel let out a breath, and the lines in his face smoothed. "The midwife said that such would mean the babe was strong and would be well."

That was something to celebrate. Karin again took great comfort in it. She reached for her husband's hand.

Stepping closer, he lifted it into his with all the tenderness she had come to know from him. Something passed over his features. Something unpleasant.

"What is it?" She didn't realize the words had been spoken aloud until they were.

"I do not want to burden you." His words were short, but something about them cut her.

"My body may be in want of a healer's minding, but I am not so fragile." As much as she tried to keep her tone soft, she feared there was a bite to it as well.

Pavel looked to their clasped hands.

She squeezed his fingers, hoping for his attention once more.

He did, after some moments, look to her again. And in watching her eyes, he seemed to seek something. But what? Some assurance of her words? She did not know.

At last, he pressed a gentle kiss to her hand. "I will leave you to your rest."

She firmed her grip on him. "Pavel, do not treat me thusly. Speak plain. Let me bear it with you."

He glanced down at the space between them, but nodded. "The unrest grows. There is now much tension, much conflict between our brethren."

"Between the Hussites?"

His gaze found hers. "Yes. The lines between the factions deepen."

She frowned. Such tidings indeed. "And Zizka?"

"He returns to the front. Rosenberg has been made to see reason. The general does not think there will be more trouble on that front. And thank God for that. Sigismund's support within Bohemia has been snuffed out."

Karin bit at her lip to hold back the words that rushed to the surface. Words that would confirm Pavel's regret at not being among the men that neutralized Rosenberg. Of not joining Zizka now. Not doing what he could to reunite their people.

They may fight for the same cause, but what would come of the tension between these fractured groups? Would the Hussites become little more than a field full of children, segmented by their minor differences? She prayed they would continue to rally under a united cause when called upon.

"Karin?" His brows furrowed. What did he see in her eyes?

She could not tear her gaze away from his. Not even to hide her thoughts.

He reached to her and wiped at a tear. How had she not known of its presence?

"Tell me," he urged.

"I...only fear for your regret. That you will one day find you resent having stayed when..."

He pulled back.

She pushed on, "...you should have gone where you were needed."

"No, Karin." His eyes flashed. "You were right. I am needed here. With you. You are everything to me. What..." Emotion choked off his words.

She tugged at his hand.

He seemed to gather himself. "What would I have done had something happened to you? Had you been lost to me?" His voice was thick.

She swallowed. How might she respond to such? *Lord, how to make him see?*

But God...

Freeing her hand from his, she lifted it to his face. "No one can measure their days or mark their last hour. Your presence here does not prevent my end nor lengthen my time. No more than I can yours. Regardless of how we may wish it. Only God has such power. And there is where we place our lives. And each other."

He searched her features for several seconds. What was in his head?

After some moments, he turned into her hand and pressed a kiss to her wrist.

"Rest, my love," he said as he rose. "For your sake and the babe's."

She wanted to speak further, to know that he understood, that he heard her. But she watched him release her hand and walk out of their chamber with nothing further.

What had become of his faith?

How had everything gone so wrong so quickly? Radek's brooding had filled much of the afternoon. After the interchange in the solar, the men had been dismissed for Hana's sake and to give the baron a moment to consider the words spoken.

Could Radek allow such to proceed? For Sir Ivan to use Hana only to gain lands and a title? How could he have been so blind? Of course, others might see the opportunity and seize it!

Now as the evening meal approached, his ire only increased. He would have to face the man. If he were one for prayer, it would certainly be that the man was seated far from him. For he might have little control over his actions should Sir Ivan say the wrong thing. Or look at Hana as if he…

It would just be best if Radek not have access to the man.

Radek stepped into the Great Hall. Many had settled into their seats. He scanned those present and did not spot Sir Ivan or Hana among them. Did that mean the two were together? That thought did not sit well either.

"Lord Miklas? Radek?" a familiar voice spoke behind him.

He turned. "Pavel Krejik? Is it you?"

Radek moved toward his friend to grip his arm in greeting. So elated, it took a moment for him to remember that the last time Pavel had seen him was at the Battle of Vitkov Hill before he…before he had made his way to the Royalist camp.

What did Pavel know? What did he think of his friend who had defected?

"My friend," Pavel's words were warm and sincere. "It is good to see you!"

Radek nodded, unsure in the moment of how to proceed. "I am pleased to see you again, as well."

"I have many questions." Pavel's features betrayed his confusion. Even so, he drew nearer. "And there is much to tell."

"And I, you." Radek found he was ever so eager for his friend's ear and good advice. As if he were a parched man who had found a spring in the desert. Movement near the stairs drew his attention from his friend.

Hana appeared.

On the arm of Sir Ivan.

The two conversed with ease and all pleasantness.

A growl rumbled in Radek's chest. How could he endure such?

"Radek? Are you well?"

He was pulled back to the moment by Pavel's entreaty. Turning to his friend, he did what he could to put on a smile he did not feel. "I am. As I said, there is much to share."

Pavel's furrowed brows lifted only just. "Let us not delay further, then."

They moved toward the tables, taking their seats at the high table with the other nobility. It did not escape Radek's notice that Sir Ivan was granted a place beside Hana. Nor did he miss Hana's glance in his direction. Was that hopefulness in her eyes? Longing? Did she desire him still? Or had his dismissal cut her too deeply?

The meal was spent listening to Pavel's stories. Radek ached for his friend and what he had endured. Even as he was quite distracted by the exchanges between Sir Ivan and Hana. Did she engage him thusly to get a rise out of him? She must know how it would affect him.

"I cannot help but notice that your mind is...elsewhere." Pavel took a bite of meat and tossed a glance over his shoulder to where Hana sat. Had Radek been so obvious?

Radek stared at his trencher. "It is...difficult to explain."

Pavel offered a half grin. "I think not. Perhaps the situation is difficult, but I think I can quite easily understand what is the way of things."

Radek's face heated.

"Are you of a mind to win her for yourself?"

Radek's gaze leveled on his friend. Dare Pavel be so forward?

"There is no sense in pretense. Only two options remain to you—let Sir Ivan have the lady, or fight for her hand."

Looking back to his food, Radek wished for a way out of this conversation.

"I know you may not wish to speak of it. And I understand. But there may not be time to think long on it. If you care for the lady half as much as you appear to, I would urge you to make your feelings known to her."

His gaze jerked to Pavel's. "You are rather confident in your assessment."

Pavel did grin then. "Oh yes, my friend, I am." He leaned forward on his elbows. "Tell me I'm wrong."

Radek looked at Hana. He could not lie to Pavel any more than he could himself. His feelings for Hana were real. And deep.

He could not let her go.

Eva listened as Zdenek and the baroness spoke. There was much she didn't understand...leaving precious little that she could speak to.

The baroness was Lord Krejik's mother—Pavel's mother—one and the same as Zdenek's dear friend that fought alongside them at Vitkov Hill. How had they encountered her here? Was Pavel in Tabor with General Zizka as well?

As they continued to discuss their next course of action, each sharing what information they had, Eva and Zdenek became aware that Zizka had left Tabor. What would that mean for them? Would they follow? It seemed unlikely as of yet.

For Pavel had come through and left his mother at this inn on his search for Karin and Baron Krejik. The baroness had not garnered the courage to leave. But she had neared the point of deciding to backtrack to Duke Novak's castle and wait there.

They concluded that Zdenek and Eva would see her there and hope to reunite with Pavel. Then they would make their plans to rejoin the Hussite army.

Zdenek turned to Eva and offered her one of his half smiles. She returned it. He had not been himself of late. Not for far too long. The thought gnawed at her that perhaps this encounter with his father had taken the light-heartedness of her husband from her forever. That, she could not abide.

She became determined anew to see him whole again. Beneath the table, she slid a hand into his, lacing their fingers.

His eyes widened ever so slightly.

Her cheeks warmed at the sudden intensity in his gaze, but she did not look away.

Zdenek did, however. After only a few seconds, he pulled his gaze away and regarded the baroness once more. "How soon can you be ready to leave?"

"Within the hour, if need be. But as great as my need, I will stay it, for I know you must have rest after your journey." She glanced first at Zdenek, then Eva, and back again. With a knowing smile.

Zdenek's features colored a bit. "My lady, do not worry with my comfort, I—"

Baroness Krejikova waved a hand. "I more think of your lady wife. Have a thought for her." The woman lifted an eyebrow.

Now, the redness on Zdenek's face deepened to become more discernable.

"It is not that I do not consider her, my lady, rather I..." He caught himself, and allowed the sentence to trail, unfinished.

"Of course." The baroness smiled. "As well you should." She glanced about the room. Many of the men had finished their meals and now seemed more engaged in conversation. "Too long I have kept you from your meal. I would have you take my captain's room after you have eaten your fill."

"I thank you, my lady," Eva said. It was more than they could have asked for.

The baroness nodded as she rose. As she did so, the men nearby got to their feet, hands on weapons.

"They mean well," the baroness intimated. "But I grow weary of their vigilance."

Eva smiled as the baroness moved from the table and up the stairs. The woman was all grace and confidence. Would Eva ever be such? If this was what it meant to be a noblewoman, perhaps Eva wouldn't measure up. Was Zdenek's father right? Did he deserve more?

Pressure on her hand drew her attention back to her husband. As their eyes met, his smile fell and he released her hand.

Did he see something there? Something she was unaware of?

"It is best we eat and you are settled for the night," he said simply.

Would he not stay with her? After all these weeks of separation, would they not reunite? Did he not wish to?

Zdenek left to secure bowls of goulash for them. Then they ate in silence.

Many times, Eva thought of something to say, some conversation to put forth. But, in the end, did not have the courage.

They finished and the innkeeper took their bowls.

"Her ladyship mentioned you would take the room alongside hers."

Zdenek rose. "Yes, I wish to see my wife to her rest." He extended a hand toward Eva.

She took it and allowed him to escort her up the stairs and to the room recently occupied by the captain of the baroness's guard. That gave her pause. Was it the Krejik guard? Or the Novak guard? From all that was shared this eve, the things she understood and the things she did not, she found herself uncertain.

Zdenek inspected the room.

Though it seemed well enough to her. It was simple, but comfortable. A bed, a stand, a candle, and little else to recommend it —but what more did she need?

"I shall leave you to your ablutions." He moved toward the door.

Her heart pounded. She did not want him to leave. Would there forever be this barrier between them? Was he not ready to bridge it?

"Husband?" she called out before she could think further on it.

He halted, already at the door. Did she imagine it, or was his chest heaving?

"I..." She turned to show him her back. "Am not certain I will be able to work these laces without a handmaiden."

His eyebrows shot up. And the deepening of his breathing was discernable. "What say you, wife?"

She swallowed. "I would ask, my lord, for assistance with the laces of my dress." Turning her head so she faced away from him with only her back to him, she also pulled her hair over her shoulder. Now, the bindings of her dress were fully exposed to him.

The moments passed. Too many. Then footfalls sounded on the boards as he neared. She felt the heat of his body behind her before his hands touched the ties of her laces.

She prayed that he would answer her boldness, her risk, with his own.

For some moments, he worked the bindings. Would he only do as asked then step away? Was he too changed by their time with his father?

The dress loosened. And her heart dropped.

And then a finger traced along the skin of her upper back.

She held her breath.

He stepped closer. Hands covered her shoulders and his lips touched her neck once, twice...and a husband and wife rediscovered one another.

Hana allowed Sir Ivan to escort her to the donjon. Had it been her imaginings or was Radek particularly unsettled by her attentions toward the knight? Then why did he not make more effort to intervene? It did not make sense to her.

She had expected he would stop what he would perceive as a growing relationship. Or did he not care as much as she thought? Was he willing to let her marry the knight?

Frowning, she continued to feign interest in the man's tales of battle. For she did not wish to hear of it in the least. Her mind was only on Radek. On the anger and hurt in his eyes. Was it real? Or did she only wish it to be so?

"Duke Novak has done well with his lands."

"Oh?" Hearing her father's name pulled her from her reverie.

"Yes." His gaze was on the grounds around them, or at least what was visible from their spot on the wall of the keep.

She glanced around. Were they alone? "Sir Ivan, I fear we should return to the Great Hall. My father would not like us being here unchaperoned."

He let out a breath. "Interesting words."

One of her brows rose. What could be his meaning? "Sir?"

"It is naught to concern yourself with."

"I would have your meaning, Sir Ivan."

He gave her a long look. "It is only that I would not expect you to be worried about being unchaperoned, lady."

She dropped her hand from his arm as her face heated—in part from shame, in part from the anger rising. "I assure you, I am every bit a lady and wish to safeguard my virtue."

Sir Ivan glanced at the horizon again. "Very well. As you wish... we shall rejoin the others."

"That is not necessary. I can make my own way back to the Great Hall."

"Lady Hana, do not be so upset. I did not intend to—"

She whirled on him then. "I am certain I can discern what you intended. I bid you good night, Sir Ivan."

Even as she moved off, he called after her. "You may have spirit now. But I warn you to be cautious, lady. Your father has yet to determine which of us will have your hand. And Lord Miklas does not appear interested."

That gave her pause. But only for a moment. Then she picked up her skirts once more and pushed off back toward the safety she found inside.

# CHAPTER 19

Pavel looked out over the inner bailey. His father's life still hung by a thread. The healer was not forthcoming about his thoughts on the matter. What would come of it? Was Pavel ready? What if his father never wakened? If Pavel never had the chance to speak with the man again?

And what of Karin? She had regained consciousness, yes. And the midwife had given them much hope. Still, he was not ready to celebrate.

He deserved every last bit of guilt he levied upon himself. If only he hadn't attempted to leave. That mistake had cost...nearly everything.

For certain, he would not maintain his sanity if he were to lose her. It had surprised him how close his grief over their previous loss still lay on the surface. Had he not moved past it? How much longer would it plague him?

A commotion below shook him from his thoughts. Several horse riders appeared. Among them was a noblewoman, whose form he would recognize anywhere—his mother.

He stood for a moment, caught in indecision. Should he watch what became of the contingency? Or make haste to his mother's side?

The desire to speak with the baroness won out, and his steps found him passing through the donjon and out to the larger space. Guards spoke with the baroness and the other men with her. Another lady was astride nearby, but her focus was opposite, and he could not discern her identity.

It mattered not. Pavel's eyes were on his mother.

"I must speak with Duke Novak," she demanded. "At once."

The guard did not appear ready to comply.

Pavel could not keep silent. "The Baroness Krejikova has requested your lord be notified of her presence."

She turned, her hair trailing. Had his voice given him away? Of course, it had. This was his mother.

Her eyes were wide as they set upon him. "Pavel!"

She struggled to dismount.

He was by her side in a moment, assisting her to the ground.

Then her arms were around him. "I feared the worst," she breathed into his ear as she held him tighter than he thought possible.

He permitted the embrace longer than he normally would. And found solace in his mother's care for him as much as she did in him.

And when he pulled back, he noted that the guards continued to watch the interchange.

"Have you not been tasked with seeking your master?" Pavel's tone was no longer kind.

"Yes, my lord," the man's response was short and pushed out.

As they retreated into the keep after their errand, Pavel turned back to his mother.

Her eyes glistened. "Praise God! Have you found your father? And Karin?"

He wished it were possible to delay such a conversation. "Yes."

Concern filled her eyes, and her brows furrowed. "What do you not say?"

He thinned his lips. "There is much to say, Mother. But not here."

"Lord Krejik!" Another voice cut into their reunion.

He whirled. And came face-to-face with Zdenek Ambroz and his Eva. His face alight with one of his largest smiles.

How? Where? What brought his friend and his mother together? By what trick of fate was this? Whatever was at work, Pavel was thankful.

Radek knew he should not. But he did. Though his reasons were weak and did not stand up against good sense, still he proceeded. A fool's errand.

He could no longer keep himself away. All that remained for him was her...his every thought, his every movement, even the beating of his heart.

And so, he moved about the grounds of the castle, searching, hoping against hope that he would find a moment with her. Just a moment. There were things that needed to be said.

But she seemed to have disappeared altogether. Vanished. Even his quiet inquiries were met with disappointment.

His last chance was to search the stables. Her presence there would indeed be curious. He cared not...only that he find her.

He cut through the gardens in his effort to expedite his mission. As he brushed past the rose bushes, he nearly missed the figure sitting by the far wall.

It gave him pause.

A lone woman, hunched over as she sat, almost folded in half. Her shoulders shook. Her light hair had been pulled up. It was not the gentle waves he had come to expect of his Hana, but he was certain he had found her.

Holding his breath, he caught the soft sounds of her crying. It drove a sharp pain through his center. What had caused her such distress?

But he knew—it was his due. In part, at the very least.

Dare he approach her? Disrupt her as she worked through these difficult things?

Could he not?

Would he do so without warning her of his presence? How to do so without startling her?

There was little working out in his mind as he became drawn to her as if moth to flame. And then he stood over her.

As if of its own accord, his hand reached for her shoulder.

The contact was gentle, but she jerked away. She looked up at him. Her features reddened and swollen by her emotional display.

He watched as surprise moved across her eyes before she looked away. "What...what do you here?"

"I could not stay away." His words were out before he could stop them.

She peered up at him, a question within the hazy blue-green of her eyes. "Do not use me ill, my lord. I fear I cannot—"

"Use you ill?" What did she think? After all this time? That he had misused her?

She turned to the side. "If you must speak, I bid you do so and be on your way. For I find I have not the strength left for games."

He sat in front of her, his brow creasing. Within the depths of him, everything pulled inward and down as if by a great weight. The tearing of his insides seemed real. And he had earned it.

Reaching forth, he touched her face.

More tears made trails down her cheeks. "Please. I can bear no more."

Her pain stabbed at him. How could he sit idly by and watch such an assault on his senses? When everything within him cried out for him to do something?

Scooting toward her, he gathered her into his arms. The press of her body against his only dampened the ache within. This weight would not be alleviated by something so simple.

He would not leave her with only his embrace.

"Hana," he spoke into her hair. "I have been a fool."

Her body shook as her sobs overcame her again.

"Forgive me." A tightness filled his chest. Would he be able to continue? He must.

Her hands found the front of his tunic and clung to him.

"I needed to find you...to tell you..." Emotion stole his words. He paused.

She quieted. Was she holding her breath? He feared she had until she spoke.

"What? What must you tell me?"

"I will fight for you. For us."

A cry burst from her lips—a mixture of joy and something more.

He pulled back to look into her eyes. They would give him the strength to continue.

Cupping her face, he searched her features for any hint that she wished him away. There was only relief. Could it be?

She moved her hands over his shoulders and arms.

"I will not lose you. Not to Sir Ivan. Not to any man."

He set his forehead against hers.

She sniffled and held his wrists. "Radek," she whispered.

His gaze became drawn to her lips. As was his mouth soon after. And so, a kiss once again sealed their future.

Or what they hoped would become of it.

Eva watched the noblewoman sleep. How was it that even ill and in a worrisome rest, the woman still appeared regal? Did these women ever frumple? Or did they always look just so with nary a hair out of place?

The woman stirred.

Eva pressed the cooling cloth to her face. As she pulled her arm back, green eyes stared at her.

It gave her a start, and she jerked a little.

"My lady!"

The eyes became curious. "You are not a maidservant."

How did this woman know that? Eva could not be certain. She had not the proper training to hold herself as a woman of noble standing nor to address others in such a way that would place her in that station.

"Are you not?" The woman's confusion seemed to deepen.

"I..." Eva swallowed. "I am not sure what you mean, my lady."

Pavel's wife glanced at Eva's dress. Ah yes, the clothing. That must be what set Eva apart. She attired herself as a noblewoman. Perhaps merely a costume, but it marked her all the same. How long before this woman discovered she only acted the part?

"Why does a lady attend me?"

The woman's voice was kind. There was no judgment there, only interest. Eva became convinced they might be friends. Dare she hope? She had become one for taking risks of late. Her boldness with Zdenek last eve had met with success. Perhaps she should take another chance.

"I am the wife of Zdenek Ambroz."

Recognition lit the young woman's face.

"I was given to understand that you know my husband."

The lady's mouth turned up in a smile. "Yes, that is true. Your husband has been a great friend to my husband and myself. He is a good man."

Eva looked down, unsure how to respond to such fine words from a lady such as this.

"It speaks well of you that he regards you so highly."

Eva peered through lashes at the woman. Those same green eyes spoke kindness to the recipient of the lady's compliment. "I thank you, my lady."

"First..." The woman shifted to sit and pressed a pained breath out through clenched teeth.

Eva was on her feet in a moment, assisting the woman, who was not as delicate as she appeared, to a sitting position.

Nodding her thanks, the lady caught her breath and set her gaze on Eva once more. "Now then, first, you do not need to address me so formally. I am Karin. How might I call you?"

"Eva, please." As she sat back in the seat by the bed, she wondered how it would be possible to interact with this fine beauty as if they were indeed intimately acquainted. It did not seem possible.

Karin stretched out a hand toward Eva while the other lay on her enlarged stomach. "Tell me, Eva, what news have you of my dear friend?"

What was there to say? How much should she share of their time at his father's home? Her face heated at the very thought.

She glanced at Karin. The lady watched her with an expectant gaze.

"I fear I do not know what you wish to hear, my la— Karin." Calling the woman by her Christian name still did not seem right.

"I am certain my husband was much relieved to see his friend."

Eva nodded. "As was Zdenek."

"How did you find yourself stationed here at my bedside?" Karin's features again scrunched in a quizzical way.

"Your lord husband is so very worried after you," Eva spoke truthfully. "He wished to remain by your side himself, but he took the Baroness Krejikova to see her ailing husband."

Karin's eyes widened. "The baroness is here?"

"Oh y-yes," Eva stuttered, stumbling over her words. How could she forget that Karin had no way to know that? "She arrived with us just this morning."

Karin reached for Eva's hand, clutching the stranger as if they were already great companions. "Praise God! And thank Him for the provision of you and Zdenek!"

"Yes, praise the Lord indeed!" Eva agreed. "But I fear you give my husband and me too much credit. Her numerous guards would have brought her back had they the notion to."

"But it was not they that did so. It was you. And Zdenek. Can you see? You were the instrument used by God to reunite a mother and son...soon a husband and wife. Do not dismiss your usefulness in God's hands."

Eva watched the woman, though nothing but sincerity shone on her features. Was it true? That God had used even her as a vessel? Didn't Eva believe that at one time—that she had been a tool in the Hussite army? Fighting in God's war? Had she let Zdenek's father take all of that away from her?

More—would she continue to let him? Or would she let go of the lies and seek the truth at the Source?

Her mouth widened. "That is true."

Karin squeezed her hand. "Of course. God is ever able to use the willing."

Eva watched the lady in front of her and indeed hoped that this was only the budding of a lifelong friendship.

Pavel held his mother's arm as he walked her through the final corridor. They had been silent for some time.

He opened his mouth to speak but found that no words would suffice. Nothing could truly prepare her for what she would see of her husband.

The thought to pray crossed his mind, but he dismissed it. He wasn't as keen to raise a request when it seemed God had removed himself from Pavel's life. Perhaps he should not begrudge the Lord as much. An Almighty God did have the right to do as He saw fit.

Soon enough, they arrived at the door that served as the final barrier. Pavel sensed his mother's trembling through her arm. He turned slightly to look at her.

She played at the fabric of his sleeve for a moment. "Why do we delay?"

Pavel closed his eyes, wishing he did not have to endure the next moments. Perhaps he should send his mother in alone? No, that would be heartless indeed. She needed him, by her side. To lean on, to comfort her.

And so, he pushed the door open and led her into the space.

The baron was laid out as he had been the last time Pavel was within. A coverlet hid a good portion of his injuries. For that, Pavel was grateful. There was no reason his mother needed to see the extent of the injuries.

Her hands fell from Pavel's arm, and she moved toward her husband.

As he watched, her hands moved from her chest, to her opened mouth, to clutch her chest again, to then hover over the baron's body. She seemed not to know what to do with them.

At last, she set tentative hands on the baron's face. She did avoid touching the places where there were bandages.

"Alex...what...?" she managed. "Oh, my Alex..." Her voice was so tender. And loving.

Pavel became aware that he may be intruding on a private moment. Should he leave and bid the healer do so as well?

The healer stepped closer to the baron and baroness. "My lady, I do not believe he knows pain."

Tears poured down her face. "Will he..." She tried to speak, but was cut off by her sobs.

She wiped at the moisture on her face and took a deep breath. "Will he wake?"

Pavel feared this question. He had tried to warn his mother. But he still worried that she would seek the answer from the healer.

The man dropped his head. "He has not, Baroness. It is unlikely that he will."

She closed her eyes, as if that would staunch the welling of tears. Pavel became certain the moment would be better suited if he and the healer stepped out.

He lay a hand to the man's shoulder and indicated that they should do so. But as they neared the door to the room, a great gasp filled the space.

Pavel turned.

His father's body shook.

The baroness let out a cry and put hands to his chest. "Alex!"

In a moment, the healer was beside the baron. His hands moved expertly over his patient's body, but they did not keep Pavel's attention. For his gaze had caught on his father's face. And the eyes that had opened.

Baron Krejik's mouth moved ever so slightly.

Pavel stepped toward the bed as his mother placed fingertips to the baron's lips.

"No, my lord. You do not have the strength to speak."

The baron's eyes were rapt on his wife's face, his gaze clear and set. A moment passed between them. Something that Pavel could not describe.

"Always, my love," his mother took Baron Krejik's hand and pressed it to her heart. "I will always love you. Be at peace."

Pavel could not look away as his father took three more measured breaths, then ceased all movement. And was gone.

# CHAPTER 20

Hana knocked on the door to her father's solar. As she waited for the baron to respond, she couldn't help but smile. The feel of Radek's kiss upon her lips from that morning was still fresh. As was the comfort of his embrace just hours ago. Her stomach flipped inwardly. How could she ever have doubted in their connection? It was solid and sure.

"Come," her father's voice boomed even through the door.

She reached for the latch, but the large wooden door swung open before her. And she then faced Sir Ivan.

What was he doing here? Ingratiating himself to her father? A sick feeling filled the bottom of her stomach. Gone was the fluttering; now there was only a solid, thick weight.

She searched the room beyond him. Her father was indeed seated at his desk within the room.

"Father?" Though she wanted to say more, she bit at the inside of her mouth to hold her words back.

"Hana," he greeted her. "Sir Ivan was just on his way out." He gave the man a meaningful look.

She only wished it contained a menacing undertone. Why was it more companionable than she'd like? Had Sir Ivan's scheme to woo her father worked?

The door shut, and she was left in the room with her father. She swallowed hard and glanced at him.

He sat and caught her eyes. "I had expected you to seek me out sooner."

She blinked. Had he? Did he know she would speak on her own behalf? That she would not quietly accept his choice for her? Would she? If he, in the end, chose Sir Ivan, would she acquiesce?

Perhaps he did know her well.

"Father, I..."

He held up a hand. "You have a strong spirit, Hana. And I have indulged you for far too long. This recent dalliance with the Hussite army, leading to your capture, has far and above taught me better. For what I believed was true and what *was* true of your situation, as it seems, was quite different."

"Father, I wasn't—"

His eyes were hard. "I am not finished." He walked to the window and looked out. "Now, this situation...it put you in a precarious, dangerous position, which allowed you be captured."

She could do little more than sigh and concede his point. "Yes, Father."

"And so, I find myself somewhat grateful that it has come to this. For it is time you were married. You need someone to watch over you. To mind you. Far better than I have."

"But, Father, you—"

He held up his hand again. "I will not be absolved of my guilt in the matter. It belongs to me, and I will have it."

She drew in a ragged breath.

"I believe you have come here to share your thoughts on the man I should choose for you." He raised a brow as he looked at her.

"Yes, Father."

"And I will tell you that I care not."

Her eyes became so wide they stung.

"Your thoughts on what was best for you have not served you well. Rather, time and again, you prove that your rashness and ill-conceived notions will land you in terrible trouble again and again. I neither trust your judgment..."

"But I—"

"Nor your heart," he raised his volume to speak the last words.

She stepped back. Indeed, perhaps it would have been better had he slapped her. Her eyebrows furrowed.

He closed the space between them. "Hana," he said, his voice soft as he raised a hand toward her. Then, as if he thought better of it, he let it fall back to his side. "I am not unfeeling of your plight. Just the opposite. I will do what I can to make the best match for you. But for the right reasons."

Her lip trembled. She realized that all of her shook.

Something passed in the baron's eyes that she could not name. Then he turned his back to her and returned to the window. "That is all."

She wasted little time removing herself from the room that had become suffocating. And she didn't stop running until she closed the door to her chambers. Then she sank to the floor and let the hot tears come.

Zdenek returned to the stables. The ride had been much needed to clear his thoughts. His reaction to all of Pavel's news had not been helpful to his friend. Least of all, the fact that he homed in on the piece about Radek.

His friend was here? Within these same walls? How was he to respond? What was he to say? A wave of uncertainty overwhelmed him, and he had to get out to where there were open spaces. He couldn't face Radek yet. Not until he had a better handle on himself.

So much had passed since he last saw his friend. Too much.

Between the contention with his father, his challenges with his marriage, the other happenings within their borders, and Radek's defection...was it not enough?

*God...*

So, he had prayed in the solace. And found the respite he sought. If he wasn't ready to face his friend now, he would never be.

He passed his horse off to one of the stable hands and moved toward the inner bailey.

Did Radek know of his arrival? Had Pavel told him as well? Would his friend avoid him? Or did Radek wish to seek him out?

There were these and many other questions that needed answers. And there was only one way to find those.

Zdenek stepped into the donjon and wondered at where he might cross paths with Radek. Might he wait until the next meal? Perhaps that would be best. A neutral place to come face to face.

As he entered the Great Hall, Zdenek sensed something was not right. Everything was solemn. A somberness hung in the air. Had something happened to one of his friends? To one of the women? Eva?

His heart pounded, the beats coming hard and fast. He scanned the large room.

There. By the hearth—his Eva.

He crossed the space in a few breaths and wrapped his arms around her.

She went easily into his embrace, letting out a muffled cry as he pressed her to himself.

"I'm sorry," he whispered. "I worried."

She nodded. "It is the Baron Krejik. He is pained no more."

Pavel's father?

Zdenek drew back and sought her gaze. The emotion welling within him was difficult to understand. His friend's loss was part of it. A realization of his father, also truly gone, was another. Grief settled into his heart—grief for two fathers, now beyond reach for two sons.

Eva set a hand to the side of his face. "Zdenek?"

Had she seen more in his eyes? He delved into hers for a moment then pulled her into his arms once more.

Radek watched his old friend find solace in the arms of his wife across the room. It gave him reason to ache. For Zdenek? Or Pavel?

There seemed to be more to the sadness in the scene before him than the death of the baron. What had passed for Zdenek in the last months? What had he and Eva endured?

Oddly, there was a renewed feeling of loneliness in him that he had no knowledge of it. For he had missed these months with his friend. And for what? He had not found what he sought in the Royalist camp.

But he did find Hana.

Was that what he was meant to find?

If he believed that, he would have to believe there was a greater power at work. And he wasn't sure he could.

Fingers grazed his. He looked to his side.

Hana stood next to him. And though she did not look at him, he saw the sadness in her eyes. Had this death, too, been hard for her?

He took her fingers in his, pressing them gently, hoping she might take strength from him.

When he lent his gaze back to the Great Hall, he sensed eyes upon him. And his attention was drawn back toward the hearth.

Zdenek had found him.

The fire in his gut burned so great, Pavel was certain it would never be extinguished. Nothing would make it right. Nothing. Ever.

He stood in a field, screaming at the top of his lungs. The only reality became the sting of his knees when he fell to them, the burn of his lungs as they ached for air, and this torrent of emotion that would not stop.

How he found himself here seemed a blur. He had been with his mother at that moment. That horrible moment. The moment when all became before and after.

Then he was here.

And the pain.

The searing pain that ripped through him, allowing a flood of raw emotion to pour through him. And it would not stop. He couldn't rebuild the wall. It would never stop.

He would never hear his father's voice. Or see those eyes shining upon him. The man would not lay a hand on his grandchild and bless the babe.

They had been robbed. And the thief had not even been cunning.

But their help, their hope, had either not bothered to bend an ear to their cause. Or did not care to.

Either way, that trust was shattered.

# CHAPTER 21

Karin spoke the words of the hymn that were necessary. But she felt numb. Though she wished more than anything for a way to support her husband.

She had only been allowed out of her chamber to attend the funeral mass, not the vigil.

Pavel had been absent from their chambers and gone from her almost the entirety of the time since his father's passing. He was angry. And he was hurting. Both to be expected, for certain.

And he was quiet. So very quiet.

Karin looked past him to his mother.

The baroness, though her features showed signs of her mourning, turned her face toward heaven. And through her tears, she said the words that told of God's part.

She had lost her husband, but not her faith. Could Karin say the same for *her* husband?

Pavel's arm came around Karin, and he assisted her to stand. The service was concluding.

She went through the remainder of the mass with reverence,

thanking God for the baron's life and for His provision in letting the baroness have a last moment with him before his passing.

Then Pavel urged her toward the aisle. He supported her such that she could lean heavily on him.

Though not her preference, she was, in truth, not so healed that she could refuse his attentions. Such stubbornness would be to her detriment.

They filed out of the chapel and toward the Great Hall. The meal would not be one of celebration. It would be somber and quiet.

However, as they neared the donjon, Pavel steered her toward the stairs that led to the chambers on the upper level.

She put a hand on his arm. "Do you not wish that I join you at the meal?"

He sighed. "I think you've been out of bed quite enough today. I would see you returned to your rest."

"I am quite well, husband," she assured him, offering him a sweet smile. "I would like to stay with you. By your side."

"That is not necessary." He continued to lead her to the stairway. Why would he so disregard her wishes? "I am more concerned after your wellbeing."

"But I—"

"If not for yourself," he cut her off with a raised voice, "then will you not think of our child?"

She quieted. He had never spoken to her thusly. Biting her lip to keep from speaking further, she only nodded.

Conquering the stairs with great effort and less speed than she should, she could not fault him for his assessment. It took some time for them to return to their chambers.

He did not cease until he settled her onto the mattress.

"Pavel, I don't want you to worry so."

He shook his head. "Don't do this." His eyes were icy as they found hers. "You and our child are what is left to me."

A fresh sadness fell over her. Why must he think such? Did he think he alone was responsible to protect her from anything and everything? That he even could?

"Pavel, it isn't—"

"I won't lose you, too." His tone was harsh, but the last word was strained by emotion.

She nodded.

He turned away quickly and walked to the door. "I will have viands sent up for you."

Then he was gone.

The mood of the entire afternoon was sedate. How else could it be? Eva had not known the man, but she was saddened for the loss. She remembered that pain quite well. Her mother's death still felt fresh... especially today.

Zdenek drew her nearer than he had needed to at mass, had held her hand as often as possible during the meal, and even now suggested they might take a stroll.

As they came to the inner bailey, they crossed paths with Radek. Where had he been? Hadn't he sat only five seats away at the meal? How had he been out here and then returning already?

Radek's eyes lit with recognition as he neared. He turned to the side. Did he seek some manner of escape? Was he so resistant to speaking with her husband?

Zdenek, too, stiffened. She felt the muscles in his arm tighten.

What might she do? These two friends must, at some point, share words. It could not be avoided for much longer, if at all.

Radek seemed to decide the same. He adjusted his path to intersect with theirs.

Eva noticed Zdenek slowed their pace and halted. She looked to his face. There was a tautness about his features. As if he were unsure how to proceed.

At last, Radek stopped just short of where they stood. "Lord Ambroz."

There was a quick intake of breath beside her as her husband fairly bristled. Must Radek be so formal? Or did he only tread with as much care as possible?

"Lord Miklas," Zdenek returned.

"I..." Radek's words faded for a moment. His eyes flicked to Eva. Perhaps he wished this interchange take place apart from her presence. Such could not be helped. "I hope you have been well."

"As well as can be expected." Zdenek's reply was short.

Why did he respond so? Was he trying to be contentious? She pressed fingers into his arm. Would that communicate her support?

Radek's face darkened as his brow dropped. "As can be expected?"

"It has been...difficult. The *weather* has been unkind these past weeks."

Eva became more uncomfortable with the glares the men now exchanged. Their interchange was becoming more strained. Zdenek's temper flared close to the surface.

"Has it?" Radek's tone sharpened. "The sun has beat on my efforts as well."

Zdenek quieted for a moment. "Perhaps then, you should not have been out where there is no hope of shade."

Radek's eyes narrowed. "Would you not see? The shade offered no respite for me."

Eva wished she had remained within the keep. The men grew more guarded and their voices all the more stern.

Zdenek let out a breath. At last, someone would relent!

"You have but two choices: the shade or the sun. And you must abide your choice."

"And you with yours. As you said, it has been difficult for you. I cannot say I am altogether surprised the shade is not everything it should be."

Zdenek's eyes narrowed. "There has been little of the shade.

What you fail to take note of, or search out, is the great storm the shade could not withstand."

Radek looked to Eva.

She turned to the side, unwilling to come into the thinly veiled discussion.

"If you would tell me, I would know. As it is, I heard of no such bad weather. Not from you, nor any other. Yet, I am supposed to possess such knowledge?"

"That is not what I said." Zdenek's words cut then. "I didn't think you cared to know. You have made every effort to avoid me since our arrival here. What sin have I committed against you? It was not I that ran away."

At last, all effort at a pretense had fallen.

Radek's features became stony. "It is not because I care not." He looked at Eva, perhaps again wishing for her absence, and then to the ground before glaring at Zdenek once more. "You cannot know how difficult..."

Zdenek's eyebrows rose.

"I did not run away."

"Then what would you call it? For the whole of the Hussite army regards it treacherous."

"And you?"

The lines around Zdenek's mouth eased a bit. For a moment. "I don't know how to see it. My friend did not favor me with much to see otherwise."

"You know I was challenged with Zizka's efforts."

Zizka's efforts? What could he mean? Eva did not understand.

"There is a price in war."

"But must there be such compromise?" Radek shot back.

"That is not my decision to make. God is with General Zizka, and he does as he sees fit."

For certain, Zdenek spoke true. Eva had seen it to be true. How could Radek not? Even after all *he* had seen?

Radek shook his head. "A soldier through and through."

Eva stepped between the men and turned to Zdenek. "I bid you, my lord husband. I do not think there will be resolution to be found here today."

When his gaze settled on hers, it softened. "You speak wisely, wife." Then he shifted his focus to Radek. "It is regrettable, my friend, that there is nothing for you in the shade or the sun. For I do not know where you will go, where you shall find your peace."

Radek stared back at him.

"And, as much as you may doubt me, I do hope you find it."

Radek looked off toward the donjon. What was in his thoughts? Would he not respond?

After a few moments of silence, Zdenek offered his arm once more to Eva. "Come, wife, let me get you back inside. Out of this heat. It has been a long day."

She nodded, her heart heavy for her husband. And wishing more than anything that there could have been more resolution between the two men.

Pavel avoided the baroness. He did not wish to speak of some things which they must. He did so loathe putting much before her in the midst of her deep grief.

How did she fare? With regret, he realized he had not been so attentive to his mother these past days. So caught in what went in his mind, in his heart.

His mother was in his care now. And he must do better.

Pavel walked the corridor of the upper level and as he passed the master's solar, he saw that the door was open slightly. It gave him pause.

As he neared, he picked up on the voices within. One, indeed, being his mother's.

What would she be doing in the duke's solar? Had they business to discuss that would not include him? What might that be?

He inclined his head to better listen.

"...you were a good friend to my husband, and to myself." His mother's voice, clear and without hitch. How was that possible?

It was the duchess that responded. "I don't know how you have held together so well. You are a standard none of us mere mortals could hope to attain to."

"You speak more highly of me than I deserve. I have had moments of deep sorrow. When the tears will not stop and my body aches terribly. But I also know that I was given a gift."

The duchess scoffed. "A gift? For your husband to be beaten? To hold to the edge of life for so many days, and then die in your presence?"

"To have that last chance to speak with him. Can you not see? God kept him for me to speak final words to him. If that does not tell of mercy, I don't know what does."

"You think in puzzles."

"How can you not see God in it? My husband was always going to die. But God's grace allowed him to sleep and not feel pain. And to awaken in the one moment that mattered. To me."

Pavel backed away from the door. He would hear no more. How could his mother think such? That his father's passing was mercy? Grace? From God?

His pulse thrummed so loud in his ears he could hear nothing else.

That could not be true. The man had lain in a horrible state for weeks. At the very limits of life and death. Only to breathe his last on his wife's arrival.

But then...it was the timing she spoke of.

It was true that he was always to have succumbed to his wounds. If Pavel were honest, he had known it from the first time he saw his father after the attack.

Perhaps...his mother's faith was not misplaced.

But if he took that leap...believed that God was even in this pain, even in this death...he would have to trust God with Karin.

The very thought made him ache.

Could he?

He wanted to maintain control. *His* control. But it was nothing more than illusion. A haze he cast for himself over the reality of the situation.

If some ill seized Karin, he could no more stall it than hold the moon back.

Trust God or not, it was in His hands alone. What He offered Pavel was peace.

And hope.

The chapel was silent at this hour. The day was giving way into evening and the earth prepared to rest. But Radek did not think he would be able to calm his anxious heart. Not for rest, not for anything.

Why had he let Zdenek bait him? He understood his friend's sense of injury. The man probably thought Radek had abandoned him.

If only he could understand that Radek wished it were different, that he might be able to fight alongside his brother, his friend as before. But he could not.

Still, he had found himself challenged by Zdenek's words...

*"There is nothing for you in the shade or the sun. For I do not know where you will go, where you shall find your peace."*

The words rang truer than his friend could know. They stung deeper than he could have imagined possible. Radek had nowhere to go, no side to align with, no allies in this war. Where *did* he belong?

What use was it? The question had plagued him for weeks. And he still had not found an answer.

Why did he think he would find it here?

He spun and moved to leave the sacred place.

"What can I do for you, my child?" an older voice called from farther in the space.

Radek looked back over his shoulder. Had he not been alone?

A figure shuffled in from the opposite side, near the altar.

"It is nothing. I did not mean to impose." He stepped toward the exit again.

"There is no imposition when it comes to the Lord's sanctuary."

Radek cringed.

"He welcomes all who would seek to know Him. To find peace."

Radek paused. How could this man possibly know? He turned to face the old priest, now standing by the kneeler at the front of the room.

"What do you seek?"

Radek watched him as the room became dimmer with the descending sun. What *did* he seek? Was it peace? Or to satisfy his curiosity? An answer to a challenge? Perhaps to please Hana in his efforts?

No, this much he knew—he had come out of his own volition. He *was* curious. Of all that had happened, it seemed to lead to this place, this point—would he seek further or continue to walk away? Might there be acceptance with this Almighty God or was he forever to be on his own?

"You have a great burden you will not relinquish, my son."

The words did not judge. Nor did they invite argument.

Radek fought the tightness in his chest. He did want to release it all. Could he? "How can you know what is in my mind?"

"Do you think you are the first battle-weary man I have seen? The first man caught between faith and wounds dealt by the church?"

Radek let out a long breath. How could this man understand so well and yet not know even his name?

"Come," the priest bade, holding up a hand. "Seek, and you will find."

Radek creased his forehead. Was it so simple? He moved to the front, toward the altar. Perhaps it could be. Perhaps...

Opening the door to their chambers, Pavel slid through. Would Karin be sleeping? He hoped not. His heart was heavy. And his need for her great.

As he entered, he heard her voice. Was someone else within?

His eyes caught on Zdenek's wife by the bedside. The woman and Karin spoke quite amiably with each other. When had this friendship developed?

He could not begrudge it. Rather, he found himself thankful.

The women quieted as Karin's eyes met his.

Soon after, Eva noticed him. She said something in hushed tones to Karin and pressed her hand then stood and moved toward the door, nodding to Pavel as she did so.

He offered her a small smile as she passed.

Once Lady Ambrozova closed the door, Pavel moved closer to his wife. Her expression had become more neutral. No longer did her face hold the light it had moments before.

He took the seat just vacated. The silence stretched between them.

"Karin, I...wish I was better...with my words."

She looked to him. Her green eyes filling with light from the setting sun's final rays streaming in.

"These last days..." His voice hitched.

Reaching for his hand, she spoke. "I know. They have been impossible."

He nodded. "Yes."

"I only want to help you carry that burden." She winced.

Why must he invite further pain? "I know. But I don't want to cause you distress."

"'Tis not distress to be a wife to a very loved husband." Her eyes spoke the truth of her words, but her mouth twitched on one side. More pain?

He came to sit on the edge of the bed, slowly, careful to watch for any sign of injury to her person. She seemed to welcome the closeness.

Gathering both of her hands in his, he leaned forward. "I have not been...so trusting. Or as faith-filled."

She watched him but offered nothing, giving him space to share his heart.

"I thought that *I* needed to do more. That *I* had to..." His words again trailed. "But that is not the way of it. God is our anchor, our protector, our keeper. And I...can do nothing without Him."

She leaned in and pressed a kiss to his hands. "I am glad to hear you say it."

He let out a breath. And all the tension in him melted. "So, you will forgive a thoughtless man his foolish words?"

"Yes, my husband. And more. I will love him for the man he is. The man God is making him into."

Something warm swirled in him and filled his chest. He captured her lips, so close to his.

When they parted, she grimaced.

Still?

He put a hand to her face. "Do you hurt?"

Her eyes caught his. She did not speak for some moments. Then she said, "I fear I do. I have had pains now for some hours."

"Pains?"

"Yes." Her eyes were sorrowful. And her hands pulled from his to rest on her stomach. "And the baby does not move."

He widened his eyes.

Another pain took her, and her body stiffened.

Pavel rushed to the open door and called. "Send for the midwife! And the healer! The Lady Karin is unwell!"

A faint response came back from some distance, and then there was much movement about below stairs.

Satisfied that others would see to it, Pavel returned to Karin's side. She had maneuvered in the bed, slid until she was lying on her side facing him, curled around the babe.

Her hand shot out to grab for his. "The pain is worse. Something is wrong. It is not yet time."

Was it not? How did the months add? Pavel did not know. How should they? He scanned her body but was helpless. There wasn't anything he might do to alleviate her suffering. And he was gripped with fear. Would they lose the child? What of Karin?

The tortured minutes seemed like hours until the midwife first, soon followed by the village healer, entered the room.

After a short examination, the midwife, with brows knit, turned to Pavel. "She labors. The babe comes."

Was that supposed to bring him some relief? It did not. Watching his beloved wife in such pain was the worst thing he could imagine.

"What...will she be all right?" he managed.

"Women have been birthing since God created Eve. She has that in her favor."

"But, it is not time. I—" Karin protested.

The midwife set a hand on Karin's forehead. "It does not always happen as we wish it. No matter our timetable, this babe will make his or her appearance before this time tomorrow."

Was that her answer? It did not reassure Pavel.

The healer put hands to Pavel's shoulders. "Come with me. It is best we remove ourselves from the chambers."

He wanted to shrug the man off, but he thought better of it. A birthing chamber was no place for a man. While he ached to stay with Karin, to offer any comfort he might, he did not wish to be in the way.

As he rose, he leaned over her and pressed a kiss to her forehead, which had become clammy. It didn't seem right.

"Is there naught I can do?" he beseeched the midwife.

"Pray." The woman gave him but a moment of her attention before shifting her focus back to Karin.

And that was all he needed before tearing himself from his wife and allowing the healer to remove him from the chamber.

Radek paced the solar. How long would Hana's father keep him waiting? Long enough for Radek to second guess his actions. Did he do the prudent thing? He was unsure. But for certain, he did what he must. For Hana.

The door swung open, and Duke Novak entered.

Radek dipped in a slight bow. "My lord duke, I thank you for seeing me."

"Lord Miklas," the duke said as he nodded. "I wondered myself if I would."

Radek set his jaw. Had the man already determined his course? And Hana's fate? Would there be any changing it?

Regardless, he must fight for her. For them.

"My lord, I do not think I have made clear my intentions toward your daughter." Radek stood as straight as possible. He would face this boldly and with as much courage as he could.

"I believe you made your thoughts on the match quite clear." Duke Novak lifted a brow. "At least, it seemed so."

"Forgive me. I fear my...reaction may have been misleading."

"Oh?"

"Yes. I wanted to ensure that you knew there is much I could offer your daughter. Much I can provide to keep her comfortable, make her life easy."

The duke's brows came together. "Comfortable?"

"Yes. My family has holdings, lands, great..." His voice trailed as he watched the duke's interest wane.

"What does she need of comfort? She will be provided for in either choice, will she not? My lands will be awarded with my daughter's hand."

Of course. Radek blew out a breath. He went about this rather badly. For he was not Sir Ivan—it was not the lands nor the title that mattered to him. It was his care...his *love* for Hana that drove him to stand here today. That burned within him with a desire...a *need* to win her hand at all cost.

That was what set him apart. That was what would have to make the difference to Duke Novak. Because, in the end, that was all he had to offer—his heart.

"Lord Miklas," the duke said on an exhale. "It is true you have all these things, but I don't know if you have real interest in this contest for my daughter."

"Duke, if I may, I would like to tell you a story."

# CHAPTER 22

Hana crept up the stairs. Her father's solar was, once again, her destination. What would come to pass in the next moments? She had been summoned. Was it time? Had her father made his decision?

She stopped at the large oak door and took in a deep breath.

"Your father has requested my company," a voice said from behind her.

Her stomach churned. She felt ill. As she turned to face Sir Ivan, she feared she would not be able to contain her emotion.

He stood only a couple arms' lengths away, a smug smile upon his lips. "I take it, then, that your father has seen reason."

She swallowed against the bile rising in her throat. "Then he will know you care not for anything but your own gain, sir knight."

His eyes became wide. "Is that so?"

He did not appear threatened. Only amused. Why did this not concern him?

"You suppose your father is not aware of my desire to raise my own prospects in marrying you."

She stepped back, hitting the wall of the corridor.

He let out a little laugh. "You cannot think your father so fooled to suppose that I wish for your hand because I was so besotted by your beauty? Or your wit perhaps?"

Her face burned. She looked to the floor. How could she bear it? Did her father consider her so little? As nothing more than a piece to be bargained with?

Sir Ivan stepped closer. "You have much to learn, Lady Hana." His eyes moved over her features. "You *are* lovely."

She wanted to slide further, but there was no escape.

Shaking his head, he gave her the space she sought. "If only your head wasn't so full of fanciful notions." He pushed out a breath. "Perhaps you will learn in time."

His gaze on her was meaningful. Did he intend to threaten her? That by his hand she would learn her place?

He reached to the side to the door's latch and opened the way to the solar, and her fate.

She remained where she was, watching as he stepped within. After he disappeared through the door, she thought she heard a grunt.

What might have brought that from him? Was something amiss? Had something surprised him?

She pressed her hands against the wall, pushing her body free of it, and moved through the opening.

Her father stood by the window at one end of the solar with Radek. It appeared as if the two had been deep in conversation.

Her heart raced. Was this reason to hope? Had Radek come to speak with her father? To fight for them? Or had her father called on Radek to explain the way of things?

Hana tried to meet Radek's gaze, but he seemed to avoid her eyes. Why?

Instead he glared at Sir Ivan, his features darkening. Was Radek so put out with the man? For sooth, that did not portend good things.

Her newfound hope fell, and the heaviness filled her once more.

She regarded her father as he stepped to the center of the room, looking first at Sir Ivan, then to her.

There was nothing to be had for her timidity. She would be brave. She *would*.

Taking a step forward, she sought her father's gaze. "My lord, you called for me."

"Hana." The duke extended a hand in her direction.

She slid her fingers into it.

"The time has come for you to know what will be of your marriage arrangement." His eyes moved over her, then to Sir Ivan. But did not slide to Radek.

A thickness filled her throat so much so that it became difficult to swallow. What would she do? Refuse her father? That wasn't possible. Would she be able to escape into the night? How could she do so and prove herself the reckless lady her father supposed her to be? Would Radek even have her if her father promised her to Sir Ivan?

She sucked in a breath, only then aware she had held back from taking one. "Yes, Father?"

"I have given this much thought. As marriage is not something to be entered into blindly. There is much to consider. Your situation, the qualities of each man, the benefit to you and your future children, my grandchildren..." The duke's smile broadened at that. "And I do so wish a marriage that may be in some part happy for you, that will produce grandchildren for me."

She nodded but felt as if she balanced on the edge of a precipice. Her gaze had dropped to the floor, and she could not force her eyes elsewhere.

"Hana," her father said, giving her hand a gentle tug.

She shook her head. Could she bear it?

"I will have you look at me." His words were simple and firm.

Despite her desire to hide her emotion, to keep the worst of it disguised, she did as requested and raised her face, setting her gaze on his.

"It is my best judgment that you would be most suited, and more successful, in a union with Lord Miklas."

The shaky breath that came out of her was soon followed by tears.

"My lord." Sir Ivan spoke. Then his lips flattened.

The duke glared at the knight. "Sir Ivan, I will forgive the outburst. But I have made my decision. And it is final. I thank you for your concern for my daughter and her wellbeing. However, her future with Lord Miklas is set."

Sir Ivan's face reddened, and his muscles tensed. "Yes, my lord."

"You are dismissed."

The knight turned.

"Just one more thing, sir knight."

Sir Ivan halted.

"A man's daughter is not a pawn to be maneuvered as if in a game of strategy. Least of all, one that is so beloved."

The knight clenched his fists. He would not dare strike, would he?

"Yes, my lord." The words were pressed out.

"That is all. You may have your leave." Duke Novak waved a hand, and the knight was forgotten. Though Hana knew he was watched by her father's man-at-arms until after he left the room.

But not by her. No, her eyes were only for Radek. As his gaze had settled on her at last.

It took everything in her not to cross the space and throw her arms around him. Before she could decide if that was permissible, Radek moved toward her.

He took her hands in his and drew her closer. "I told you," he whispered.

She nodded. He had told her...and indeed he had fought for her. In the wilderness he had fought her barriers, in the mountains he fought with his life against her captors, and today he had fought with cleverness and with his heart. And had won.

His prize?

Her heart and her future.

When would it be time? How long was long enough? Zdenek looked out over the grounds of the castle yard and could not make sense of the way his conversation ended with Radek.

His dear friend had made a decision, and Zdenek couldn't live with it. But was it his to live with?

Perhaps, it was time that he and Eva moved on with their own lives. Too long, they had been gone from their purpose. Too long, they had been distracted from the efforts of the Hussite army.

That was where they needed to be. That was where they were needed.

There they must return. And soon. After all, had they not come to Tabor seeking General Zizka? What was to keep them from continuing on that mission?

"You are great at many things, my lord husband." The voice of his dear wife called from behind.

He smiled but resisted turning to face her just yet.

"But I had not known that secreting away was one of them. Until now."

The sound of her footfalls and the way her voice carried belied that she neared as she spoke. Once she had come within arms' reach, he turned and welcomed her into his embrace.

"I might say the same of you. Where have you been?"

Her grin warmed him.

"I wanted to speak with Lady Karin."

"Ah. You have become well acquainted with the lady?"

"Yes." Eva's eyes brightened. "She is as gracious and easy to know as she is lovely."

Zdenek nodded. He knew the same to be true. "As are you, my wife."

She laid her head against his shoulder. Did she shy away from his compliment? Or was this only her sweet humility?

He stroked her hair. It would not be fair to delay broaching the subject. "I have something to ask."

"Yes?" She pulled back, and her gaze found his again. "Is it so serious?"

He offered a small smile. "It is nothing to fear."

Her worry seemed to be only partly sated.

"We came to answer a call for aid."

The haze of confusion in her eyes melted to understanding.

"And, though I am much relieved we have been here for our friends, that call is still in place."

She nodded. "Perhaps, it is time for us to follow it."

He traced the side of her face. She was so strong, his Eva. Her courage astounded him. Truly, she was his partner in every way. "Yes."

"Then we shall. Can all be prepared by morning?"

He smiled once again. "If necessary."

"The need is great. And we have been much delayed, have we not?"

"Yes. And I would linger with you several more nights in the privacy of this fine castle if I could. But I will take but one more night."

She pressed up on her toes and met his lips.

The running footsteps alerted Zdenek to the presence of another. He released his wife far sooner than he wished to.

A maidservant rushed for them, with breaths heaving. "Lord Ambroz!"

"Yes?" He looked to Eva. Concern had found its way into her features once more.

"Lord Krejik beseeches you and your lady wife to come."

"What could require such haste?"

"Lady Krejikova labors. The midwife is with her."

Eva's eyes widened.

"Show us where Lord Krejik is." Zdenek kept a firm hold on Eva's arm. Perhaps offering comfort as much as seeking it.

The young woman nodded and turned back in the direction she had come.

Though this should be a welcomed, celebrated moment, it seemed anything but.

Radek held Hana's hand as he led her from the solar. He could not be happier. Everything he could have hoped for and dreamed of had come to pass.

More so, Hana was happy. Could God be so kind?

Yes, God. These first tentative steps were strange, fresh, and new...but very real.

And he needed to speak with Hana.

Her gaze was on him. The streaks on her face evidenced tears had filled her eyes. Now, she was aglow with life and...love? Indeed.

"Hana," he said, pulling her to the side in the Great Hall.

He glanced about. A handful of servants lingered, preparing the space for the evening meal. It might not be the best situation, but it would have to suit him.

"I must speak with you."

Her eyes danced in the light.

He wanted to lose himself in the flickering brightness within the hazel. And he would. But not this moment.

"God has blessed me doubly today."

Her brows arched.

"He met me at my point of need. And He granted me favor with your father."

She waved a hand. "This I know."

"You do?" How did she know? Surely, the priest had not...

"I mean only that I know about my father's favor on you."

Of course.

"What do you mean that God met you at your point of need?"

"I did not believe. I did not think Him true. But I know now that He is. And He is good."

Her smile filled her face. "How? When? I wish to know everything."

He put a hand between them. "I understand. And I will share what I can. But there is something that I must tell you now."

"More to tell? Something more wonderful? What can be better?"

He licked his lips. How to go about this? Taking her hands in his and facing her once more, he looked into her eyes. "You know that I love you."

"Yes." The word came slowly. As if she were uncertain.

"I do. So much. And we will wed. The banns will be read and the date will be set. And I will be back. I will marry you."

"Back? Where...where will you go?"

He drew in a breath and let it out. "I must go and make amends with my father."

"Your father?" Her features contorted.

"Yes. I know you may not understand. But before I can move forward, I have to reconcile what is behind."

He watched several emotions play across her face.

She squeezed his hands. "I will not lie. I wish it were not so, but I trust you. I trust what is between us."

His heart warmed and, if possible, his love for her deepened even more. He leaned forward and pressed a kiss to the side of her face. "I will return. And we will wed."

"There is no doubt."

A cry went out through the large room.

Radek and Hana turned toward it.

"Lord Krejik has a son! The Lady Karin has given him a son!"

Hana looked to Radek. "Your friend, Lord Krejik? Their babe has come?"

How many hours had Pavel sat, crunched as he was, folded in prayer. Then a maidservant had come from his and Karin's chambers announcing that a boy had been born.

Such relief had overcome him. A warmth filled his chest and expanded until there wasn't room for anything else.

"How is the Lady Karin?" he called after the woman.

But she had closed the door.

For certain, she would have spoken thusly if there was concern for his wife.

A son. *His* son.

Zdenek clapped him on the shoulder. "You are blessed, my friend."

"Indeed."

Eva beamed at him, but remained silent. Her eyes turned to Zdenek, however. It was not difficult to see the longing in them.

Pavel could not remain still. He walked the floor outside the chambers back and forth. He had spent some of the hours in waiting doing just this before weariness found him praying.

The sound of movement on the stairs alerted him that others came. Soon enough, Radek and the duke's daughter appeared.

Radek and Zdenek exchanged a hard look before Radek crossed to Pavel.

"Congratulations! Your son is a gift," Radek said, reaching for his arm.

Pavel nodded. Then glanced at Zdenek and then the door separating him from Karin before resuming his pacing.

"Why are you not at ease?" Zdenek asked. "The hard part is over. Your child is well."

"I know not." Indeed, Pavel could not discern why he was ill within. Something unsettling had taken hold of him. And he could not shake it.

"Perhaps it is nothing more than the newness of it," Radek offered.

Pavel looked to his friend. Maybe he was right.

Both Radek and Zdenek watched him. Neither looked at the other. And they stood some distance apart. It seemed strange. Maybe not. Nothing was right in that moment to him. Nothing.

The door creaked.

A maidservant came out, bearing a wriggling bundle. She moved straight to Pavel. "Your son, my lord."

Holding out her arms, she made a move to pass the babe to Pavel. The baby was so small, but whole and active. His hands moved, seeking. And the tiny features scrunched—perfect and beautiful, yet so unaware of the difficult things of life.

Unsure how to proceed, Pavel only stared.

Eva came alongside him and urged him to open his arms for the child.

Once his son was cradled against his chest, something altogether indescribable overcame him—joy and peace wrapped in this tiny bundle.

Could that be possible?

But what of Karin?

He looked up.

The maidservant stood where she had been, watching him.

"What of Lady Karin?"

The woman remained silent. Notably so. Her eyes shone. Was there moisture in them?

Pavel noticed the blood upon her person. And a lot of it.

"My wife." He stepped toward her, voice breaking. "How does she fare?"

"The midwife is with her," the maidservant said, her words small and quiet. "She does what she can."

The height to which Pavel's heart had soared seemed impossible as it plummeted to depths it had not known.

"What she can?" he repeated numbly.

"I'm sorry." She backed up and slipped into the room, closing the door behind herself.

Pavel slammed into the door and gripped the latch. It was locked.

The baby in his arms cried. His son. Cried.

He stepped from the door. What was he to do with the crying infant?

Eva and Zdenek were beside him in a moment. Small hands helped him bounce the baby—Eva's. Her fingers moved over the baby's face and head, soothing him.

Zdenek's hand was on his back. But there were no words. What words could there be?

His eyes burned. Everything hurt.

As the seconds passed, Radek came to his other side. Again, with no words, only his presence to offer as solace.

And so they three, who had journeyed much in these few years, stood together as one among them faced an impossible future.

*Keep reading for a preview of the next book in The Lady of Bohemia Series!*

*Thank you, dear reader, for reading along with me! If you enjoyed this story, I would sincerely appreciate if you would submit a review. It would mean so much to me!*

**To read more about these characters, follow along with The Lady of Bohemia Series. Find it at:**

https://saraturnquist.com/lady-bornekova-series/

# Author's Note

Hello, Readers! Thank you for reading along with me. Pavel and Karin's story has become so dear to me. It has become both difficult and exciting to journey with them through the (fictionalized) telling of the Hussite Wars.

For those not familiar with Czech history, the Hussite Wars were sparked by the martyr of Jan Huss. Huss opposed some of the practices of the Catholic Church in his day. I generally tell people to think of Marin Luther, but before Martin Luther. In fact, Huss's ideas and writings inspired Luther. Though, Huss himself was inspired by John Wycliff. The Hussite Wars, if I could boil them down, were religious civil wars between the Hussites (followers of Huss's teachings, opposing the Catholic Church in a sense) and the Catholic Church. This conflict lasted fifteen years.

There is not as much movement forward in that conflict during this book. Following the Battle of Vitkov Hill (which is represented at the end of *The Lady and the Hussites*), there was much civil unrest and General Zizka, as in this novel, was busy chasing down the threat posed by Ulrich of Rosenberg. Ulrich, a supporter of the outside forces opposed to the Hussites, had been responsible for the torture and murder of several priests.

Ulrich of Rosenberg's hand in the lives of my fictional characters is, of course, fictional. With the exception of General Zizka and references to characters that remain "off page," all of the characters in the story are products of my own imagination.

Singing greeted Karin as she awoke—a soothing lullaby. Bright light filled her vision, a harsh contrast to the gentleness of the melody. Where was she? What time of day was it?

Her eyes adjusted to the sunlight in the room, and she remembered. She had been settled in chambers within Duke Novak's castle. This room in which she labored and nearly died became her only refuge. Her return to health had been taxing and long. So long.

She turned in the direction of the voice. A maidservant sat, rocking a baby. Karin's vision cleared as she blinked. It was *her* baby. Hers and Pavel's.

A weak smile spread Karin's lips but slightly. God was good. She had been to the very brink of death. And survived. As had her son. It was a long-fought victory, due in no small part to many prayers lifted on her behalf.

The nursemaid continued to sway and bounce the small bundle. After several seconds, her gaze drifted to Karin. And the older woman startled. Was she so surprised to see that Karin had awakened?

"My lady," the woman said as she stood and drew near. "How do you fare?"

Karin closed her eyes and made an inventory of her body, taking care as she shifted her limbs to assess their state. A sharp pang stole her breath when her movements reached her abdomen. Beyond that, a dull ache seemed to pervade her whole being. Despite this, she found only gratitude. "All is well. There is some discomfort, but I cannot complain."

The woman's brow furrowed.

Just then, the babe cried, distracting them both from any further discussion.

The servant's warm brown eyes met Karin's above the babe's blue ones that squeezed shut. "I think he is hungry."

Karin nodded. "Help me sit." She maneuvered her arms to pull herself upward.

"My lady," the woman protested as she took another step toward Karin. "I can fetch the wet nurse, I—"

"No." The word was not gentle. They had been through this. It was a kindness to be sure, but Karin wished to care for her child in this way.

The nursemaid frowned.

"I assure you; I am well enough." Karin grimaced against renewed pains, due in no small part to her movements. "Just help me."

The older woman set the babe on the bed—several inches from the side— and turned to assist her mistress.

But the infant's wails intensified.

With features drawn, the nursemaid stepped back toward the infant. Then to Karin. Only to turn back to the child.

"Please," Karin seethed. "Make haste!" She had not the time nor the patience in the moment for the woman's well meaning but confused intentions.

Proving herself capable, the woman helped Karin raise herself into a seated position. Then propped a pillow behind Karin's back.

"Now, my son." Karin motioned for the babe.

"Aye, my lady." The servant scooped up the infant and brought him over.

Though Karin's arms felt weak and useless when she lifted them, she downplayed the pain as the nursemaid laid the child in them.

Moments later, and with a bit of maneuvering, the babe nursed and was content once more.

Karin sighed and let her head fall back. Why must everything be so challenging? She parted her lips to ask that Pavel be summoned. But she stopped herself before the words formed. Her husband had returned to the heightened conflict with the Royalist army. The war hadn't stopped because of her delivery and subsequent difficult recovery.

Sigismund still grasped for control over the Czech lands. And the power he had lost in their forfeit. And so, a month past, he marched back into Bohemia in an attempt to retake ground previously lost. Even now, General Zizka—completely blinded in his last battle—led the Hussites to intercept the would-be king and his army. Zizka's men—a cobbled together contingency of peasants, farmers, merchants, and warriors—would make every attempt to push the invading force out. If Zizka's successes up to now were any indication, it would be done. And quickly.

Pavel had needed some convincing that Karin was well enough for him to resume his stand with General Zizka. After all, Duke and Duchess Novak would see to her comfort and safety. She had been loathed for him to depart, yet it was she who insisted he go. Knowing her husband, he would never forgive himself if the conflict at the front turned for the worse in his absence. However, all she could think now was that she would never forgive herself if Pavel were to be injured or...she couldn't even piece the words together in her mind.

She put a stop to the errant thoughts that would lead to naught but worry. God was with Pavel...and with the Hussites. Had He not proven faithful already?

The nursemaid bustled about the room, straightening this and that. Perhaps only attempting to give Karin and her child some space.

She lifted Karin's psalter from a nearby table. "Shall I have someone read to you?"

Karin looked at her briefly and then back down to her son. "I do not wish to disturb Father Dominik."

The servant woman nodded but ventured further. "If only there were others who could read Latin."

Karin's gaze caught the woman's before her attention returned to her work. The nursemaid spoke the truth. Precious few were educated enough to read the Holy Writ. Karin's parents had seen to that in her tutelage, for which she was grateful.

The thought struck her. What would it mean if her son—if all—could read the precious words of the Holy Writ for themselves? To no longer rely on priests and bishops to impart the Scriptures to them? The idea spread wings within her as if preparing to take flight.

But she suppressed even this. It was forbidden to transcribe the sacred writings. Only...

The Catholic Church no longer held authority in these lands. Would there, then, be a chance...a hope that someone could ink these ancient words into Czech?

Karin watched her son. The babe had fallen asleep nuzzled against her body. She covered herself and held him close. With the lightest touch, she traced a finger down one side of his face, admiring the chubby features. Angelic. Her chest expanded as it always did when she held her son—a piece of Pavel and of her, evidence of their love.

She marveled anew at the life in her arms that had not an inkling of the conflict around them. Such innocence. Would he ever know these things that created distance and hardship for his parents? Would he know *why* they sacrificed? Would he understand? Perhaps...in time. Would that be best? Or dare she hope to preserve his ignorance of these hard things?

She sighed, considering the name that seemed big for the small child— Jaromir.

Her fervent wish had been to name their child after Pavel's father. A deeper pain surged through her at the memory of he who had accepted her as his own flesh and blood. He was gone and would never see his grandson. Pavel, however, had determined that Alexander would be the boy's second name. He wanted for his son to represent the peace they fought so fervently for. And so, they chose Jaromir for 'fierce peace.'

It was fitting, she decided. The name suited him.

Karin only then realized she hummed—the same tune the nursemaid had just earlier sung to the babe. And though Karin's arms had since tired, she could not make herself relinquish her son.

A knock on the door broke her reverie.

Her gaze darted to the nursemaid, now across the chamber.

The woman, likewise, looked at Karin.

"I am able to receive," Karin said, nodding as she permitted a smile to touch her features.

The nursemaid strode across the room as Karin readjusted the top of her gown for better coverage.

"Yes?" The gruff voice of the nursemaid spilled into the hall. Was she so put out that someone would disturb her charges? Karin found comfort in the woman's concern for them.

Craning her neck, Karin spotted a younger woman who worked to find her voice. The words seemed to crowd her mouth as her tongue shifted within and her lips twisted.

Karin sensed the growing frustration of the nursemaid. The older woman's body fairly radiated her ire.

After several moments, the servant in the hall managed to state her purpose. "I have a missive. For the Lady Krejikova."

The nursemaid jerked her head and moved aside, permitting the servant girl entrance.

Karin maneuvered Jaromir so she could receive the letter. But as she struggled, the nursemaid again intervened and plucked the rolled paper from the girl's fingers.

The nursemaid then shuffled the young servant back into the hall, dismissing her with the flick of her hands, and closing the door. She turned and moved toward her mistress. "Shall I take him, my lady?"

Karin hesitated. She did not wish to end this moment with her son, but her heart ached to see what news the missive bore. Even from this distance, Pavel's seal was visible.

The letter must hold information about his wellbeing. Now desperate for whatever the papers contained; she motioned the woman over.

Time slowed as the nursemaid set the missive on a side table and collected Jaromir.

His face scrunched and, for a moment, it seemed he might wake. However, his features soon smoothed as the older woman commenced her swaying.

It was all too much. Even distracted by Jaromir, her heart raced to discover the contents of the letter. Now that the babe had settled, she stretched to the very extent of her ability to reach for the message. Indeed, her muscles protested the action.

Ignoring it, she tore at the seal. Her eagerness for word of her beloved almost led to ripped parchment. Soon enough, the stamped wax gave way.

She searched the pages, her first fears quelled as she recognized Pavel's writing. He was well enough if he could write, wasn't he? Calming herself, she forced her gaze to still and focus.

Pavel first offered words of love and of hope that her health continued to improve. They were a balm to her heart. Then he spoke of the soldiers and their preparations for battle. Zizka had marched on the town of Zatec to push out the Royalists, who had a tenuous hold on the town. The enemy had halted their barrage and pulled back.

Karin paused. Would the Royalists turn tail and flee? After all their efforts, they would pack up and retreat so quickly? Perhaps Sigismund's fear of Zizka's abilities was greater than anticipated.

She glanced at the date. Some time had passed since Pavel pored over these words. Had the Hussites overcome? Or been defeated?

Karin prayed for the former and hoped that her husband would not have known combat in the days that followed. Oh, how she prayed.

**To read more, find *The Lady and Her Secret* here:**

https://saraturnquist.com/the-lady-and-her-secret/

# The Lady Bornekova (Book 1)

The red-headed Karin is strong-willed and determined, she tries to keep her true nature a secret to avoid being deemed a traitor by those loyal to the king.

Karin and her father butt heads over her duty to her family and the Czech Crown. However, her heart soon becomes entangled though her father intends to wed her to another.

The turmoil inside Karin deepens and reflects the turmoil of her homeland, on the brink of the Hussite Wars.

# The Lady & the Hussites (Book 2)

Karin and Pavel have found their way safely to his parents home, but things are not as well as they seem. There are secrets between them. A wall goes up. And then Pavel is called into battle.

Radek and Zdenek find themselves pulled into the conflict despite their best efforts to remain neutral, while Stepan finds himself ready for bloodshed.

With tensions mounting within their circle and throughout their country, what will become of Pavel and Karin? Can they find their way back to each other?

# The Lady & Her Champion (Book 3)

She needs someone to fight for her. He needs to be rescued.

Karin and Pavel have become separated by war and the destruction of his family's home. When Pavel hears of Karin's predicament, he rushes to his beloved. But what will he find?

Will the pull to remain by her side be stronger than the tug to return to the front lines?

While the Hussites maintain a tenuous hold on their lands, will internal conflict prove their undoing?

# The Lady & Her Secret (Book 4)

She seeks the forbidden. He struggles to find peace.

Karin and Pavel are at last reunited. But her desire to take on a task long prohibited has Pavel worried for her safety and that of his new family. She strives to keep her work a secret while he faces his own fight—one of a warrior weary of battle.

While the Hussites wrestle with internal conflict, will the enemy take advantage of their vulnerability...and overtake them?

# The Lady & Her Mission (Book 5)

## COMING SOON

# Acknowledgments

There are many people who have played a part in this book's publication. Many more than I could remember. So, to everyone who asked after the process, let me talk about it, or share my characters and story in development, I thank you. You are part of this work in a very real way.

I want to thank Word Weavers Page 13. This group of wonderful people listen to and read my work each month, giving me valuable feedback that shapes the scenes and hones my skills. The encouragement and camaraderie are a bonus!

My Advanced Reader Team, you all are more appreciated than you know. You make my writer heart so happy!

Hannah Conway, my writing mentor, you are part of every book in so many ways—through advice and letting me brainstorm. You continue to inspire me.

Cindy Smith, your feedback has been more valuable than I can say. Thanks for the plotting sessions and all the support you give so tirelessly.

My editor, Julie Sherwood—I can't say how much you enhance my work through your efforts. You have a gift for kicking my butt.

Cora Graphics, you did it again—another amazing cover. Getting a new cover from you never gets old.

VerBull Photography, thanks for getting my "good side" :-)

My husband and number one fan, this quarantine has given us good days and bad days...maybe more of one than the other, but you still helped make this happen. Thanks for helping my dreams come true more and more every day.

For my sister, you make me want to be better. For my dad, you make me feel so good to have achieved this dream of writing. For my mom, I will love you forever. And for my kids, you give me every reason to smile.

Last, but certainly not least, my readers, you give me a reason to keep writing.

# ABOUT THE AUTHOR

Sara is a coffee lovin', word slinging, Historical Romance author whose super power is converting caffeine into novels. She loves those odd little tidbits of history that are stranger than fiction. That's what inspires her. Well, that and a good love story.

But of all the love stories she knows, hers is her favorite. She lives happily with her own Prince Charming and their gaggle of minions. Three to be exact. They sure know how to distract a writer! But, alas, the stories must be written, even if it must happen in the wee hours of the morning.

Sara is an avid reader and enjoys reading and writing clean Historical Romance when she's not traveling.

Please follow along with her journey through her newsletter at:
http://saraturnquist.com/list

**Happy Reading!**

facebook.com/AuthorSaraRTurnquist

instagram.com/sararturnquist

x.com/sararturnquist

youtube.com/@SaraRTurnquist

pinterest.com/sararturnquist

# ALSO BY SARA R. TURNQUIST

**STANDALONE NOVELS**

*The General's Wife*

*Trail of Fears*

*Off to War*